FRANCIS V...
THE DEATH ...

Francis ... ...n
1906 at ... He was
the younger ... ...grapher Hallam
Ashley. Vivian ... a decade as a painter
and decorator b... ...ecoming an author of popular
fiction in 1932. In 1940 he married schoolteacher
Dorothy Wallwork, and the couple had a daughter.

After the Second World War he became assistant editor at the Nottinghamshire Free Press and circuit lecturer on many subjects, ranging from crime to bee-keeping (the latter forming a major theme in the Inspector Knollis mystery *The Singing Masons*). A founding member of the Nottingham Writers' Club, Vivian once awarded first prize in a writing competition to a young Alan Sillitoe, the future bestselling author.

The ten Inspector Knollis mysteries were published between 1941 and 1956. In the novels, ingenious plotting and fair play are paramount. A colleague recalled that 'the reader could always arrive at a correct solution from the given data. Inspector Knollis never picked up an undisclosed clue which, it was later revealed, held the solution to the mystery all along.'

Francis Vivian died on April 2, 1979 at the age of 73.

The Inspector Knollis Mysteries
Available from Dean Street Press

The Death of Mr. Lomas
Sable Messenger
The Threefold Cord
The Ninth Enemy
The Laughing Dog
The Singing Masons
The Elusive Bowman
The Sleeping Island
The Ladies of Locksley
Darkling Death

FRANCIS VIVIAN

THE DEATH OF MR. LOMAS

With an introduction by Curtis Evans

DEAN STREET PRESS

Published by Dean Street Press 2018

Copyright © 1941 Francis Vivian

Copyright © 2018 Curtis Evans

All Rights Reserved

Published by licence, issued under the UK Orphan Works Licensing Scheme.

First published in 1941 by Herbert Jenkins Ltd.

Cover by DSP

ISBN 978 1 912574 27 8

www.deanstreetpress.co.uk

FOR

MY WIFE

INTRODUCTION

SHORTLY BEFORE his death in 1951, American agriculturalist and scholar Everett Franklin Phillips, then Professor Emeritus of Apiculture (beekeeping) at Cornell University, wrote British newspaperman Arthur Ernest Ashley (1906-1979), author of detective novels under the pseudonym Francis Vivian, requesting a copy of his beekeeping mystery *The Singing Masons*, the sixth Inspector Gordon Knollis investigation, which had been published the previous year in the United Kingdom. The eminent professor wanted the book for Cornell's Everett F. Phillips Beekeeping Collection, "one of the largest and most complete apiculture libraries in the world" (currently in the process of digitization at Cornell's The Hive and the Honeybee website). Sixteen years later Ernest Ashely, or Francis Vivian as I shall henceforward name him, to an American fan requesting an autograph ("Why anyone in the United States, where I am not known," he self-deprecatingly observed, "should want my autograph I cannot imagine, but I am flattered by your request and return your card, duly signed.") declared that fulfilling Professor Phillip's donation request was his "greatest satisfaction as a writer." With ghoulish relish he added, "I believe there was some objection by the Librarian, but the good doctor insisted, and so in it went! It was probably destroyed after Dr. Phillips died. Stung to death."

After investigation I have found no indication that the August 1951 death of Professor Phillips, who was 73 years old at the time, was due to anything other than natural causes. One assumes that what would have been the painfully ironic demise of the American nation's most distinguished apiculturist from bee stings would have merited some mention in his death notices. Yet Francis Vivian's fabulistic claim otherwise provides us with a glimpse of that mordant sense of humor and storytelling relish which glint throughout the eighteen mystery novels Vivian published between 1937 and 1959.

Ten of these mysteries were tales of the ingenious sleuthing exploits of series detective Inspector Gordon Knollis, head of the Burnham C.I.D. in the first novel in the series and a Scotland Yard detective in the rest. (Knollis returns to Burnham in later novels.) The debut Inspector Knollis mystery, *The Death of Mr. Lomas*, which was published in 1941, is actually the seventh Francis Vivian detective novel. However, after the Second World War, when the author belatedly returned to his vocation of mystery writing, all of the remaining detective novels he published, with two exceptions, chronicle the criminal cases of the keen and clever Knollis. These other Inspector Knollis tales are: *Sable Messenger* (1947), *The Threefold Cord* (1947), *The Ninth Enemy* (1948), *The Laughing Dog* (1949), *The Singing Masons* (1950), *The Elusive Bowman* (1951), *The Sleeping Island* (1951), *The Ladies of Locksley* (1953) and *Darkling Death* (1956). (Inspector Knollis also is passingly mentioned in Francis Vivian's final mystery, published in 1959, *Dead Opposite the Church*.) By the late Forties and early Fifties, when Hodder & Stoughton, one of England's most important purveyors of crime and mystery fiction, was publishing the Francis Vivian novels, the Inspector Knollis mysteries had achieved wide popularity in the UK, where "according to the booksellers and librarians," the author's newspaper colleague John Hall later recalled in the *Guardian* (possibly with some exaggeration), "Francis Vivian was neck and neck with Ngaio Marsh in second place after Agatha Christie." (Hardcover sales and penny library rentals must be meant here, as with one exception--a paperback original--Francis Vivian, in great contrast with Crime Queens Marsh and Christie, both mainstays of Penguin Books in the UK, was never published in softcover.)

John Hall asserted that in Francis Vivian's native coal and iron county of Nottinghamshire, where Vivian from the 1940s through the 1960s was an assistant editor and "colour man" (writer of local color stories) on the Nottingham, or Notts, *Free Press*, the detective novelist "through a large stretch of the coalfield is reckoned the best local author after Byron and D. H. Lawrence." Hall added that "People who wouldn't know Alan

Sillitoe from George Eliot will stop Ernest in the street and tell him they solved his last detective story." Somewhat ironically, given this assertion, Vivian in his capacity as a founding member of the Nottingham Writers Club awarded first prize in a 1950 Nottingham writing competition to no other than 22-year-old local aspirant Alan Sillitoe, future "angry young man" author of *Saturday Night and Sunday Morning* (1958) and *The Loneliness of the Long Distance Runner* (1959). In his 1995 autobiography Sillitoe recollected that Vivian, "a crime novelist who earned his living by writing . . . gave [my story] first prize, telling me it was so well written and original that nothing further need be done, and that I should try to get it published." This was "The General's Dilemma," which Sillitoe later expanded into his second novel, *The General* (1960).

While never himself an angry young man (he was, rather, a "ragged-trousered" philosopher), Francis Vivian came from fairly humble origins in life and well knew how to wield both the hammer and the pen. Born on March 23, 1906, Vivian was one of two children of Arthur Ernest Ashley, Sr., a photographer and picture framer in East Retford, Nottinghamshire, and Elizabeth Hallam. His elder brother, Hallam Ashley (1900-1987), moved to Norwich and became a freelance photographer. Today he is known for his photographs, taken from the 1940s through the 1960s, chronicling rural labor in East Anglia (many of which were collected in the 2010 book *Traditional Crafts and Industries in East Anglia: The Photographs of Hallam Ashley*). For his part, Francis Vivian started working at age 15 as a gas meter emptier, then labored for 11 years as a housepainter and decorator before successfully establishing himself in 1932 as a writer of short fiction for newspapers and general magazines. In 1937, he published his first detective novel, *Death at the Salutation*. Three years later, he wed schoolteacher Dorothy Wallwork, with whom he had one daughter.

After the Second World War Francis Vivian's work with the Notts *Free Press* consumed much of his time, yet he was still able for the next half-dozen years to publish annually a detective novel (or two), as well as to give popular lectures on a plethora of intriguing subjects, including, naturally enough, crime, but also fiction writing (he published two guidebooks on that subject), psychic forces (he believed himself to be psychic), black magic, Greek civilization, drama, psychology and beekeeping. The latter occupation he himself took up as a hobby, following in the path of Sherlock Holmes. Vivian's fascination with such esoterica invariably found its way into his detective novels, much to the delight of his loyal readership.

As a detective novelist, John Hall recalled, Francis Vivian "took great pride in the fact that the reader could always arrive at a correct solution from the given data. His Inspector never picked up an undisclosed clue which, it was later revealed, held the solution to the mystery all along." Vivian died on April 2, 1979, at the respectable if not quite venerable age of 73, just like Professor Everett Franklin Phillips. To my knowledge the late mystery writer had not been stung to death by bees.

Curtis Evans

PROLOGUE

HE WAS A little old man with shrewd grey eyes. He had a yellowish goatee beard, a moustache with waxed points, and bushy eyebrows. His nostrils were twitching and his lips quavering when he called on the Chief Constable of Burnham early that fine June morning. He allowed himself no more than the front edge of the chair with which he was provided and each time his eyes met those of the Chief Constable they retreated behind their lids like the horns of a snail.

Sir Wilfred Burrows, a bluff and mountainous globe with surprisingly small feet, knew his visitor to be the owner of a prosperous business out on the Desborough Road where he combined the functions of newsagent, stationer, bookseller, and tobacconist; a mild little man who had never taken any share in civic duties or responsibilities and who had, therefore, never fallen foul of Sir Wilfred's impatience with local legislators, or earned the commendation of more broad-minded citizens.

Sir Wilfred noticed his visitor's uneasiness and made a show of attending to his morning mail in order to give him time in which to control himself. He meanwhile passed casual remarks about the weather, the chances of the County Eleven in the forthcoming match against Yorkshire, and the possible outcome of the present match at Worcester, until at last, deeming the time to be ripe, he smoothed his circumference, ran the gold chain that garlanded it through his podgy fingers, and smiled with all the reassurance of a man who was about to boost the merits of some vacuum cleaner he was trying to sell.

"We hope it is nothing in the nature of a complaint that has brought you along, Mr. Lomas," he remarked affably. His voice boomed from deep within a massive chest, and as he boomed so he beamed, with an expansiveness that embraced the whole of humanity.

Mr. Lomas wriggled on his inch of chair. His beard quavered ridiculously as he tried to force words from his throat. He opened his mouth twice, only to close it again, and Sir Wilfred found himself looking behind Mr. Lomas's ears for a pair of gills. Mr. Lomas eventually gripped the arms of the chair and leaned forward. "I am being poisoned, Sir Wilfred!" he said dramatically.

Sir Wilfred blinked and made unintelligible noises. He was not too sure that he had heard aright. "Poisoned! Poisoned, did we hear you say?"

"I am being poisoned," Mr. Lomas repeated.

Sir Wilfred gave a short laugh.

"Come, Mr. Lomas! Poisoned! Come now! I mean to say . . ."

"I am being poisoned," Mr. Lomas said once more, this time in a more assertive, dogmatic voice.

Sir Wilfred was not at all sure of himself. He massaged his right cheek thoughtfully, and then his eye brightened.

"Poisoned, you say? Well, perhaps you are right, but who would want to poison you, Mr. Lomas? Tell me that. And for why? Oh yes, we must have a motive, you know! People don't go about poisoning other people without a good reason. It wouldn't make sense, would it? You're sure that you aren't imagining things?"

Mr. Lomas's beard shot upwards to point at the Chief Constable like an accusing finger. "You—you are questioning my sanity! This—this is scandalous! I will report it to the Watch Committee. Indeed I will!"

Sir Wilfred grimaced. His opinion of the Watch Committee as a functioning body was far from complimentary; they were far too officious and critical.

He coughed behind his hand and chased an idea to its logical conclusion.

"Look here," he said after a pause; "suppose you tell me the whole story from start to finish?"

"Oh, what's the use?" Mr. Lomas complained. "You won't believe me! I can see that clearly. You don't want to believe me!"

"Of course we believe you," Sir Wilfred hastened to assure him. "You simply bowled us over. After all, y'know, we hear a good many stories here that would astonish a layman—but poisoning! Anyway, we can hardly venture to express an opinion until we have heard the story, can we?"

He beamed, realising that his logic was faultless. "Oh well," said Mr. Lomas wearily, and by a vague gesture intimated that he was prepared to try anything once. "You may know my shop on the Desborough Road," he began. "I live in the house next door—they are connected by a doorway in the wall of the living-room. A woman comes in to clean for me each morning, and has done so ever since my dear wife Jennifer passed away. That was five years ago. I am comfortably well off and I was hoping to retire within a few months and enjoy the money for which I have toiled and saved."

"Quite, quite!" murmured Sir Wilfred.

"All that is beyond my reach now," Mr. Lomas said hopelessly. "My time is short."

Sir Wilfred shifted impatiently and toyed with the gold pince-nez which he wore in the office, more for effect than for any assistance they could render him. He suddenly exclaimed:

"Good gracious, man, there must be at least a dozen years left to you! How old are you? Not a day older than fifty-nine, I'll be bound. And the span of a man's life is three-score years and ten."

Mr. Lomas flushed at the compliment and gave a faint smile of pleasure. He straightened his black knitted tie and in a more confident tone revealed his age. "I am sixty-five, Sir Wilfred," he said. Then the worried frown reappeared on his brow. "A few weeks ago I would have agreed with you about the years left to me, but now I can count them on the fingers of my two hands. The years? Nay, the very days! I am being poisoned, slowly and remorselessly."

He fell silent, and Sir Wilfred had to prompt him with a murmured "Yes?"

"It is essential for my peace of mind that the villain who is doing this to me should meet his just punishment, and so I come to you to-day to put into your hands such little evidence as I possess. There is little enough of it," he admitted ruefully, "but you, who are an expert in such matters, will be able to see an elephant where I can only see a fly."

Sir Wilfred grunted non-committally, although secretly pleased at the return compliment.

"The poison is being introduced surreptitiously," Mr. Lomas went on in a hushed and dramatic tone. "I am completely at a loss to understand or explain how it is being effected. My habits are simple ones, and it is seldom that I depart from a daily routine. Logically, therefore, it should be comparatively easy for an expert such as yourself to find the solution."

The Chief Constable smiled again and stroked into place the few strands of light brown hair that remained with him.

"I rise at half-past five each morning," continued Mr. Lomas, happier now that he had a seemingly attentive audience. "I make my own breakfast. My dinner and tea are supplied by the Desborough Road Café, each meal being brought to the shop by a waitress who later collects the tray. After closing the shop I call at the Golden Angel, there meeting my friend Steadfall, the chemist. Together we go to the Commerce Club in Devonport Street, and play snooker or billiards. I leave there shortly after ten, and, if the weather allows, walk home for the exercise. I mix a malted milk drink and sip this in bed. I am usually asleep by a quarter-past eleven."

He caressed his beard and looked covertly at Sir Wilfred.

"It would seem from these facts that the poison is either introduced into the food sent by the café, or into the drinks at the Angel or the Commerce Club—and I have to admit that both possibilities are fantastic." The Chief Constable twirled the point of his pencil on the blotting pad, but found himself unable to raise his eyes for fear of betraying his thoughts.

"Your—er—symptoms?" he mumbled. "They may indicate the nature of the—er—poison."

Mr. Lomas pursed thin, puckered lips.

"Ah yes, the symptoms!" he exclaimed. "Have you ever experienced an intense excitation of the nerves? Have you, Sir Wilfred, a man in normal health, ever fancied that insects were walking about under your skin? Have you?"

Sir Wilfred was shocked into meeting Mr. Lomas's eyes. He shivered, in spite of the warming rays of the morning sun that streamed across the room. "God forbid!" he ejaculated.

"Have you ever known a sudden burst of energy to sweep over you, making you feel like a man of twenty-five again, with all a young man's urges and desires? And later to have known this transient rejuvenation replaced by an abject, almost abysmal state of depression, so that suicide seems the most desirable prospect on earth?"

Sir Wilfred frowned. "You're sure this isn't a nervous disease, Mr. Lomas?"

"Of course it is a nervous disease, brought on by the poison," replied Mr. Lomas.

"You have consulted a doctor?"

"No, I have not done that," Mr. Lomas admitted, "but I did consult my friend, Steadfall, about my condition—and without stating my suspicions. He gave me a tonic which only served to intensify the excitation. Later he suggested a bromide. That increased the degree of depression when I was experiencing the trough of the wave."

"Ah!" exclaimed Sir Wilfred with an air of understanding. Into his mind swept memories of delirium tremens, as exhibited by drunks who had occupied the cells on the lower floor.

"Look here, Mr. Lomas," he said softly. "I think we are getting somewhere at last. Now tell me; ever see animals running about the shop? Y'know! Rabbits, and rats, and all that sort of thing?" His fingers imitated the pattering of tiny creatures across the table.

Mr. Lomas's nostrils expanded angrily. "I am a temperate man!" he barked.

"Oh, quite, quite!" Sir Wilfred exclaimed as he recoiled from the little man's wrath. "No offence, you know! I just wondered. Have to take everything into account. Doesn't do to miss anything!"

He scratched his ear and muttered something beneath his breath that was not at all complimentary to his visitor.

"You know," he said aloud, "we could do something for you if only you could provide us with the smallest shred of direct evidence. But you can't, and that makes it most damnably awkward. What you have described are undoubtedly neurasthenic symptoms. Take my advice and see a doctor. I'm afraid you've come to the wrong place. Poisoned? No, it won't do, Mr. Lomas. Really, it won't do!"

Mr. Lomas's shyness vanished before his anger. He rose from his chair and stamped his feet like a petulant child. He was trembling from head to foot. He fixed his gaze on the lampshade and addressed it as though the Chief Constable was not present.

"It serves me right. I should never have come. I forced myself to come against my better instincts. I never had a great opinion of the city police—nor of any other police for that matter. I doubt their integrity, have nothing but contempt for their intelligence, and regard with deep pity their restricted and parochial outlook. They find it impossible, in their blind self-righteousness, to believe that anyone in this city could or should descend to the poisoning of a fellow creature. But when I am a body, lying mute in the city mortuary, then they will be interested! I shall be a case, something over which the morbid can bend with bated breath." He tottered to the door, and Sir Wilfred followed him, protesting.

"Do try to be reasonable, Mr. Lomas! Who would want to poison you? Who *could* poison you?"

Something akin to fear crossed Mr. Lomas's wizened features. Then he giggled nervously.

"You are perhaps right, Sir Wilfred. Who would want to poison *me*, an old man with one foot in the grave. Who *would*, Sir Wilfred?"

The Chief Constable took a deep breath and remembered the dignity of his position. "The matter will be handed to our criminal investigation department, to be dealt with by them. You will hear from us at a later date."

"Later?" queried Mr. Lomas as he shuffled into the corridor. "Not too late, I hope!"

Sir Wilfred Burrows returned to his desk. He plaited his fingers and assumed an attitude of deep thought. He drew the memorandum pad toward him and pushed it away again. Twice he rose and walked to the window, and twice returned to the desk and the pad. At last he unscrewed his fountain pen and made a brief note, leaving it in a conspicuous position where it was likely to be seen if Inspector Knollis came while he was out.

"The whole thing's too ridiculous for words," he exclaimed aloud. "Poisoned indeed! In Burnham . . . !" Then he remembered that he had an appointment at the nineteenth hole in an hour's time, and it is to be feared that all thoughts of Mr. Lomas slipped from his mind as he took putter and Silver King from a cupboard and, by an act of imagination, transformed the carpet into a green.

CHAPTER I
THE BODY AT WILLOW LOCK

Inspector Gordon Knollis knew nothing of Mr. Lomas's troubles until eleven o'clock that same night when the telephone bell startled the peace of his suburban home. He was reading by the fire, enjoying the one hour of the day which he could normally call his own. His wife was sitting opposite, also reading. Now and again they looked up to smile at each other, each fully satisfied with the silent company of the other.

"You are not interested in your book, dear," she said when he had looked across at her for the seventh time. "Anything on your mind?"

"No, not really," he replied. "I was just thinking. Silly in a way, but I was wondering why I became a policeman, and then a detective. It's the first time I've asked myself in twenty years."

"Because you were meant to be a detective, of course, Gordon. You are a good one, aren't you? And you are happy in your work."

"I've been fairly successful, I suppose," he mused, "but that isn't the point. I wasn't cut out to be a detective. I always wanted to be an engineer, to take things to pieces and put them together again; I always wanted to know how things work, and why they work."

His wife smiled. "Doesn't that prove that you have a flair for detection? You deal with men's minds, motives, and desires. You dissect their actions, theorise on why they do this, and that, and the other; on how they could have done this, and that, and the other. You are just as much an engineer as if you were dealing with engines and machinery."

Knollis nodded slowly. "I suppose you are right."

"Of course I am right. In any case," she added slyly, "you look like a detective."

This was the truth, for Gordon Knollis looked more like a detective than anything Hollywood could produce in its most enthusiastic moments. He might have been taken from stock. He was lean, and had a long inquisitive nose that was destined to be thrust into mysteries whether mechanical or psychological. His eyes were of a cold grey hue, mere slits through which he regarded the world with suspicion. They were forbidding until the creases at the corners were noticed, but it was seldom they came into play unless he was relaxing in his wife's company or playing bears with the two infant versions of himself who were now safely tucked up in the nursery above them. Knollis's major trait was patience, a fact thoroughly appreciated both by his wife and by the officers with whom he worked; it was his patience that had enabled him to rise from a uniformed constable on beat to the head of the Burnham Criminal Investigation Department. He was now forty-one years of age, and eminently satisfied with his lot.

"That is a disability I have to overcome with each new case," he said quietly. "Witnesses and suspects alike tend to close like oysters when I approach them. It needs a deal of tact and patience to persuade them to open up."

His wife smiled, and then glanced at the clock. "Eleven, and night-cap time. I think I'll have milk to-night."

Knollis grinned boyishly and reached for the decanter. A moment later he had to lay it aside, for the telephone bell had sounded in the hall. He grimaced and left the room. He was smiling wryly when he returned. "Premises entered, Gordon?"

"Worse than that, dear. River Station asking me to go out to Willow Lock. Male cadaver recovered from the water. Circumstances suspicious. They've 'phoned for Dr. Whitelaw instead of waiting until they get it to the mortuary, so it sounds grim. You'd better go to bed. There's no point in waiting up for me. Heaven knows when I'll get home."

He slid into his outdoor clothes and went to the garage at the rear of the house. He sped the car through the almost deserted city streets, through the magnificent city square, and then turned eastwards. Ten minutes later he gained open country and his foot came down on the accelerator. Twenty minutes after leaving his home he drew up outside the ancient whitewashed inn, The Ferryman, at Willow Lock. He left his car in the parking-ground before the inn and walked along the towpath. Through the dim mid-June twilight he saw a group of men gathered on the river bank, and at their feet a still, prone figure. The police sergeant saluted as he joined them. "Suicide?" Knollis asked shortly.

The sergeant eased his peaked uniform cap and scratched his head. "I'm blessed if I can decide, Inspector. That is why I asked you to come out. We were doing the nightly river patrol and saw this fellow half-submerged as we came up to the lock. He was tight up against the lock-gates as if the current had carried him there. Good job it didn't sweep him round the point and over the weir or he might have got to the Humber before he was found."

"Identification marks?" Knollis next asked.

"Well, we've been through his pockets, and various documents seem to suggest that he's Ezekiah Lomas, the newsagent on Desborough Road. And that's rummy, because if I remember Lomas rightly he was a bearded man, and, well, you can see for yourself, Inspector." Knollis knelt beside the bedraggled body while a constable focused the light of a torch on the features. He ran the back of his hand over the right cheek.

"Yes, he's been shaved, and very crudely," he agreed. "And the only apparent reason for that would be an attempt to delay identification. And yet you say that he carried documents bearing his name and address?"

"There was a wallet in the inside jacket pocket," the sergeant explained. "It contained a wireless licence, tobacco licence, two bills, a receipt, and a circular. All bore the name of Lomas. They were sodden, of course, so we've put them in the locker over the engine to dry out." He nodded towards the police craft moored to the bank.

Knollis got to his feet and slowly regarded the group. It consisted of the river patrol sergeant and his constable; the remaining three people were civilians. Two of them were roughly dressed and appeared to be awed by the circumstances. The other, a tall clean-shaven man, seemed to be a commercial traveller. He was possessed of an abundance of self-confidence and replied with equanimity when Knollis asked who the civilians might be.

"My friend on the right is the lock-keeper," he said. "Our other companion is the waiter at the inn. My name is Lester, George Lester; I am staying at the inn for a few days. We gravitated to the spot when we heard the sergeant calling for assistance. We helped to take the body from the river. Rotten business, isn't it? I wonder why the poor devil did it?"

Knollis's eyes narrowed. "Did what?"

"Jumped in. Made a hole in the water. Committed suicide. I take it that that is what happened?"

"There's no proof that he did," Knollis said shortly. "It doesn't do to jump to conclusions, Mr. Lester."

"Then you think that perhaps—" Lester began, but Knollis cut his question short with an imperative gesture. "Can any of you definitely identify the corpse?" The waiter stepped forward.

"I think I can, Inspector. I'm sure that it's Mr. Lomas. He was in the bar-parlour to-night, and he wasn't shaved then. He left ten minutes before closing time and he wasn't too steady on his pins. He'd had a lot of whisky before he came to The Ferryman. I think he had, anyway. He reeked of it."

"At what time did you find him?" Knollis asked the sergeant. "How long after ten minutes to ten?"

"It was exactly a quarter to eleven when we spotted him. We were on the point of turning back."

Knollis turned as the police surgeon's car swept round the corner and came to rest beside his own. Dr. Whitelaw, a gaunt loose-limbed Irishman joined them with no more than a muttered greeting and a nod to Knollis. He went straight to work on the body. There was deep silence for a time and then he looked up and was about to speak. Noticing the civilians he changed his mind. He ordered the sergeant to get the body to town.

He dusted the knees of his trousers and then took the Inspector by the elbow and led him some distance from the group. "The fellow was doped, Knollis. It may have been self-administered, and there may have been foul play. I can't say which with any degree of certainty until I've had him under a decent light. I don't like the looks of him at all. I take it that we'd better let Bunny know?" he said, referring to Sir Wilfred by his nickname.

"He's been shaved since ten minutes to ten," Knollis remarked non-committally. "He was moustached and bearded until then and has been these past twenty years. "The doctor showed interest. "You've identified him?"

"We think he is Lomas, the Desborough Road stationer and newsagent. He carried documents bearing that name."

"Wait here," said the doctor. He strode back to the body and examined the features closely. "I think you are right," he said on rejoining the Inspector. "I wasn't expecting that item and so it escaped me. Most unusual! I knew him slightly, a secretive little man I always thought him. He has a son in Desborough, Lawrence Lomas, the dental surgeon. Very clever fellow, I believe. And the daughter, she is companion to Mrs. Geoffrey Gregory out at Fountains. I've heard my wife speak of her. A rather old-fashioned spinster with more than a trace of the early nineteen-hundreds about her manner. Very prim and proper.

"She's going on for forty now. Rather a pathetic figure I understand. Psychopathic trauma—y'know, permanent mental wound as a result of being jilted. You never know what such people will do. Very unstable. Funny thing, that, Knollis. She, and people like her, let one event ruin their lives when two or three sittings with a decent psychotherapist—or the application of her own common sense—would put her right. I'm often tempted to study for the business. Very profitable I'm told and yet the money doesn't pull somehow. Still all this is irrelevant. The old man is dead and you'll have to notify the next of kin. Hateful job! I always shrink from it."

"I shall send for them," said Knollis. "You never know, especially after what you have told me about the daughter."

Dr. Whitelaw permitted himself a smile. "Good heavens, man, you aren't thinking of Gertrude Lomas as a potential suspect, are you? The old suspicious Knollis! Suspect everybody, including the corpse. Oh well, I'll get back to town and warn Devlin to expect a boarder at his mortuary. See you later."

Knollis saw the body taken aboard the craft and then drove back to town, pondering on the case as the black tar-macadamed road passed beneath his wheels. Death was a horrible business at the best, but he had to admit to a certain exhilaration at the prospect of the investigation which would have to be set in motion. He was satisfied that there was more in the case than met the eye and it would be a welcome break in his normally undisturbed routine. Housebreakings and bicycle-stealings were apt to get monotonous after a while, mainly because the guilty parties were always such fools and left too many traces behind them.

This was different. It would mean the taking apart of Lomas's life, considering the people and the elements connected with it, analysing and analysing, and then, when the analysis was as complete as it could possibly be, the still more fascinating business of piecing it together, bit by bit, until it was possible to read the riddle of his death from the finished picture. He was as sure that Lomas had met with foul play as he was of the rising of to-morrow's sun. Lomas had been murdered, disposed of, done to death, or call it what you will. There was practically no evidence of that as yet, but he felt it in his bones, and Knollis set great store on his intuitions.

He rang to Sir Wilfred Burrow's house as soon as he reached his office. "Recovered a stiff from the river at Willow Lock," he reported laconically. "Identification not positive, but believed to be one Ezekiah Lomas, of Des—"

He broke off as a pungent exclamation burst in his ear.

"Really did die?" he echoed. "Do you mean that you know something about it? All of it? Wait until you've put a pair of trousers on? Well, it would be advisable, sir."

He rang off, asking himself what blasted mess Bunny had created this time. If it wasn't one thing it was another, and somehow it always managed to concern the detective staff. Then he lifted the inter-office telephone and asked for two members of the mobile section. "Take a car each and bring Lawrence Lomas from Desborough, and Miss Gertrude Lomas from Fountains. Break the news gently and use your tact. Don't tell 'em too much, and keep your ears open. Bring them here. If I'm not in, take them to the mortuary to identify the old man, or otherwise, and then return 'em with all speed."

He went up to Sir Wilfred's office and occupied the waiting period by trying to decipher the scrawl on the memorandum pad. He gave it up as a bad job.

Sir Wilfred arrived ten minutes later, puffing and blowing from his exertions on the stairs.

"Two hellish flights," he grumbled. "We'll get a lift installed when the Watch Committee find time to do anything but criticise the department." He grinned feebly and became serious. "Lomas called on me this morning. See, I made a note of his visit!"

The Inspector gazed at the pad. "So that's what it is about! I've been trying to translate it into English for the last ten minutes."

"It's plain enough," the Chief Constable said irascibly. "Doesn't it say 'Re Lomas. Tell Knolis.' That's what I wrote, anyway."

"I spell my name with two L's," Knollis remarked.

"What the devil does it matter? I abbreviate. Always did. Saves time. Phew—I haven't got my wind yet! Here, get out of my chair, Knollis, there's a good fellow. My legs ache. Done eighteen holes to-day. Most damnable course. It was made for steeplechasers instead of golfers. And then those stairs—!"

When he was in possession he leaned back and rested his hands where his lap should have been. He regarded the memorandum pad reminiscently. "Yes, Lomas called on me this morning."

"I'm beginning to understand that," said the Inspector. "Reminds me of Lord Emsworth."

"Emsworth? Emsworth?" murmured the Chief Constable. "Can't say that I ever met him. Who was he?"

"He was related to the Empress of Blandings," replied Knollis with unsmiling lips.

"You don't say! Good lord! Fancy that! Where's his place? Anywhere that I know?"

"Out at Wodehouse Eaves," said Knollis. "Still, we can skip that for now."

"Yes, I suppose we can," mused Sir Wilfred. "Emsworth? The man escapes me. Anyway, Lomas called this morning, paid me a visit, you know!"

"If you feel like returning the call," said Knollis, "you'll find him on the cold slab in Devlin's kitchen. Whitelaw will be removing his works by now, so you'd better hurry if you'd like to meet him in one piece."

"Whitelaw can't do that without an autopsy order from the coroner!" Sir Wilfred exclaimed indignantly. "The devil he can!"

"I'm sorry," sighed Knollis. "I was too literal. Lomas is dead and cold."

"Poisoned," Sir Wilfred said in a flat matter-of-fact voice. "Poisoned, Knollis."

The Inspector glanced curiously at his chief.

"You must have misunderstood me when I 'phoned. He was dragged from the river at Willow Lock."

"I heard every word you said," Sir Wilfred replied in the placid manner of one who knows all the true facts. "I tell you that he was poisoned. He came to tell me all about it this morning. The poor chappie was very upset."

Knollis gaped, and then gulped. "Who was upset?"

"Lomas, of course! Good lord, Knollis man, I've told you four times that Lomas called on me this morning. Who the devil do you think I'm talking about? He was being poisoned. Been goin' on for weeks. He's had hysteria fits and heaven only knows what. Trouble was that I didn't believe him. Thought he was off his rocker, y'know . . ."

He plunged into a detailed account of the visit, concluding: "Thought it was neurasthenia, and now, good lord, it's all true. We've muffed it, Knollis! Muffed it!"

"I refuse to be dragged in," said the Inspector.

"It will recoil on the whole police department," complained Sir Wilfred.

Knollis stared through the window, out into the translucent summer's night, at the cupola of the Council House, around which the Corporation Pigeons, as they were known, sported and played during the daylight hours.

"You aren't listening to me, Knollis!" There was a volume of reproach in the complaint.

Knollis turned his head. "I was listening, Sir Wilfred. You rang a bell in the memory department. Will you please repeat Lomas's symptoms as he gave them to you?"

"He experienced an intense excitation of the nerves, and felt as if insects were walking about under his skin. Why do you ask?"

"Your telephone, please."

Knollis snatched it from under the Chief Constable's nose and asked the night staff in the Records and Library Department to send him the copy of *Forensic Medicine and Toxicology*, by Mann and Brend. "To Sir Wilfred Burrows's office," he added.

"I don't like that row of esses at the end of my name," said Sir Wilfred. "It sounds like a beehive."

"It's good grammar, anyway," retorted Knollis. "Better than missing letters out of mine."

When the book arrived he consulted the index, found a page, and pushed the book across the table, his finger indicating a passage he wished Sir Wilfred to read.

"I thought I'd remembered it correctly," he said with great satisfaction.

Sir Wilfred read:

> A symptom of cocaine poisoning, known as Magnan's symptoms, is produced by disturbance of sensation: the patient complains of feeling as though grains of sand, or small round bodies, or in some instances worms, were under the skin. The will-power is lost; he becomes irritable and quarrelsome, and may learn to indulge in alcohol to excess.

The night-shrouded city was silent, but the silence in the office was almost tangible for the next few minutes. It was at last relieved by a long-drawn sigh. "Cocaine!"

"I'm told that he drank a deal of whisky both at The Ferryman and before he arrived there," said Knollis. Sir Wilfred dipped into the pages.

"Cocaine, it says here, is partly soluble in alcohol. Whisky is almost the same thing—or is it, these days?"

"Willow Lock, you will remember, is only a few yards from the inn."

"He could have fallen in while one of these bouts was in progress," the Chief Constable muttered.

"But then he wouldn't have been in a condition to shave himself, would he?"

Sir Wilfred's jaw dropped. "What did you say?"

"He was facially nude. Moustache, beard, and eyebrows had been shaved. But for papers which were found in his wallet he wouldn't have been recognised immediately."

"That's a queer complication! But why . . . ?"

The Inspector shrugged and turned again to the window.

"We can only speculate as yet," he said.

The Chief Constable strode across the room, his hands clasped behind his back. "It doesn't make sense, Knollis! It doesn't make sense."

"Murder cases never do at first," Knollis said gently. "What sense can be made of a man who is found in a river after being poisoned? On the face of it the whole thing is absurd." Then he smiled. "It will come right. It only needs patience, infinite patience. It is just a riddle set by one man, and what one man has devised another can unravel."

Sir Wilfred seemed to be eased by the assurance. "Quite, Knollis. We can do it between us, I'm sure."

Knollis bit back a cynical retort. "We'd better go down to the mortuary, sir. And I would like to suggest that nothing is said to Whitelaw with regard to the poison until he has made his preliminary report. He suspected that Lomas was doped, but no more."

Sir Wilfred thought the point over, and then nodded. "Yes, I think I understand that, Knollis. Leave him to say how Lomas came by his death, instead of preparing his mind for what he will find, eh? Yes, that is a sensible suggestion. I agree with you. After all, he may have met his death by drowning."

"He may," Knollis said dryly.

As they descended to the street the Chief Constable said: "Y'know, Knollis, I'll feel guilty to the end of my days about this. If only I'd paid more attention to Lomas's story we might have been able to save his life—and a lot of trouble for ourselves."

"I wouldn't let that worry you," Knollis said comfortingly. "If it does prove to be murder, and the murderer is as slick as most of his kind, then the odds are that we could have done no such thing. I have a feeling that it was too late even when Lomas called on you. His man was there, active. All we can do now is make sure of getting the blighter and handing him over to Teddy Jessop for the nine o'clock walk."

"We'll do that, Knollis. We'll do that, won't we?" the Chief Constable enthused.

Knollis shrugged his shoulders. "Depends on what Dr. Whitelaw has to tell us."

They found Dr. Whitelaw bending over the remains of Mr. Lomas as they entered the mortuary. He was wearing a white smock and rubber gloves. All his attention was concentrated on the naked corpse, and he did not notice the newcomers for some seconds. At his side stood a weedy little man with popping eyes. He was collarless and had a long stringy neck and a huge Adam's apple that projected like the stump of a sawn-off bough.

Sir Wilfred herrumphed, and the doctor looked round and grimaced. It was a close night, and the sweat stood on his forehead. He withdrew a thermometer from under the body and consulted it. "Rotten night for this work. It confuses the issue. We'll have him in the ice-chamber when I've done, and the sooner the coroner is informed the better. An autopsy will be necessary. You've realised that, I dare say?"

Sir Wilfred simulated surprise. "Autopsy? Why so? Plain case of suicide, isn't it? He was found in the river."

"So are fish, and old boots, and tin cans," Dr. Whitelaw replied caustically, "but that hardly proves that they threw themselves in."

"Well, no," the Chief Constable admitted reluctantly. The doctor became grave and his manner brooked no contradiction. "He was dead when placed in the water. I am sure of that, but an examination of his lung tissue will prove it beyond doubt. That being the case, you have three possibilities to consider: murder; natural death with attempt to disguise same; or suicide with a similar attempt to conceal the true cause of death. And you can add, in any case, an attempt to delay identification."

"What, in your opinion, was the true cause of death?" asked Sir Wilfred. His eyes were fixed upon the body and seemed incapable of moving from it. Knollis stood by, silent, a cold smile upon his lips.

"Poisoning," said the doctor in a decisive tone.

"And the poison?"

"Cocaine."

The doctor shot a keen glance at the two men. "You've dissembled long enough. You know more than you have said. Out with it."

Sir Wilfred looked helplessly at Knollis as if for advice. "Well, Knollis?"

"Better tell him now, sir. It's your story."

The Chief Constable recounted the events of the morning once more, winding up with an apologetic: "Never thought there was anything in it, y'see, Whitelaw. Most damnably stupid of me. And now he's . . . dead!" His eyes wandered back to the greyish-white form on the slab and the little man who was fussing round it; there didn't seem to be much difference between them somehow.

The doctor did not heed his lame explanation. He was staring at the remains of Mr. Lomas. "Cocaine bugs!" he commented. "Well, I can't say that I'm surprised, although I certainly didn't think he'd reached that stage—not from a superficial examination like this. He must have taken a great deal on board, and he must have been taking it a deuce of a time."

He turned to Knollis, wagging the thermometer as he made his point. "You'll be able to trace the source of supply, and then you'll know whether the stuff was self-administered or otherwise. Judging by the story he told Sir Wilfred it was not, but you never can tell. Cocaine addicts are queer fish, and they may run to a persecution mania. There are no set rules you can follow."

"I've been thinking, Whitelaw," Sir Wilfred remarked ponderously. It might have been a rare act by his manner. "I've been thinking," he repeated. "I take it that, if the deceased was insured for any great sum—of a small one for that matter—the policy would automatically become null and void if it was proved that he had taken narcotics, knowing that they were undermining his health and would eventually cause death?"

"What a peculiar question for you to ask," the doctor said with surprise. "You know the facts as well as Knollis or I. It would be tantamount to suicide."

"And anybody interested in his will might be expected to stage an accidental death in the hope of forestalling the otherwise inevitable cancellation of the policy?"

"That is quite possible," Dr. Whitelaw agreed. "At the same time you must take into account the possibility that he was overcome by the drug. In parenthesis I should add that his organs would still betray the amount of cocaine he had been in the habit of consuming. Still, he may—and I do say may—he may have died on the bank and slipped into the water after death. I'll be better able to discuss that when I have all the pathological details to hand."

Knollis was taking no part in the discussion, being occupied with an examination of the body. "The shaving was a darned rough job," he commented.

The doctor beckoned to Devlin, the mortuary attendant.

"You've shaved a good many corpses in your time?"

The little man's Adam's apple went up and down like a yo-yo as he replied, with a good many gulps: "Literary 'undreds, sir."

"And you have examined this body?" the doctor asked in the manner of an examining counsel.

"I 'ave, sir," Devlin replied in an emotional voice.

"Then kindly tell the Chief Constable and Inspector Knollis whether, in your considered opinion, Mr. Lomas was alive or dead when shaved, and whether, also in your opinion, he was standing up, lying down, or sitting at the time."

Devlin gulped, moistened his lips with a pointed tongue, and blinked through watering eyes. He wiped his mouth with the back of his hand and cleared his throat as if he was about to recite sentimental verse.

"Gen'lemen, in my considered opinion 'e was shaved arter death, and while lying down in a recumbent position," he averred emphatically.

Knollis suddenly became aware that Devlin had large protruding ears and that they waggled as he talked. He restrained an impulse to giggle.

"Anything else, Devlin?" asked the doctor.

"He was shaved dry, sirs. I c'n tell that by the way the 'air lies, and the patches what has been missed or gone over. It takes a practised 'and to shave a stiff and this—this is a rotten job of work and I don't care who done it!"

"Well, there you are," said Dr. Whitelaw, "and you may regard Devlin as an expert witness. His evidence completely demolishes the theory that Lomas slipped into the water after death without assistance, and as a result of his body complying with the laws of gravity. As I see it at the moment, Lomas was poisoned, shaved after death, and placed in the river. He is full of whisky and the post-mortem examination will undoubtedly prove that cocaine was in the alcohol. The murderer worked on him with a lavish hand, one so lavish that it may eventually prove to be his undoing."

"He may have got it at The Ferryman," Sir Wilfred murmured uncertainly. "Er—Whitelaw! You will be able to tell, within fine limits, the amount of stuff absorbed?"

"I shall remove his stomach and certain other organs and send them to the Home Office laboratory," replied the doctor. "Their report will satisfy your question."

Knollis produced his notebook and pen.

"How long has he been dead?"

The doctor hesitated before replying.

"Well, we are not so dogmatic on that point as we used to be. It was nearly half-past eleven when I first saw him. He had been dead more than an hour, but not longer than an hour and a half."

"So that he was dead before half-past ten, but no earlier than ten o'clock? That right?"

"Between ten and half-past? Yes, I'll stand by that."

"I'd like to ask a further question," said the Inspector. "How often do you find it necessary to prescribe cocaine?"

"Seldom, Knollis. I cannot remember doing so for over eighteen months. Why do you ask?"

"According to the story Lomas told Sir Wilfred, his best friend was John Steadfall, the Desborough Road chemist."

The doctor raised his eyebrows. "You are aware that cocaine is unobtainable from a chemist other than on a doctor's prescription?" he asked tartly.

"Yes, I know that," said Knollis, "just as I know that his books will show the amounts received from the wholesale suppliers and the amounts used in the prescriptions. I'm wondering if there can be ways and means of circumventing the official regulations."

"Pharmacists are men of upright character, Knollis," the doctor retorted.

"There are black sheep in the whitest flock," Knollis commented lightly.

"You can rely on the integrity of the profession! "Dr. Whitelaw stripped the gloves from his hands and threw them down, his annoyance showing clearly on his tight-pressed lips.

"I have to suspect everybody," said Knollis. The thrust at his suspicions had not disturbed him.

The doctor prepared to leave.

"There are two facts about the cadaver that may interest you, Knollis. His upper molars and bicuspids have recently been extracted, probably one at a sitting—which indicates nervousness on the part of the patient or a weak heart. He has, as you can see for yourself, an appendix scar. There is a possibility that cocaine may have been prescribed after his removal from hospital. Again, he may have acquired a taste for the stuff while in hospital, if, that is, it was found necessary to give hypodermics. There are no visible signs of hypodermics being given, but there is an odd chance that microscopic examination of skin sections may reveal them. Mind you, I'm not at all hopeful. I'm merely supplying you with the facts which my medical knowledge enables me to give. One other point! Even if he had hypodermics in the past the poison that finished him was taken by mouth and not subcutaneously. That, I think, is all, and I will bid you good morning—you very suspicious fellow!"

The Inspector once more cast a keen eye over the body and then asked Devlin for the contents of the dead man's pockets.

The mortuary attendant led them to a miniature office at the rear of the building. Here a sergeant was cataloguing the items taken from Lomas's clothes. "What have you, Bates?" asked Knollis.

Bates was his right-hand man, a stolid and unimaginative aide who knew how to obey orders without question, a conscientious and literal-minded sergeant of the old school.

"Brown leather wallet, bunch of seven keys, some silver and coppers—detailed in the official list, pipe, pouch, box of matches, wireless licence, tobacco licence, letters, two bills, and a receipt."

"Nothing exciting, eh? Well, I'll have the keys. We shall be taking a look round the Desborough Road premises before breakfast. I'll need you, so return to headquarters when you are through with this job, and bring the collection with you."

He and Sir Wilfred walked out to the street. The north-eastern sky was aglow with the pearly light of the false dawn. The streets were those of a long-deserted city. There was no sound but the soft swish of hose-fed water as the city cleaners worked in a nearby court.

They stood by Sir Wilfred's car for a time, each concerned with his own thoughts.

"Murder is damnable," the Chief Constable said at last.

"You are satisfied that it is murder?"

"I can see no alternative, Knollis."

"And the motive?"

"Ah yes, the motive! We must have a motive. Why was Lomas poisoned? That's the question, eh? He said I should be asking myself that."

"It's a pity he had no suspicions beyond the one that led him to believe that he was being done to death."

"I think he had," the Chief-Constable said surprisingly. "He was almost vindictive when he told me that he had come in order to make sure that the murderer received his due reward. Looking back to the interview I see Lomas in an entirely different light. I wish you had been present, Knollis. Ah well, you weren't, and we are going to be busy. I'll see the man's lawyer and bank manager for you in the morning, while you follow up Lomas's movements. You are in charge, nevertheless, and I put myself at your disposal."

"I shall give Dawes and Slater that assignment," said Knollis. "There are certain other important matters that will demand my attention."

Sir Wilfred sighed. "I know! I know!"

They drove back to headquarters, there to be told that Gertrude and Lawrence Lomas had been taken to the mortuary.

"Must have taken the Brownlow Avenue route," said Knollis. "And that gives us time for a cup of tea, for which I'm more than ready."

"And me," the Chief Constable said heavily. It was evident that he was greatly affected by the tragedy.

CHAPTER II
THE AFFAIRS OF MR. LOMAS

When a messenger informed Knollis that the Lomases had returned from the mortuary and were about to be shown into his office, he gave orders for them to be detained for a few minutes. "I'll go down and see them for myself. Then we'll have them in one at a time."

"You're surely not suspecting them, Knollis?" the Chief Constable asked with amazement.

Knollis smiled, but only with his lips.

"And why not? Patricide is not such an uncommon crime, and you don't solve murder cases by trusting everybody."

"I know," said Sir Wilfred, "but after all . . ."

"One at a time, if I'm conducting the investigation!"

"All right! All right! Have it your own way!" agreed Sir Wilfred. "You can hardly suspect me because I was in bed at the time."

Knollis halted at the door, smiling grimly.

"So you may have been, but the man had confided in you and you were in possession of vital information which you failed to pass on to my department. Now does that make you an accessory after the fact? It is a moot point."

He left the Chief Constable gaping and went down to the waiting-room.

Gertrude Lomas, a spinster of thirty-nine, was sitting in a corner, sobbing quietly into a square of lace, while her brother looked on with true masculine helplessness. She was dressed in dove-grey, with a hat of the same colour that was rendered startling by the addition of a scarlet humming bird with glassy eyes. She was slim, and well-figured. Knollis decided that in other circumstances she was likely to attract the attentions of men of her own age, or would have been, but for the elusive air of frumpishness that surrounded her. At the moment she was a despairing, overwhelmed woman with little or no thought for her appearance.

Lawrence Lomas was about four years her junior. He was clear-eyed and fresh-complexioned. His jaw was tight, but Knollis, from long experience, recognised signs of moral weakness in the curve of the chin and the sloping angle of the jaw. There was no physical deterioration visible however, and as he rose to meet the Inspector his height became apparent, as did the breadth of his shoulders. It was extremely likely that he had been athletic in his younger days.

"This—this is a shocking affair, Inspector," he muttered.

"Terrible," said Knollis gravely. "I understand that you have seen the deceased. Do you identify him as your father?"

At this stage of the investigation he could not afford to be other than strictly formal in his manner.

"Yes, he is my father. Gertrude and I are agreed on that in spite of the—the unusual appearance of his face. Inspector, there are several things we should like to ask. Why, for instance, was he—"

Knollis jerked his head doorwards.

"Perhaps we could leave Miss Lomas for a while?"

Lawrence Lomas glanced at his sister, hesitated for a second, and then reluctantly followed the Inspector.

"It would scarcely be kind to discuss the affair in her hearing," Knollis said in explanation. "I think we will join Sir Wilfred Burrows in his office."

After introducing the two men he settled to the questioning of the dead man's son.

"Can you suggest any reason why your father should have died in this way?"

"The whole thing is a mystery to me," Lawrence Lomas said earnestly. "His affairs, as far as I know, were in perfect order and he should have had no business worries. In fact there was every reason to believe that he was looking forward to a happy retirement. I am completely puzzled. Why, for instance, did he shave? And why—"

"When was the last occasion on which you saw your father alive?" asked Knollis. He made a pretence of looking at his notes, while in reality he was covertly watching Lomas.

"See now, it would be last Wednesday morning. I was in town on business and so I called at the shop. He was all right then, of course—!"

"He appeared to be in good health and good spirits?"

"Oh quite!" replied Lomas. "He was laughing and joking and seemed as fit and energetic as a man many years younger. I was amazed at his vitality."

"How often did you see him?"

"Oh, about once a month as a general rule—until lately. He has been coming over to my surgery once a week. His teeth badly needed attention, and I was treating him. He was inclined to be afraid of pain, like so many people who have had little or no experience of it. Even the thought of it would make him wince, and so the treatment was perforce spread over a long time."

"Your father made a will?" Knollis murmured.

"A will? Yes, he did that. He consulted me about it some three months ago. He told me that the one then in existence was made before my mother died, and he thought he would ask his solicitors to draft a new one."

"His solicitors are . . . ?"

"Morgan and Caine. My father and Caine have been friendly for years. He is of my father's age, you know, and they were schoolboy friends."

"Who are the beneficiaries?"

Lawrence Lomas hesitated. "Well," he said uncertainly, "I can't say with exactitude, because I don't know whether the new will was actually completed and signed. If it wasn't, and the old one is valid, then Gertrude—my sister—and I share the estate equally. On the other hand, if the new will is in existence, everything goes to my sister without a single reservation."

Knollis looked up. Sir Wilfred gave vent to a significant if tactless "Ah!"

Lawrence Lomas turned on him with a twisted smile. "Your surmise is inaccurate, Sir Wilfred. It was I who suggested that my father should cut me out completely and leave everything to Gertrude."

Sir Wilfred gaped. "But why on earth that?" Lawrence Lomas stared fixedly at the desk calendar as he replied.

"My sister occupies a rather lowly position as companion to Mrs. Geoffrey Gregory. I, on the other hand, have a fairly prosperous practice in Desborough. Now I made the suggestion to my father for several reasons. Firstly, it is not becoming that my sister should be in such a humiliating position. It—it—"

"I think we understand," Knollis interrupted. "It reflects on you. Suppose you continue with the other reasons."

Lawrence Lomas flushed under the implied snub and went on: "My father was a queer man, with queer ideas. He spent a lot of money on my education and made me work like the very devil to become something of which he could be proud. You understand?"

Knollis nodded. He did understand, understand how the attitude had been transferred from father to son.

"He was out for reflected glory, something to make up for his own comparative lack of success. He refused to do the same by my sister, saying that she would doubtless marry just when her education was complete and all the money spent on her would be wasted! Well, she never did marry. There was a love affair that crashed and she lost her interest in men. In any case, the old man was wrong, because she would have made an ideal bluestocking. She was always the brains of the family. She helped me a great deal."

"So you suggested to your father that it was time he compensated her for his short-sighted policy of past years?"

"I knew that he could not have many more years to live, and that by the time he died Gertrude would be getting past the age when she could efficiently carry out her duties as a companion or governess. With my father's money as a dowry she could probably find herself a husband, or, alternatively, settle down in some quiet back-water, living the life of a retired gentlewoman. You see," Lawrence Lomas added, "I thought it out this way. We could have left things as they were, but my father will not have a great lot to leave, and a half-share would not have been enough for Gertrude's needs, and while I could have assisted her from my own share it would have tasted like charity to her, and I did wish to avoid that if at all possible. What was more, by persuading my father to leave her everything I could—well, I could rid myself of a mental discomfort that has afflicted me ever since my father put his foot down on her ambitions years ago. I always had the feeling that I had succeeded at her expense."

"This is all very frank," Sir Wilfred remarked in a disapproving tone.

"It is better for you to hear the frank truth from me than a garbled version from other sources," Lawrence Lomas replied defiantly.

"How did your father receive the suggestion?" asked Knollis. He was anxious to avoid trouble at this stage.

"Well, I may be wrong, Inspector," said Lomas, "but I do think that some such idea had been running through his mind and that he was only afraid of me opposing it. I saw the relief in his eyes when I made the first tentative suggestion. He pretended to quibble, but I knew him, and played up to him. He was letting himself down easily by pretending to allow me to persuade him. As we were both working to the same end I was fully prepared to play his game and let him save his face. To the best of my knowledge and belief he went to see Caine some days later. He said he would do so, anyway."

"What was the extent of his estate?" Sir Wilfred asked.

"I'm not at all sure," Lawrence Lomas frowned. "He was a thrifty man up to the time of my mother's death, and he should have been worth two or three thousand then. He had a wild period after that, and it lasted for some time. For some months he drank heavily and neglected the business. Then he appeared to come to his senses and take a fresh hold on life. Still, as far as the financial matters are concerned his solicitors are the best people to approach."

"Has he ever displayed suicidal tendencies previous to this week?"

"My father? Commit suicide? Good lord, Inspector, no! I've never heard him mention the subject." Lawrence Lomas paused and stared at Knollis. "Previous to this week, you say! Did he—"

"He saw Sir Wilfred early yesterday morning."

"Told me that at times suicide seemed the most attractive prospect on earth," Sir Wilfred supplied.

Knollis, watching his man closely, felt certain that a flash of relief showed in his eyes.

"Good lord! My father!" he muttered.

"Did he ever indulge in pernicious habits?"

"Pernicious habits? Such as, Inspector?"

"Well, narcotics, drugs."

"Good heavens, no! He liked a drink of beer or whisky, but he was no toper—apart from the short period I have mentioned. As for drugs, well, the whole suggestion is preposterous. What makes you ask?"

Knollis lifted his shoulders. "Just a routine question. You need attach no importance to it."

He rang a bell for a messenger. "Please show Mr. Lomas to the waiting-room."

He jerked his thumb in the direction of the side stairs. To Lomas he said: "We are grateful for your assistance. It is unfortunate that we have to bother you at such a time, and I can assure you that we shall get in touch with you just as soon as any definite information reaches us." As soon as the door closed the Inspector snatched the inter-office telephone. "Bring Miss Lomas up the main stairs. I don't want her to meet her brother."

"You should get results," the Chief Constable commented. "You are the most suspicious man I've ever met. Er—by the way, Knollis! This Emsworth fellow you mentioned. Would he be kin to the Dorset Emsworths? I'm sure I've either met the fellow or heard something about him."

"Related to the Blandings," Knollis replied, and repressed an inclination to chuckle.

Sir Wilfred shook his head. "Damned if I can get it. It keeps coming and going, y'know. Oh well, I shall remember when this case is over and my mind is free again. How are we doing up to now?"

"Lawrence Lomas is a bad liar," said Knollis. "He first tells us that his father's money should have made his sister independent for life, and in the next breath says he has no idea how much he was worth. He can't have it both ways, now can he?"

Sir Wilfred blinked. "I say! So he did! No, he can't. We'll get him, Knollis! We'll get him—!"

"It doesn't necessarily follow that he killed his father," Knollis pointed out drily. "It just means that all along the line he is interested in the money and doesn't want us to know it. In fact, he may be trying to conceal the truth from himself. Further to the point, he is a rotten snob. It's his own pride he is thinking about and not his sister's welfare. And," he added slowly, "there may be another reason for his self-sacrificing action. We'll see about that as we go." They rose as Gertrude Lomas was shown in.

She looked round with surprised eyes. "I thought my brother was still here—!"

Knollis also contrived to look surprised.

"You haven't passed him? Then they must have shown him down the other flight of stairs. Anyway, he will be waiting below. Please take a seat, Miss Lomas." Her eyes were dry now, but her pallor that of death itself. Knollis decided to cut the interview as short as possible.

"You will realise," he said, "that there are certain questions we must ask you even at a time like this?" She nodded vaguely, as if not understanding. "Had you seen your father during the past week?"

"A fortnight ago," she replied jerkily. "I came into town with Mrs. Gregory, and she gave me leave to visit him."

"He was in good health?"

She shook her head. "No, Inspector, he was depressed. I was worried about him. He told me that he had been suffering from bouts of depression of late, and was wondering whether to see a doctor. He brightened considerably before I left and so I put his condition down to living by himself in such an old house. It is very dark, and dismal."

"Yes, that is quite possible," said Knollis. "You will realise that, considering the circumstances surrounding his death, we have to allow for the possibility of causes other than accidental ones?"

Again she nodded vaguely.

"Lawrence said something about that, Inspector, but he wouldn't do that, I'm sure—!"

Knollis hesitated and then took the plunge.

"I'm sorry to have to break this news to you. There are grounds for the belief that he was murdered. All the available evidence points to such a possibility."

Gertrude Lomas caught at the arms of her chair as she leaned forward with incredulity written on her pale features.

"Murdered! My father! Surely—surely there must be some mistake!"

"Can you think of any person possessing a motive for the killing of your father, Miss Lomas?"

She sank back in the chair. "He was an old man, Inspector Knollis! He had no enemies! I—I cannot understand—!"

"To whom will his money go?" asked Knollis. He hated the necessity that compelled such questions, but forced himself to continue in the interests of justice. "Perhaps you can tell us whether he made a will?"

"Lawrence and I were to share equally," she replied dully. "He made a will long before mother died. All his effects were to be hers—"

She broke off.

"No, that is not quite right. Mother, you see, was inclined to let money slip through her fingers. Father was too careful. I don't understand these things properly, but I believe that my mother was to have the interest on his money and the profits from the business as long as she lived, and the business and the capital in the bank—is that right?—were to remain in trust for Lawrence and myself. We both regarded it as an unsatisfactory arrangement, and if mother had outlived him we should have tried to make matters easier for her. I'm afraid that neither Lawrence nor—well, mother was so gentle with us!"

"And you three hung together to compensate each other for your father's harshness?" suggested Sir Wilfred.

Gertrude Lomas seemed to realise that she had been guilty of disloyalty to her father. She tried to retrieve the situation as best she could.

"He was not really harsh," she said, "but mother was so generous that I suppose he seemed harsh to our childish minds. We never wanted for essentials, but he would not spend money on luxuries or the little things that could have made life brighter."

"I see," the Chief Constable replied ambiguously.

"I wonder, Miss Lomas," said Knollis. "Did your father ever hint at a second marriage? Was there another woman in his life after your mother's death?"

"Good gracious, no!" Gertrude Lomas exclaimed in a shocked voice. "He would never have dreamt of such a thing. And if he had, then Lawrence and I would have put a stop to it. But father really did cherish my mother's memory."

Knollis disbelieved her, and rose as a sign that the interview was at an end.

"I thank you for your assistance, Miss Lomas, but we must not detain you longer. You are in need of a rest after this shock. You may rest assured that we shall do everything in our power to clear up the riddle of his death."

She flashed him a half-fearful glance, thanked him, and left the room to rejoin her brother.

"Well," said Sir Wilfred, "that was a queer interview!"

Knollis grimaced. "It's too early to say anything yet. We've barely scratched the surface of the case. But we can say that Lawrence is a liar and a snob, and that Gertrude possesses remarkable powers of recovery! We—"

He broke off as Lawrence Lomas burst into the room and stood panting before the desk.

"You didn't tell me that my father was murdered," he exclaimed hotly. "You deliberately led me away from my sister in order, as you put it, to spare her feelings, and then you get her in here and reduce her to a state of collapse by telling her that my father was murdered. Don't you think that I was the one to be told that?"

Knollis raised mild eyes to his accuser.

"I thought you had realised the truth, Mr. Lomas. After all, you are a thinking man, and when you consider the circumstances surrounding the finding of the body it is rather obvious, isn't it?"

Lawrence Lomas's lip quavered. He lowered his eyes.

"I—I suppose it is," he stammered. "Murdered!"

He suddenly turned and ran from the room.

"A peculiar man, Knollis!" said Sir Wilfred placidly. "Very much upset!"

"Or afraid."

"H'm? Afraid? Of what, might I ask?"

"Oh, murder," said Knollis. He smiled enigmatically.

Sir Wilfred grunted, and drew golf-balls on the blotting pad. After a period of meditation he asked Knollis what were his immediate intentions.

"The examination of Lomas's premises. I'm putting Dawes and Slater to trace his movements. They can hardly start before nine o'clock, but I can do a lot of useful work before then. I shall take Bates."

"Then I'll return home for a few hours," said the Chief Constable. "I'll see Morgan and Caine in the morning, and perhaps the bank manager as well. Give me a ring if anything important turns up, please." The Inspector went down to his own office, where he was joined by Sergeant Bates, a tubby fellow with ginger hair and a short-clipped moustache.

Bates grinned affably. "Where is it, Inspector? The Desborough Road?"

"You've guessed it, Bates. Get a car round and collect my murder bag. We could do with some tinned sleep, but as our scientists have not yet succeeded in producing that miracle we'll prop our eyes open while we work." The Inspector then sent for Dawes and Slater and issued his instructions. "Get moving by nine o'clock. We know by what Lomas told Bunny that he had a certain number of calling places. We can now add The Ferryman. Start from there and work backwards."

He dismissed them on these meagre instructions and went out to join Bates.

Lomas's house and shop were half a mile from the city centre, standing cheek by jowl on the long straight road that led from Burnham to Desborough, a borough and market town. They were remnants of an older Burnham, shabby in appearance, like two bemittened old ladies of reduced means, and like two old ladies of another age they stood hand in hand, bewildered by the evidence of modernity about them and yet determined to ignore their surroundings for the sake of the traditions they held dear.

The shop was double-fronted and had quaint bow windows which were glazed with small panes of green-hued bottle glass. There were three stone steps leading up to the shop door, each hollowed by the countless feet that had tramped up and down during the decades that Mr. Lomas and his predecessors had done business in the premises. The panelled walnut door was hinged in a crumbling stone arch, from which hung a decrepit and ancient bell-pull.

The Inspector pushed the key in the lock and turned it, then stood in the doorway for a moment as the door creaked backwards into the shop. The dim morning light filtered reluctantly through the tiny panes and gave the shop a strange quality of weirdness. At any second Knollis was prepared to see the thin grey ghost of Mr. Lomas appear behind the counter, to fold a magazine with meticulous care, ring a coin on the modern till, and pass the change across the scratched mahogany counter.

The Inspector shook the fancy away and strode into the shop. He lifted the hinged section of the counter and walked on. Then he came to a sudden halt, swearing vividly and standing on one leg to hold his shin in both hands.

"Run into something?" Bates enquired naively.

"No, you ass. I'm playing hop-scotch!" Knollis barked. In an instant he apologised for his show of temper, explaining: "I fell over that blasted box."

Bates turned the rays of his torch on the offending case. It was painted black, and was padlocked, and had white letters stencilled on its lid.

"It says it is the Postal Library, Inspector."

"Then I wish the old man had posted it before he died," Knollis grunted. "It's fetched blood—just."

"I'll lead the way, having a torch," said Bates.

Beyond the shop was a storeroom, heavy with the smell of paper, tobacco, and damp. There was a door on their right. Knollis pushed it open and found a switch. As he pressed it down an aged lamp, long past its span of usefulness, cast a reddish glow round the room, a mere apology for light.

"What a hole," Bates commented.

Knollis crossed to the sole window, which overlooked the main road, and plucked the nigger-brown curtains aside. A moth fluttered away in alarm.

The room was living-room and sitting-room combined, and was furnished in a style reminiscent of the earlier days of the century. In one corner stood a solemnly-ticking grandfather clock, its case dull and dirty. On the hearth lay a rough-cut cloth rug from which the dust rose as they walked over it. There were horse-hair padded elbow chairs on either side of the hearth, black-upholstered, each decorated with a flamboyant antimacassar. A heavy plush cloth of the colour of deep red plums covered the table. The legs of the table were stockinged.

In the recess formed by the chimney breast and the inner wall of the room hung a three-cornered cupboard, its inlaid door smeary with finger-marks. Under the window was an oak bureau, and on it rested a multitude of objects; a begrimed aspidistra pitifully lacking water, a glass jar half full of Turkish Delight, two pipes and a tobacco jar, a tattered dictionary, a dusty goldfish bowl filled with odds and ends, and a perpetual calendar.

Over the slate mantel hung an oil-coloured photo-graphic enlargement of a young woman. She was wearing a high-necked striped blouse and a straw hat with a low crown and wide brim.

"His wife as a girl, eh?" said Bates, following Knollis's glance. He regarded it sentimentally.

"She was a pretty kid, anyway," the Inspector remarked.

He lowered the flap of the bureau and groaned on seeing the chaos within. The pigeon-holes were crammed with an assortment of bills, statements, advertising leaflets, price-lists, publishers' and wholesalers' catalogues, and business letters. There was not the faintest sign of order or system.

The Inspector was a tidy man by nature and the mess made him wince. He was also conscientious and so he drew up the chair and settled to his task. The conglomeration was eventually resolved into heaps of classified matter, each of which he tackled in turn, and as he finished them they were handed to Bates to be packed ready for transport to headquarters. At last he closed the flap. "Nothing there of any importance. Let's see what the drawers can do for us, Bates."

In the top drawer he found a batch of newspaper cuttings. The first one was from the *Burnham Courier* and described the funeral of Lomas's wife in fulsome detail. The others, culled equally from the *Courier* and the *Burnham and District Echo*, were In Memoriam notices. There were two for each of the years since her death, one from each paper, and were obviously inserted to coincide with the anniversary of her demise.

"'After a long illness nobly born,'" Knollis read aloud. "I hate that kind of thing. I suppose I should need a psychologist to explain why, but it always makes me feel sick, and I want to kick somebody. May be due to the traditional English dislike of emotional display. I never could stick sentimentality, and especially when it is platitudinous."

"I can't see why you object," said Bates stolidly. "A very nice thought that is. It isn't as bad as long words like sentimentality and platitudinous, anyway!" Knollis looked at his sergeant with astonishment. It was seldom that he expressed himself so forcibly.

"We'll skip the subject if you feel that way," he replied. "I wouldn't tread on your corns for a pension." He lifted the cutting, revealing the next in line. "Here's another. 'In memory of Jennifer Lomas, who passed from this life five years ago. In death she still survives.' H'm."

"That means he never forgot her," Bates informed him. "Even when dead she still lived—in his memory. See?"

Knollis turned pained eyes on his aide and emitted a deep sigh that might have meant anything.

"And yet another. 'In Memoriam. Jennifer Lomas. Died Ninth June, Nineteen Hundred and Thirty-Five. Safe at Last.' Quite a change!"

"Not so nice as the others," said Bates. "Except for that last bit about being safe at last. He meant that she was safe from outrageous fortune and all that. Shakespeare. But it's not so good. Too blatant, as they say. No feeling in it."

"They?" queried Knollis. "Who are they, Bates?" Bates sought for a word, but self-expression was not his strong point. "They," he repeated. "Them—people!"

"I know," Knollis murmured sorrowfully. "I was going to say that if you hadn't managed to get it in first. Do you know, Bates, I'll bet you like Madonna lilies!"

"And I do, Inspector. As nice a flower as comes. You'll not find as nice a bloom anywhere except in a . . ."

"Cemetery," suggested Knollis as he worked his way through the cuttings. "Believe in cremation, Bates?"

Bates was definite. "It isn't natural, Inspector. A second cousin of mine was cremated and we never felt satisfied, but there wasn't anything to be done about it. Now if he'd been buried, and then we'd have decided—What is it, Inspector?" he asked when he saw that Knollis was not listening.

Knollis's eyes had narrowed to slits and he stared at the wall with unseeing eyes. "What's the date, Bates? Ninth or tenth?"

"Ninth last night. Tenth this morning. Why, Inspector, you don't think . . . ?"

"You remarked that this notice was much colder in tone than the previous ones, Bates. You are a good detective. Now be a better detective and tell me why it should be colder. See, it is dated for June last year. And what does the year Thirty-Eight give us in the way of sentiments? 'In Memory of my dear wife,

Jennifer, who departed this life three years ago. In death she is not forgotten.' That is the same thought in a slightly different form. He stuck his initials on this one. Here—hold 'em, Bates!"

The Inspector pushed the notices into Bates' chubby hands and went through the remaining drawers with the rapidity and skill of a pickpocket. He eventually turned to the table with a pack of photographs.

"We'll try to spread these out in chronological order, or as near that as we can."

"What are you after?" Bates asked with gleaming eyes. "Unhappy married life, and one of the family avenging her?"

"I won't say that," the Inspector replied with a subdued chuckle, "but I do sense something queer in those notices. I've never yet handled a case without finding a woman in it somewhere."

"Jersey la femme," interrupted Bates.

"Your own experience has led you to the same conclusion. A woman's desires, or a woman's unhappiness, have stimulated more than one man to commit murder. Desire and necessity are the two mainsprings of action. And somehow I have a feeling that Lomas's wife will loom large in this case."

"But she's been dead five years," Bates protested. His detective instincts over-rode his sentimentality. "I suppose you are right. Even in petty burglaries we get a man stealing to buy pretty things for his wife."

"Or food," Knollis added.

"Or food," Bates agreed. "Always makes me feel sad in a way. I know he's acted against the law and all that, but his motive might have been lots worse, and it seems a shame to send a man down the line for it."

"There's no law against procuring pretty things for one's wife, Bates. It's the way you set about the job that causes the trouble. If we all did it we'd be in the position of people who make their living by taking in each other's washing. We'd all be stealing from everybody else—and the fittest would survive."

"Well, it isn't a case of that here, Inspector. She's been dead five years, and that's a long time."

Knollis grunted. "You mentioned Shakespeare a short time ago. Remember what he made Mark Antony say about dead men and the evil they have done?"

"Learned it off by heart at school," Bates replied with a swelling breast. "The rest of it goes—"

"Oh no, you don't!" protested Knollis. "I also learned it at school, mainly because I had to learn it. No, Bates, my point is that any evil Lomas might have done, or any good that his wife might have done, was also likely to live after them. And if, as Gertrude Lomas hinted, the old boy didn't treat Jennifer too well, then there may be someone who has been waiting a long time to square the account—and picked the anniversary of Jennifer's death for the appropriate date."

"Which is exactly what I suggested," Bates pointed out. "A member of the family avenging her!"

Knollis was silent for a moment, and then he nodded. "So you did, Bates. I apologise. We'll assume a vengeance murderer, and that is the worst type from our point of view. He takes pains, and covers his tracks, and often tries to incriminate an innocent party who yet has a solid motive for the killing. Give me a hot-blooded killer any day of the week and I'll have him in jug by nightfall. That, in my humble opinion, is the sole virtue of a passion killing."

He regarded the family photographs slowly.

"Look at 'em, Bates. In this wedding group she is radiantly happy. The next one must have been taken a few years later. She is smiling here, and I'll grant that readily, but as you stare at the photograph so the smile appears to fade. It is a superficial one produced for a purpose, and at the photographer's request. It isn't genuine."

He shook his head.

"She was a disillusioned woman, Bates, and I won't have it any different. Now in the third one she has a child on her knee. That will be Miss Gertrude. Jennifer Lomas has altered yet again. She is happy with the happiness of motherhood, and yet—"

"Now who's getting sentimental?" demanded Bates. Knollis bit his lip. "Look at the photographs, blast you. Surely you can see what I'm getting at, and I'm not going sentimental either. Far from it!"

Bates fixed his eyes on the photograph in a hypnotic stare, and then opened them to their fullest extent. "I don't pretend to be psychical, and yet I think there's something in your idea, Inspector. There is something sad behind her smile, like that Monna Liza picture. She sort of—I can't find words, but I know what you mean."

"We'll look at them again, after we've slept on the thought," said Knollis. "Come upstairs with me. Search every drawer, cupboard, and wardrobe. Look for the clothes of the late and lamented Jennifer Lomas. You take the rooms at the rear of the house, and I'll go front."

Twenty minutes later he met Bates on the landing. "Well?" he asked quietly.

"Not a scarf nor a hairpin," said the sergeant.

"Same here," said Knollis. "Since his wife's death he has cleared away every scrap of clothing that might serve to remind him of her. What do you make of that, you over-romantic merchant?"

"Obvious," Bates replied loftily. "He wanted to avoid painful memories. Every time he went into what was their bedroom he would have seen something that belonged to her, and it would take him back to their long years of married life and the years of courting before that—"

"And the days when they were both teething and used to hold bubble-blowing competitions in their prams?" snarled Knollis. "That was just my idea. Memories ever green. Floreat Boloney."

"You're making fun of me," Bates complained. Knollis was contrite on the instant. "I'm sorry, Bates, old chap. I'm tired for one thing, and for another I get so darned cold—emotionally, I mean—at this job. I'm slowly losing my faith in human nature and all the better values in life. I'm too much of a realist and I threw my rose-tinted glasses away years ago."

"A disillusioned married man, eh?" Bates murmured with malicious glee.

Knollis winced. "That served me right, Bates. No. I'm supremely happy at home, but it's this darned job. We only see the worst people, and it isn't good for one's soul."

They returned downstairs, and here Knollis turned his attention to the corner cupboard. It proved to be Lomas's medicine chest. There were two medicine bottles on the upper shelf, both bearing John Steadfall's labels. Behind them were cardboard packets of herbs; vervain, skullcap, marshmallow, and elecampane. On the lower shelf was a bottle of bicarbonate of soda, one of picric acid, three iodine ampules, two tins of health salts, a phial of camphorated oil, a tube of tannic acid jelly, and a graduated glass measure, with a clinical thermometer to complete the assortment.

"He must have had shelves fitted round the lining of his tummy," commented Bates as he stared at the assortment. "It's a wonder he didn't kill himself with kindness. He must have been an ailing man."

The Inspector opened the 'murder bag' and pulled a pair of rubber gloves over his hands.

"He was getting on in years, Bates. Old men take a delight in trying to stave off death. And that is hardly consistent when one remembers how little Lomas had to live for. He was a lonely man, and an ill man and his memories do not seem to have been too kind to him. Yet Lawrence, or was it Gertrude, said that he hung on with both hands. Well, that part fits in all right with what we see here."

Bates turned away. Noticing the jar of Turkish Delight he lifted the lid. He was about to slip a piece into his mouth when the Inspector's hand closed round his wrist.

"Bates!" he said reproachfully.

Bates stared his astonishment. "What's wrong? It's only a sweetmeat. There's half a jar full!"

"You must be tiring, Bates," said Knollis; "this isn't like you. If you are really needing something to eat, then dodge into the shop and help yourself from the counter, *from the stock supplied to the general public!*"

"Perhaps you're right; perhaps I'm tired, but I'm hanged if I see what you are getting at, Inspector."

"Listen, Bates," Knollis said gently. "If our Lomas kept this jar in the house for his own personal enjoyment it would suggest that he was fond of the stuff. You get that?"

"Er—yes. That's obvious!"

"Good. Now Turkish Delight is covered with fine sugar. Further to the point they call cocaine 'snow' for a reason that needs no explanation. Anybody who knew of his sweet tooth and who wished to get cocaine inside him unawares—See the idea?"

Bates wiped his brow with the back of a gloved hand. "Phew! I guess I'm not the man I was twelve hours ago," he muttered. "Must have been half-asleep." Knollis grinned patiently. "You'll be more like your old self when you've had a nap. I don't know when that will be. Probably Saturday—and it is now Tuesday morning. You've something to look forward to."

They made a thorough examination of the shop and later carried the contents of the bureau out to the car. They carefully packed the assortment from the medicine chest in cardboard boxes and these also were taken to the car. Then they drove back to headquarters.

CHAPTER III
THE PROGRESS OF MR. LOMAS

AT NINE O'CLOCK Knollis and Bates were again outside Lomas's shop. A girl of about sixteen years of age was looking at the door apprehensively. At her feet were the morning papers, in bundles which were opened, and from which she had apparently been supplying the regular customers.

"You work for Mr. Lomas?" Knollis asked as he strolled from the car.

"Yes, but I can't get in. I'm wondering if he is ill. The shop should be open at seven o'clock."

Knollis produced the keys and unlocked the door. The girl stared in bewilderment.

"You haven't heard about Mr. Lomas?" said Knollis as he led the way into the shop.

She caught up with him swiftly. "Nothing has happened to him, sir?"

Knollis inclined his head. "I am Inspector Knollis of the city police, and I'm afraid I have bad news, my dear. Your employer is dead."

He slid an arm under her shoulders just in time and carried her to the sitting-room. He lowered her into a chair while Bates hurried for water. Later, when she was somewhat recovered, Knollis questioned her tactfully "Can you remember the time when you last saw Mr. Lomas?" he began.

"It was about five minutes to six," she replied weakly. "The gentleman called for him, and they went out together."

"Did he come back?"

"No, sir. He hadn't come back when I left. I usually go home at six o'clock, but Mr. Lomas asked me to stay and look after the shop. He said I was to bring the paper racks in and lock up if he was not back by seven. And I knew something had gone wrong when he didn't come."

"He went away with a man, you say?"

"Yes."

"Did you notice which way they went? Towards the city, or towards Desborough?"

"Towards the city," she said. "What—what has happened to him, sir?"

"He was found in the river at Willow Lock," Knollis said gently. "He died between ten o'clock and half-past. Now about this man. You've seen him before?"

"Oh yes, but I don't know who he is. He is tall, and dark. I think he was going to buy the business. Mr. Lomas didn't—I mean, was it an accident, sir?"

"I'm afraid not," Knollis replied. "That is why I am asking you all these questions. How long have you been working for him?"

"Just over two years, sir. I came straight from school." She dabbed at her eyes with a damp handkerchief. Knollis waited a moment, and then continued: "Did you do any work in the house?"

"I used to dust the room sometimes, usually at tea-times when the shop was slack."

"Mrs. Lomas died about five years ago, I believe," said Knollis. "Did he mention her very often?"

She shook her head. "He didn't like talking about her. It upset him. He used to call her 'poor Jennifer' when he did mention her."

"The shop was closed on the usual half-holiday every week, I suppose? Or did he keep it open?"

"Oh no. He used to close it dead on one o'clock every Thursday. He was very strict about that."

"Have you any idea what he did on these half-day holidays? Did he go out, or stay at home reading and pottering about?"

She could not answer that question, having no knowledge of Mr. Lomas's private life. Knollis resumed his inquiry from a fresh angle.

"There was a jar of Turkish Delight on the bureau. Was Mr. Lomas very fond of sweets?"

"He was until his teeth began to trouble him," the girl answered. "He was upset about it, because he used to be so proud of the fact that in spite of his age he had nearly a full set of teeth in his head, and perfect eyesight. At one time he was dipping into the sweet bottles all day long, but when he had been to have his teeth seen to he told me to remind him if I saw him making for them. He had got into a habit, he said, and didn't realise what he was doing until the sweetness got into his gums."

"Very interesting," commented Knollis. "How long has that jar been in this room?"

"Why, it was last Christmas. I remember him bringing it. He said it was part of his festivities."

"It was about half-full when we took it away," said the Inspector. "Can you give me any idea—no, let me put it in another way. Can you say whether Mr. Lomas had dipped into the jar during the last three weeks?" This was another question she could not answer with certainty, but she thought that he had sampled the Turkish Delight more than once because on several occasions he had come into the shop with what looked like the white sugar coating on his beard and moustache.

"You knew that he was suffering from nervous trouble?"

"Oh yes," she replied. "I called at Mr. Steadfall's shop twice for his medicine. Mr. Lomas used to slap his arms and legs as if they were hurting him. He said it was like pins and needles, only worse."

"Who was extracting his teeth? Can you tell me that?"

"I think it was his son at Desborough."

"It is possible that he went there on Thursdays after closing the shop?" Knollis suggested.

"I don't know for sure, but I think he went over in the evenings. I leave at six and I sometimes go into town to look round the shops, and on my way back I've seen him standing against the bus stop as if he was waiting for the Desborough bus. Besides, twice when I got here in a morning he was complaining about the pain in his face."

Knollis decided that he had asked enough for one sitting. He told her to keep the shop open for the time being. If the man with whom Mr. Lomas had departed on the previous evening was to call again she was to keep him talking as long as she could.

"We are getting somewhere," he said to Bates as they drove away. "We know that Lomas left the shop with his companion, and we have a good idea that the fellow was interested in the purchase of the business. It is further known that, over a period of years, Lomas has contracted a set of habits. When he needed relaxation or a drink he went to the Golden Angel or the Commerce Club. Now when men discuss business they like to do it over a drink, providing that neither are abstainers, and so it seems logical to assume that Lomas took his companion to one of his usual haunts. We'll start the trail at the Angel. While I park the car down the side-street, Bates, you hop into the kiosk and tell Franks to make observation outside Lomas's shop. If a tall man goes in and is in for some time, then he is to tail him to his home and then report."

Hotels, as such, have an atmosphere which is peculiar to them, and each individual hotel has an atmosphere that is distinctly its own. That of the Golden Angel was calculated to appeal to the tired business man who desired quietude and non-argumentative conversation—as far as the public rooms were concerned. What went on in the private rooms was nobody's business unless a disturbance was created.

The Angel was a place of low ceilings, thick carpets, and silent movements. The waiters did not merely come when summoned; they appeared at one's elbow like djinns from the bowels of the earth. And as one spoke the words fell softly and died on the spot. There were no echoes in the Angel. It was an ideal place in which to mourn.

Knollis pushed his way through the revolving doors and strode along the passages to the manager's office, heedless of the receptionist's injured air and the curious glances of the residents who wandered along with wistful faces as if in search of the sun, which, it was rumoured, had been blackballed by the old gentlemen of the smoke-room many years ago—maybe because it reminded them of their long-departed and perhaps ill-spent youth.

Knollis knocked once for courtesy's sake and walked into the office with Bates on his heels like an obedient spaniel. The bald, rotund manager was lying back in a super-comfortable chair, his flabby pink hands laid across his paunch and a beatific expression wreathed round his bland features. As Bates slammed the door, although it made no more noise than would a falling block of felt, he opened one eye warily, stared with it for a split second, and then opened the other and wriggled into an upright position.

"Inspector Knollis!" he exclaimed, as if trying to convince himself that he was not the victim of a mirage. "I was—er—puzzling out a little problem of accommodation. Pleased to see you, anyway. What'll you have?"

"Nothing, thanks," said the Inspector. "I'm sorry to butt in at this time of the day, but there are certain questions I should like to ask members of your staff. I take it that you will be able to arrange that for me, Mr. Boswell?"

Mr. Boswell strived to comprehend.

"I'm awfully sorry to trouble you," Knollis repeated untruthfully. "But it is rather important."

Mr. Boswell grasped the situation.

"Something's wrong!"

"I'll explain," said Knollis. He perched himself on the corner of the table to take the weight off his feet. "You'll have read about a Mr. Lomas being fished from the river? Well, we are interested in his movements, and we think he called here last night."

Mr. Boswell blinked.

"Lomas! That was the little man with the beard! Yes, he patronised the Angel most evenings. Usually had a few drinks in the Oak Bar. I think he was in the habit of meeting a friend there, a chemist from the Desborough Road. And you'd like to speak to the barman? Is that it?"

The manager spoke into the house telephone. A brisk little man bustled into the room a minute later. He was wearing a white jacket and looked as if he had come from his cellar in the bowels of the building. There was a strong smell of beer accompanying him.

"This is Inspector Knollis in case you don't know him," said Mr. Boswell, by way of introduction. "Please answer such questions as he may ask you, Smith. You've done nothing wrong, and so you needn't be afraid!"

"You were acquainted with Mr. Lomas, I believe?" said Knollis. "I understand that he visited your bar frequently?"

"The gent that was found in the river, Inspector? Yes, and a bad job it was. Slipped in, I reckon? Ah well, he'd had a good innings. Yes, I knew him well. He turned in about twenty past seven most evenings, as punctual as a clock. Usually left about eightish with Mr. Steadfall, what used to meet him here."

"And he called last evening as usual?"

"He did, sir. A bit earlier, too. I'd only just opened the bar—counting the change I was—and he was my first customer for once. He brought a gentleman with him, not Mr. Steadfall this time. They were on whiskies and knocked a goodish few back."

"At what time did they leave?"

"Oh, just after half-past six."

Knollis eyed his witness cautiously, and then asked: "Did you happen to overhear any of their conversation?"

The question had the effect he anticipated. Smith became wary, and then indignant, as if that was the safest attitude to adopt.

"Me overhear conversation, Inspector? No, sir! It's not my habit to listen to conversations between gentlemen in my bar. I was taught different to that."

He turned an appealing eye on the manager, but Mr. Boswell did not move a muscle. He was watching the scene with evident relish. It was a welcome break in the monotony.

"I wasn't accusing you of deliberate listening," Knollis said in a soothing voice. "I took it that, as they were the only customers in the bar at the time, you would be almost certain to overhear some of their conversation. In fact you could hardly avoid doing so. Were they talking about the weather, or racing, or business, or what? This is very important, Smith," he reminded him.

Smith cocked his head and let his tongue run over his upper lip. "Well," he said cautiously, "now you mention it and bring it back to mind, I believe I did hear something of what they was saying. Odd snatches, like. They were discussing a business transaction. The other gentleman said the price was too low."

Knollis jumped. Bates rubbed his cheek with one finger and stared his surprise.

"Too low? You are sure of that?" snapped Knollis.

"*Far* too low was the exact words, Inspector."

"You are sure that it was not Mr. Lomas who objected to the price?"

Now that his memory was challenged Smith threw caution to the winds and became emphatic, almost belligerently so.

"Mr. Lomas said: 'I'm asking fifteen hundred for it, and that includes lock, stock and goodwill.' The other gentleman was very indignant about this, and he said: 'Don't be so damned unbusiness-like. You know the price is far too low. Push it up another five hundred. He can afford it. And in the hands of a younger man the business will jump forward.' Them was the exact words. Mr. Lomas was mad at the suggestion that he was not as capable as a younger man. He passed an abusive remark—an epithet—that I would hate to repeat before gentlemen."

Knollis suppressed a smile, and asked:

"Can you describe Mr. Lomas's companion?"

"Well yes. He was tallish, and he was wearing a heather-mixture tweed suit and a grey trilby. I didn't notice him more close than that."

"And you are certain that he and Lomas left shortly after half-past six, and together?"

"I'm positive, Inspector."

"Thank you," said Knollis. "That will be all for now."

The manager raised his eyebrows in a silent question. "The receptionist," answered the Inspector.

She well remembered the arrival of Mr. Lomas and his companion, for the vestibule was almost deserted. She agreed that it was a few minutes after six, but was not at all sure of the departure time, being occupied with new arrivals from the London train.

Bates fingered his clipped moustache thoughtfully and asked a question almost before Knollis had the car moving towards Devonport Street and the Commerce Club. "Think we're on the trail of our man?"

"It would appear so, Bates," Knollis replied absently. "Although I'm damned if I can see why anyone should kill someone else who was trying to sell a business for less, presumably, than it was worth. Either there was a reason for hasty disposal, or else the business was not all it had been shown to be. Still, it is too early to start building theories."

He glanced at his watch. "A quarter past ten, Bates. I wish there were forty-eight hours in our day."

"There are," said Bates shortly.

"I'm thinking of what we have to do before nightfall. Interview the people at the cafe, the Commerce Club staff, see Lawrence and Gertrude Lomas again, get in touch with Whitelaw, go over whatever report Dawes and Slater send in, and heaven only knows what else may crop up. Anyway," he said with intense satisfaction, "we found Lomas's house vastly interesting!"

"Don't forget Steadfall," Bates reminded him. "He sounds a likely sort of fellow, that! A chemist always has stuff like cocaine lying about. He could just put a little nip in Lomas's beer and the job's done."

"Know anything about cocaine, Bates?"

"No, not much. Why?"

"Skip it," said Knollis. He grimaced, and said no more until they reached the Commerce Club.

Devonport Street lay behind the city square, a dismal backwater. One side was occupied by the forbidding blank wall of an extensive factory that specialised in the manufacture of electrical components, and its more pleasing and windowed aspects were to be found in the next street. The other side of Devonport Street presented the drab rears of two cinemas, the besmoked facades of several blocks of office buildings, and the Edwardian frontispiece of the Commerce Club.

Knollis walked over the moulting doormat and asked for the secretary. The scraggy, bespectacled official crept from his lair as if he had been in hiding or preparing to hibernate at the wrong time of the year. He timorously returned the card that Knollis had sent in and asked his pleasure. The Inspector stated his requirements while the secretary blinked, gathered his reserve forces, and tried to be helpful.

"Yes," he murmured, "I saw the report in the *Courier*. Poor Mr. Lomas. Very sad, very sad indeed. Now let me see! He spent his time in the billiards room. We will see the marker."

He pattered away on flat feet, Knollis and Bates following him down parquetted passages, up a flight of linoleumed stairs, and through a set of creaking swing doors. Over his shoulder they saw the long green tables and the low-hanging shades. At the far end of the room a lanky, collarless man was dusting the window ledges to the slow rhythm of the Song of the Volga Boatmen, accompanying himself in an alleged baritone voice. He turned almost defiantly as the secretary approached and touched his arm.

51 | THE DEATH OF MR. LOMAS

"Er—Ted. Inspector Knollis would like to ask you about Mr. Lomas."

The man flung his duster aside and strolled to meet them.

"Pleased to know you, Inspector. Morning, Sergeant! Mr. Lomas, eh? Don't know as I can help much, but I'll try."

"Mr. Lomas did call last evening?" asked Knollis.

"Why yes, that's so. Sorry to hear about him, 'cause he wasn't a bad old stick. Still, I don't suppose you've much to live for when you get to his age, and making a hole in the water isn't a long job—or so they say. Called last night, you say? That's hardly right. Not in here, he wasn't, but I know he was in the lounge. Sam—that's the waiter—offered me a shilling to lure him away. Said he was making himself a nuisance, drinking too much and arguing fit to bust."

"Did Mr. Steadfall pay his usual evening visit?"

"Mr. Steadfall? Aye, he did. Round about half-past eight. Asked for Mr. Lomas. Said he'd been waiting at the Golden Angel for him to turn up and he hadn't turned up."

"I'd like to interview the waiter now," Knollis informed the tortoise-like secretary. He thanked the marker and reminded him that it would probably be necessary to take an official statement from him at a later date.

The man waved his duster airily. "Always willing to help. That's Ted Denman. Any time that suits you, Inspector."

"He's something of a character," the secretary muttered apologetically, as he led the way down to the ground floor.

The waiter could offer more information than the marker.

"Mr. Lomas and the gentleman came about ten minutes to seven. They sat over there, in the alcove. Drinking whiskies pretty freely, Inspector."

"At what time did they leave?"

"An hour or so later. About ten to eight."

"Have you seen his companion before?"

"No, not as far as I can remember. He was a stranger."

"How was he dressed? In a grey suit?"

The waiter raised his eyes. "Grey? No, you're wrong there, Inspector. He was wearing tweeds of a mixed colour."

"And a cap and leather gloves?"

"No. Yellow gloves and a grey trilby. A full-faced man. Well-to-do, I should say. Very soft voice."

"Would you recognise him if you saw him again?" Knollis asked. "Be careful about answering, please. It may prove to be very important."

The waiter accordingly hesitated. "I might, and that is the best I can say. I didn't take particular notice of him."

"Denman says you offered him a shilling if he would lure Mr. Lomas to the billiards room. Why did you say that?"

The waiter grinned. "Ted hasn't got a sense of humour—unless it's something funny he's saying himself. I pull his leg now and then. Mr. Lomas was about the quietest member of the club. He scarcely ever raised his voice above a whisper. Mind you, he did sing a bit louder last night, but then he was well primed."

"I don't suppose you happened to overhear any of the conversation?" Knollis asked hopefully. "It would help a lot if you could remember."

"We-ell, yes, I did, Inspector," was the frank reply. "You can hardly help it when you are serving tables. I heard odd snatches and that was all. I remember Mr. Lomas saying something about eighteen hundred being nearer the mark."

"Eh?" interrupted Knollis. "*Eighteen* hundred?"

"That's right, Inspector. Mr. Lomas said eighteen hundred was nearer the mark, and the other gentleman said he was prepared to pay that figure after his solicitors had examined the books and proved them to be in order."

Knollis looked at Bates and bit his lip thoughtfully.

"Did Mr. Steadfall call for Mr. Lomas?"

"Yes," the waiter replied. "It would be about half-past eight time. He looked in, asked if Mr. Lomas had gone, and then he went out again, but I can't say whether he left the building."

"Do you happen to know Lomas's son? He is a dentist, and lives at Desborough."

The waiter shook his head, and Knollis then asked if the club boasted a commissionaire.

"We have a cloakroom attendant who also acts as doorman," said the secretary. "He may have seen them arrive and leave, if that is the information you require. In fact he must have seen them. I will take you to his room."

Here Knollis asked the same questions, and the attendant's answers agreed with those supplied by Denman and the waiter. In one respect he was more informative. He had been in the street when Lomas and his companion left the club, and could say with certainty that they had walked toward the city square. It was now that Knollis came to a temporary halt, literally as well as metaphorically.

"It is—or was—quite logical to assume that Lomas brought his companion to his two homes-from-home," he said to Bates as they stood outside the Commerce Club, "but after that? He did not return home. Now where did he go?"

"The other fellow may have taken Lomas to his pet pub," suggested Bates. "And as we don't know who he was we're in a difficulty."

Knollis entered a nearby kiosk and slipped two pennies in the box. "Please put me through to Police Box Number Eleven. This is Inspector Knollis of the city police."

He turned to Bates while he was waiting.

"I'm hoping to be able to attract the attention of the constable on point duty so that he can take a message to Franks—Hello? That Johnson? This is Inspector Knollis. I want you to take a message to Franks. He is making observation near Lomas's shop. Tell him to ask the girl in the shop if she knows Lawrence Lomas by sight, and if so will she give as complete a description of him as possible. I'll hang on till you get back."

He offered his cigarette case and he and Bates smoked until a click in the earpiece recalled him to business. He listened intently, said his thanks, and left the box.

"She may have seen him without knowing that he was Lomas's son, Bates. Lomas took all visitors, including travellers, through to the sitting room. Well, she'll be able to tell us whether she saw him at the shop or not if we show him to her. That being that, I think we'll make for River Station and see if Dawes and Slater have put in an appearance."

They returned to the car and drove to the south side of the city and the river. River Station stood on the embankment, a few yards below the long-span concrete bridge.

Knollis asked for his two aides as soon as he entered the charge room.

"Just missed them, Inspector," said the station sergeant. "They have traced Lomas back to the Bridge Hotel, and they were going along to continue inquiries."

Knollis and Bates walked back to the London Road. Two minutes' walk in the direction of the city brought them to the hotel, and here they were informed that Dawes and Slater were closeted with the manager—"Second room on the right down the main corridor, Inspector."

Sergeant Dawes smiled as he saw Knollis in the doorway.

"Lomas came here with a companion, Inspector. Landed about twenty minutes past eight."

Knollis rubbed his hands happily.

"That's better! They left the Commerce Club at ten minutes to eight, so we can assume that they took a bus. At what time did they leave?"

The manager interposed.

"I have been explaining to Sergeant Dawes," he said. "Mr. Lomas left alone. The other gentleman remained for a further half-hour. I was chatting with them in the smoke-room. Mr. Lomas pleaded an urgent engagement and asked to be excused. He left rather hurriedly."

Sergeant Dawes now interrupted.

"Lomas bought an evening paper from a newsboy along the road, and then turned down the embankment and set off at a brisk pace in the direction of Willow Lock, along the towpath. And now we come to a queer overlapping of stories. Mr. Gardner," he said, indicating the manager of the Bridge Hotel; "Mr. Gardner says that Lomas's companion stayed until well after nine. The newsboy says that he saw a man of similar description follow Lomas at *five minutes to nine*! He bought his last copy of the *Evening Mail*, He doesn't say that this man followed Lomas, but that he went the same way—down the towpath in the direction of Willow Lock. He remembers the time because he looked up at the clock on the insurance building to see whether it was worth while cycling to the circulation office for more copies. He decided that it wasn't, and went home."

"You've got his name and address?" Knollis asked anxiously, and immediately wished he had not when Dawes gave him a look of reproach. Dawes did not miss essentials.

"And the newsboy's description of the fellow?"

"Tall, full-faced, dressed in brownish-purplish- greyish suit," said Dawes. "That's his description, and not mine! He says he was also wearing a grey trilby and brown shoes."

"Gloves?"

"Yellow—wash-leather, he called 'em. He was carrying them. He rolled the paper and was slapping his leg with it as he walked away."

The manager again interposed.

"I agree with the description, but I really must dispute the time. I am confident that it was well after nine when he left. We have a loudspeaker in the smoke- room and it is switched on for all musical items and news bulletins. I am positive that the announcer had reached the sports news before Mr. Lomas's friend left me."

"Are you prepared to go into the witness-box and swear to that?" asked Knollis, fixing his eyes on the manager. "It may mean the life or death of this man, remember."

The manager fought an internal battle with his conscience and his memory. At last he shook his head slowly.

"I could not swear to it with so much at stake," he answered, "but I will go so far as to say that I have a very strong belief that my evidence is accurate. Of course, not knowing that anything untoward was afoot, and that Mr. Lomas was going out to his death, and not realising how much would depend on my observations—well, you see what I mean?"

"I understand perfectly," said Knollis. "We are always up against that factor. We will call on you again later."

The four officers walked back to River Station.

"He told Slater and myself," said Dawes, "that Lomas only stayed for a quarter of an hour. He left at twenty-five to nine. His companion is supposed to have followed at five or seven minutes past. The B.B.C. will be able to state at what time the general news ended."

"We now want to know where he was between twenty-five to nine and ten o'clock," Knollis murmured. "We still have to account for an hour and a half."

"At ten minutes to nine he passed Rose Cottage," Dawes informed him. "That is half a mile down-river in case you don't know the place. The owner was leaning over his gate, thinking about nothing. Mr. Lomas's appearance attracted his attention. He says he was hurrying like the devil and wasn't too steady on his pins."

"That's hardly surprising, Dawes," said Knollis. "The old boy seems to have indulged in a glorified pub-crawl. He started at the Golden Angel, went on to the Commerce Club, then to the Bridge Hotel, and finished at The Ferryman. He'd be pretty addled by the end of the night."

"He was in The Ferryman at twenty past nine, knocking whiskies back as hard as he could go," said Dawes. "The bar-man says he wondered whether he was trying to forget his troubles or beat the clock to ten. Anyway, he left at ten minutes to closing time and does not seem to have been seen alive after that time."

Knollis stretched himself.

"We are getting warm—even if we don't know when or why he was shaved. Now, Dawes, you and Slater go to the Burnham Omnibus Company's offices and find the conductor who took Lomas on board. Get a statement from him. You, Bates, hop off to Desborough and try the *Chronicle* office for a photograph of Lawrence Lomas. In fact get one from anywhere, and how you like. I'm going to have a private talk with John Steadfall."

CHAPTER IV
THE FRIEND OF MR. LOMAS

JOHN STEADFALL was a stout man of fifty-eight with florid features, damp hands, and a thick neck that overflowed his striped soft collar. He looked drawn and strained when Knollis walked into his shop and introduced himself. He uttered a dispirited greeting and showed him into the dispensary at the rear of the premises. "Be with you in a few moments, Inspector. Must attend to these customers first." Knollis availed himself of the opportunity to look round. There were shelves all round the room, ranging from ceiling to floor; all were packed with bottles, each with its label in abbreviated Latin, and most of which he was unable to decipher. He recognised castor oil under its *nom de guerre* Ol: Ricini, and he had a vague notion that Ammon: Spt: Aromat: was aromatic spirits of ammonia, or sal volatile. He recognised the winchesters of distilled water and the winchester of burnt sugar for what they were, but he looked in vain for Cocain: Hydrochlor. It was probably locked away, as it should be, and he gave Steadfall a mark for carefulness. He was just getting interested in a solo game of Think It Out when Steadfall lumbered through the doorway. Just then the chemist seemed too small for his clothes, like a small man who has taken the back legs of a pantomime elephant at a moment's notice. He was shrunken, bowed, almost haggard.

"I suppose you've come about Lomas," he muttered. "You want to know if I can tell you anything about him. I'm afraid I can't, Inspector."

"I understand that he was your friend, Mr. Steadfall?" Knollis stated, ignoring the chemist's protested ignorance.

"Yes, yes. He was my best friend—my only friend if it comes to that. Ezekiah and I were schoolboy friends."

Knollis fixed him with mild eyes, although his perceptive faculties were working at top speed.

"Exactly what happened last night, Mr. Steadfall?"

Steadfall looked about in a bewildered manner.

"Last night?" he stammered. "I don't know, Inspector. Indeed I don't. We usually met at the Golden Angel, but he didn't turn up last night. I waited for some time and then went to the Commerce Club. They told me that he had been there with a stranger and had gone again. I stayed for a few minutes and then went home."

Knollis rubbed his chin thoughtfully.

"We are of the opinion that he met his death as the result of foul play, Mr. Steadfall. Murdered," he said bluntly, and watched the chemist closely as he broke the news to him.

Steadfall passed a hand over his eyes and emitted a sight of unutterable weariness.

"I know! The Courier gave a hint to that effect this morning. It was the first I knew of it. It was a great shock—and it's so incomprehensible. Suicide would have been bad enough, but murder!"

"Who hated him so much that they could bring themselves to murder him in this way?" Knollis asked.

"I can't believe that anybody could do so," Steadfall replied. "That is what makes the whole thing so unbelievable. Lomas was too compromising to make enemies. In a case of this description we must be frank, mustn't we?"

He waited for the Inspector's affirmative gesture, and then continued: "I've always understood that friendship means an affection for a person even when you know all his faults as well as his virtues. Heaven only knows that Ezekiah Lomas had his faults! I knew his characteristics from A to Z. I've heard him say that a business man has no right to air his opinions. The customer must always be right. He'd agree with a customer whether he was a Conservative or a Socialist, a Catholic or an Atheist. He developed a habit of being non-committal, so much so that he was like that even with me. The attitude was constant whether he was in the shop or a public bar. And I venture to suggest, Inspector, that such people do not make enemies!"

The chemist's voice had risen to an almost hysterical pitch. He made the last statement with considerable vehemence, and now stood gazing defiantly at Knollis, and breathing heavily.

Knollis smiled. "All things to all men."

"He made his money by observing the principle," Steadfall returned in an effort to justify his friend's attitude.

"And made enemies, I'll be bound," said Knollis. "Such people are in danger of gaining a reputation for hypocrisy, and of being unreliable."

Steadfall was silent under the Inspector's cold logic, although his expression amply betrayed his resentment at this attack on his friend's character.

"Again," said Knollis, "it isn't common sense to assume that he had no enemies. Either he had enemies, or he was in possession of some information that endangered the security of the killer. Someone was administering poison and for a purpose—"

"Poison!" Steadfall exclaimed incredulously. "But I thought he was drowned!"

"Poisoned," Knollis repeated bluntly. "The police surgeon reports that Lomas was treated lavishly. See now, I believe you were treating him for nervous trouble?"

Steadfall started violently. "You are not suggesting—"

Knollis shrugged his shoulders.

"That was clumsy of me, Mr. Steadfall. I would not think of insinuating any such thing. But you were treating him?"

The chemist hesitated. "I—well, I don't know whether I should say anything about that. Etiquette of the profession, you know, demands silence and discretion . . ."

Knollis waved his objections away.

"Lomas was in possession of two bottles that bore your labels. Our analysts can soon find out what they contain, and if they contain anything different to what they should have contained, then that does not necessarily say that you are responsible. What I want to know is what you put in them, and why. I'm sorry, Mr. Steadfall, but I must insist."

Steadfall chafed his palms together and suddenly locked his fingers with a spasmodic movement. "Oh well, I don't suppose it matters now. There was nothing wrong with him really; nothing radically wrong, I mean. A touch of nervous debility. After all, he was sixty-five!"

"What did you prescribe, Mr. Steadfall?"

"Well, I won't call it prescribing, because that is a doctor's office, but I gave him a glycerophosphates mixture that I sell under my own label. I do not prepare it, you know; it comes in bulk from the pharmaceutical suppliers and I bottle it. There is a proportion of strychnine in it, about point nought-nought-three-seven per cent. And about point nought-seven-one of caffeine. It is a good bracer providing no more than the stated dose is taken. Ezekiah complained that it excited him, so I thought the matter out and knocked up a bromide instead."

"Why that?" asked the ever-curious Inspector.

"To quieten him and give Mother Nature a chance to put things right in her own way—which is always the best, you know! Ezekiah was overdoing it for a man of his age."

"Now there's no evidence to show that they were," said Knollis, "but could those bottles have been tampered with before they left your hands? I have to allow for all contingencies."

"Oh no! Oh no!" Steadfall protested.

"He mentioned his symptoms to you?"

"Well ye-es, such as were exhibited. He said he was out of sorts, off his food, and jumpy."

"Were you aware that he went to see the Chief Constable yesterday morning, Mr. Steadfall?"

The chemist's eyes answered the question before a word left his lips.

"What on earth for?" he demanded.

"To report an alleged long-standing attempt at poisoning. He was quite confident that his life was in danger."

"But—but he never mentioned this to me," the chemist protested, "and I was his best friend!"

"Well, I wasn't present at the interview," said Knollis, "but it would seem that he had reached the stage where he didn't trust his own shadow.'

"And I was his friend...."

Steadfall sought a high stool and balanced himself on it, resting one hand on the bench. He was paler now, and he blinked wearily at the Inspector. "Wh-what did he tell the Chief Constable?"

"He said," Knollis quoted slowly, "that he experienced an intense excitation of the nerves. He felt as though insects were walking under his skin."

Steadfall slid from the stool. He glanced at his hand, now clutching the edge of the bench. Then he raised slow eyes, and his lip quavered. "Insects walking under his skin! But that means cocaine bugs!"

"Dr. Whitelaw informs me that Mr. Lomas died of cocaine poisoning, Mr. Steadfall."

"Incredible! Incredible!"

The chemist thought for a few moments and then flashed Knollis a glance of curiosity. "But the Courier said he was pulled from the river!"

"Quite right. He was dead when put in the water."

"My God!" Steadfall said soberly.

"You recognised the symptoms readily," murmured Knollis.

"I studied toxicology, Inspector."

"Have you read it up of late?"

"Read it up? Why no; I have no occasion to do so."

"Do you have occasion to consult—no, I'll ask you a different question. Do you possess any books on toxicology as related to criminology?"

"My B.P. Codex, of course. I'm always dipping into that. That is the official codex of the British Pharmaceutical Society."

"Yes, I'm aware of that," said Knollis, "but you can hardly call it a book on criminology!"

"Well, somewhere I have an old edition of Taylor's *Medical Jurisprudence*, but I haven't opened it for ages. In fact I'm not at all sure where it is."

John Steadfall looked into Knollis's face and must have read the suspicion that rested there. He tugged at his collar and showed every sign of acute distress.

"I haven't read anything like that, Inspector! I swear I haven't! For God's sake, cease! I am completely innocent of Ezekiah's death. You must realise that!"

"Listen, Mr. Steadfall," said Knollis calmly. "You were his best friend. I understand that. Your position enables you to give us more information about him than anyone else can do. I am not accusing you of killing him! I need your help—all you can offer. If I know exactly how capable you were of the act, and what opportunities or otherwise you had of committing it, then I can perhaps find out whether it was possible for some other person to take advantage of your apparent capability and opportunity. Now do you see why I am asking you these embarrassing questions? Someone, obviously, poisoned him. You were his friend, and you are a chemist. Those two facts will emerge at the inquest. Popular suspicion may fix on you. I don't want that to happen for one good reason. The longer it takes to clear you, the more time our man will have in which to cover his tracks. I don't think for one moment that you are responsible. You, as a chemist, would be no more than a plain fool if you wanted to remove Lomas and did so by using poison. It is too obvious a weapon in your case. Perhaps you begin to understand now?"

Steadfall slowly nodded. "Yes," he whispered; "yes, I understand. But it's all so ghastly! He was alive and well at five o'clock!"

"You saw him then?"

"Yes. He came in the shop for a minute as he was passing. He had been to the post office."

"Lomas did not see a doctor?" the Inspector asked.

Steadfall shook his head. "No, he did not. I think I see what you are driving at, Inspector. You are wondering if I supplied cocaine on a prescription. I did not. He had none from me."

The assistant put his head round the door and asked for Steadfall's presence in the shop; a customer wished to consult him.

Knollis saw his chance, and jumped at it.

"You do stock cocaine then?" he questioned.

"A small amount, yes."

"Where do you store it?"

Steadfall indicated a cupboard behind him.

"You keep it locked?"

"Always, Inspector."

"Can I look inside, please?"

Steadfall unlocked the door, saying as he did so:

"There is only one key and I carry it about with me." Knollis looked toward the shop. "I'd forgotten! You are needed in the shop, aren't you? I'll wait if you like. I'm in no great hurry, and your customer may be."

Steadfall nodded, and left him.

Knollis closed the door silently and made a hurried examination of the bottles in the poison cupboard. On finding the one he needed he drew the cork and plunged a finger in the bottle. He touched it on the tip of his tongue and then spat in his handkerchief. Before the chemist returned everything was in place and Knollis was leaning on the bench, a thoughtful expression on his face. He affected a bland smile with which to greet Steadfall.

"You know," he said, "Lomas wasn't the only person in this city suffering from the effects of cocaine. We have quite a few addicts. I'm not suggesting that Lomas was an addict," he added hastily, "but there are at least a dozen known sniffers in the area."

This was a plain invention, but Knollis was prepared to smother his scruples on occasion if the end to be attained justified the action.

"We have overwhelming difficulty in finding how they get hold of the stuff," he continued. "I don't suppose you ever get asked to supply it illegally, and have to refuse? Or do you?"

"It's queer that you should say that," the chemist said suddenly. "Only once in my life-time have I been asked to supply cocaine without a prescription, and that was about a month ago. The very first time!"

Knollis raised his eyes from his notebook. "Oh?"

Steadfall smiled whimsically. "Queer, isn't it, that two unconnected incidents dealing with the same thing should occur within a few weeks of each other?"

"Very queer," murmured Knollis, although he had not the faintest notion of what Steadfall was talking about.

"I'm not too sure that I should tell you," the chemist went on. "If the man's story, and its implications, are true it will cause a scandal in the city."

Knollis did not comment. He had no intention of scaring his quarry by saying the wrong thing at the wrong moment.

Steadfall sighed, and then shrugged his shoulders.

"Oh well, I've gone so far that I may as well tell you the rest. I felt uneasy about concealing the business, anyway. It was, as I say, about a month ago. I was alone in the shop, for the assistant had gone out for his tea, when this fellow came in. He asked if he could speak privately with me. I am accustomed to such requests—you know!—and so I took him through to the dispensary—in here, of course. He was reluctant to come to the point, but there again I was not surprised. Most people have inhibitions when it comes to talking about certain subjects. But I talked about the weather and one thing and another, and at last became impatient and asked point blank what was the nature of his errand. He gave me a straight look and asked how much cocaine I had in stock!"

Knollis stiffened, and waited patiently.

"His question staggered me so much that I was shocked into telling him the truth. I had about five drachms. He said it was ample and that he wanted to buy it. I pointed out that it was impossible; cocaine was not sold like that. He said there were ways and means. I was to fake an accident in which the bottle was to be broken. The remains were to be wrapped in newspaper and put in the dustbin. I was at liberty to inform the police of the accident if I cared to do so. By next morning the parcel would be gone, and in its place I should find an envelope containing fifty one-pound notes."

"What is the cost of five drachms?" interrupt Knollis.

Steadfall consulted a list that hung from a nail. "Thirty-two shillings an ounce at present."

"Some profit! But continue your story, Mr. Steadfall; it interests me greatly."

"I refused to deal with him. I am jealous of my professional reputation. He then said that he could turn that fifty pounds into two hundred and fifty in less than two days. There was a certain dog running at the Burnham Stadium on the next night. It would run at five to one, and would win.

"Well, I saw the whole scheme then. He was doping second-rate dogs with long marks and turning them into winners for one race. Then they would revert to normal until they were on the long mark again. I turned his offer down flat, and expected trouble, but he just laughed at what he called my tender conscience and said he would look in my dustbin during the night in case I changed my mind. I think he must have done so, because I found the dustbin lid on the back doorstep when I arrived next morning."

"And that was the last you saw of him?" the Inspector asked anxiously.

Steadfall nodded.

"Can you describe him?"

"Yes. He was girlish in appearance, more the type to be found hanging round a dance hall than a dog-racing track. He was slim and willowy, and wore brown pointed shoes and a green suit. His hands were as delicate as a girl's, and his eyes about the bluest I have seen. As I say, he would have made an excellent girl."

"Think you'd recognise him if you saw him again?"

"Undoubtedly," the chemist assured him. "Look here, Inspector, you don't think there can be any connection—"

"One other question," said Knollis. "Were you called into the shop while he was here? Was he left alone even for one minute?"

Steadfall applied a hand to his forehead.

"I think . . . yes, I'm sure I served a small boy with something or other, but I couldn't swear to it. In any case, he could not have got at the cupboard," he said hastily. "The key was in my pocket."

"That is a comforting thought," replied Knollis with a slightly cynical smile. "I'd like your home address, Mr. Steadfall. This is a lock-up shop, of course?"

"Yes, I live at Seventy-Two, Flamborough Avenue."

"Across the river, eh! Are you on the telephone? We may need you later if we catch this young fellow you mention, and it may be at night."

"I'm in the directory," the chemist answered.

"What was the name of that dog?"

"Blankety-Blank Star."

Steadfall's worried features relaxed and a faint smile appeared. "Going to have a bob on it? Then don't! I looked in the paper, and it did win on that occasion at five to one, but it hasn't even run since."

Knollis made his way back to headquarters and into Sir Wilfred's presence. He related his progress.

"And your opinion?" murmured Sir Wilfred, when the tale was done.

"He's either lying or been burgled. It's bicarbonate of soda in that bottle. I'll get Whitelaw to knock up a prescription containing cocaine and have it sent round to Steadfall. If, on analysis, it proves to be bicarbonate we shall know that Steadfall was worked."

"Or else is wise to you."

Knollis's eyes narrowed. "Yes, I've thought of that. Anyway, I'll also circulate a description of Steadfall's girl friend and get Dawes and Slater to do the Stadium. There may be something in it."

"Managed to dig out a suitable motive for Steadfall?" the Chief Constable asked slyly.

"I haven't done with him yet," came the slow reply. "Softly, softly, catchee monkee . . ."

Knollis returned home for lunch. Whatever embarrassment Steadfall might have suffered during the long interview was fully avenged during the next hour, for Mrs. Knollis questioned her husband avidly throughout the meal. Knollis patiently supplied the answers. He grinned at her as he rose from the table. "I'm wondering if you would like a signed statement from me, dear?"

"What a wonderful notion, Gordon!" she exclaimed brightly. "I could mull over it during the afternoon—and perhaps solve the whole problem for you before you show in again."

Knollis kissed her affectionately and went to his den. He uncovered his Sterling typewriter, better known as "George," and slipped a sheet of paper behind the platen. After a careful study of the entries in his notebook he compiled a chronological table of Lomas's movements on the night of his death. It ran:

June 9th

9.00 a.m.	Lomas calls on Sir W.
5.55 p.m.	Lomas leaves shop with X.
6.03 approx.	Lomas arrives at Golden Angel with X.
6.30.	Lomas leaves Golden Angel with X.
6.50.	Lomas arrives at Commerce Club with X.
7.50.	Lomas leaves Commerce Club with X.
8.20.	Lomas arrives at Bridge Hotel with X.
8.35.	Lomas leaves Bridge Hotel alone.
8.50.	Lomas seen passing Rose Cottage.
9.20.	Lomas arrives at The Ferryman, alone.
9.50.	Lomas leaves The Ferryman, alone.
10.45.	Lomas's body recovered from river.

As far as the Inspector could see, there were two gaps in the story; the actual time gap between Lomas leaving The Ferryman and the discovery of his body, and what he was pleased to call the psychological gap between Lomas's conversation in the Golden Angel and his conversation in the Commerce Club.

On the surface it seemed quite logical for Lomas's companion to complain about the too-low price while in the Angel and then for him to accept it in the Commerce Club subject to an examination of the books, always assuming that the would-be purchaser was a man of exceptional honesty, but if Smith's story was correct then there must have been two men of almost identical appearance.

Lomas's companion in the Angel had said: "*He* can afford it," and not "*I* can afford it." Added to which was the remark culled in the Angel to the effect that in the hands of a younger man the business would develop. And all that, in spite of the coinciding descriptions given by Smith and the waiter at the Commerce Club, indicated that Lomas had changed horses between the Angel and the Commerce Club. Further to the point, if both men *were* dressed in exactly the same manner, it indicated the probability that one had deliberately copied the style of the other. Knollis was no believer in coincidence. Apparent coincidences did occur, but they only appeared to be coincidences because the connecting link was not immediately perceptible.

The Inspector threw his mind back to the interview with Lawrence Lomas. Lomas was tall, and broad, but he was then wearing a dark suit and a bowler hat, and carrying a walking stick and kid gloves. It was quite possible that he had changed during the evening. Dressed in X's clothes he would quite well fit the description given by the few material witnesses.

Knollis asked himself a question. Had Lawrence dressed himself to resemble X, or had X dressed himself to resemble Lawrence Lomas? He decided that the latter conjecture was the most likely, and the one to be borne in mind when trying to build a theory that would account for Lomas's death.

Then why, he further asked himself, had X gone to this trouble? Was there some twist in the projected purchase of Lomas's business? And if there was, how did it link up with the long-continued plot to poison Lomas?

There was yet another puzzling point. If it was Lawrence Lomas who was with his father in the Golden Angel, which seemed likely, then why had he denied seeing his father during the past few days? That asked for treatment. And for an excuse to see him? If it was Lawrence in the Angel then he must know the name and address of the prospective purchaser. He had said: "He can afford it," and that indicated a fair knowledge of his man.

Knollis allowed himself a smile of gratification. He felt that he was moving. From the mass of information acquired in the sixteen hours since Lomas's death he had already singled out at least one loose end upon which he could pull in the endeavour to disentangle the crossing and re-crossing threads of evidence. He returned to police headquarters with renewed vigour, and sought Sir Wilfred Burrows. He also was in an expansive mood.

"I've seen Caine, and also Dodson, the bank manager. Both were reluctant to divulge official secrets, but I wormed 'em out. Lomas did sign the new will. He left twenty-five pounds to Steadfall as a mark of esteem, twenty-five pounds to the Willow Lock Angling Club, of which he was a non-playing but life member, and the remainder to his daughter Gertrude. Guess how much he was worth!"

Knollis remembered what Lawrence had said, and gave that figure. "Two to three thousand?"

"Ten thousand pounds!" said Sir Wilfred. He sat back to enjoy the impression he had made. As Knollis passed no comment he went on: "Lawrence Lomas threw at least four thousand pounds away, and that puts him out of court. It is the most remarkable example of altruism I have yet encountered. What character!"

Knollis stared at the wheeling pigeons outside. "Altruism? Was it?"

"Well, I ask you! There's no way in which he could benefit now, Knollis!"

The Inspector narrowed his eyes, and smiled grimly. "I see one way in which he could have benefited considerably. And he gave me the clue to it himself!"

"Oh? And how, Knollis?" asked the Chief Constable.

"I'll explain when I'm a little more sure."

He hurried down to his own office. Bates was waiting for him. On the table lay three photographs of Lawrence Lomas.

"Get any information about him?" Knollis queried as he examined them.

"Usual stuff. Well-respected member of the community. Seems to be well off. Has a posh car. Is paying attention to a Nora Gretton, spinster, of Grove Road, Desborough. He drove from Desborough yesterday afternoon at a quarter past four, and Miss Gretton was with him. They took the Burnham Road and were seen by the mobile patrol to be driving this way. There could have been no secrecy about the trip because Lomas saluted Mosely as they passed."

"Mosely sure of his identity?"

"Well, there were two windscreens between them, but he recognised the car as Lomas's."

"Ah!" said Knollis. "Er—Bates; did you expect any secrecy to be observed?"

Bates twitched his moustache.

"Well, after the varying stories that Smith and Dixon told I was prepared to find Lomas Junior mixed up in it somewhere. I think it was him that called for the old man just before six, and that it was him that went to the Angel."

"You seem to be recovering, Bates," Knollis smiled.

"The point that is puzzling me is whether it was Lawrence that went with him to the Bridge."

"Yes, Bates, and was it Lomas or the other fellow who followed the old man down the towpath? Until I realised that there were two men I could not understand how the manager and the newsboy could have mixed the times. We can say now that there really were two men, and that one of them was playing a funny game at the expense of the other. I've been thinking it out, and if Smith reported the Angel conversation correctly, then Lawrence Lomas must be aware of the identity of the prospective purchaser—the other fellow. You and I are going to Desborough."

Bates pointed to a table under the window. "Dawes came to leave a report. He's taken Slater and they are gone out on some other lead they picked up. Dawes was very mysterious about it."

Knollis read the report:

> "Following your instructions, Slater and myself went to the Burnham Omnibus Company's offices and there obtained the addresses of the men who were on duty as conductors on Route 41, that between the city square and the bridge. We soon found our man. He is Albert Hakes, and his home is at 63, Old Mill Lane. He remembers Mr. Lomas getting on the bus at the square. A tall man called out 'Good-bye' as he did so. Three hundred yards further on this same man mounted the bus and joined Lomas on the upper deck. Hakes remembers this distinctly because he was 'fair struck all of a heap' by the queerness of the incident. He did not think it possible for the men to have raced the bus for three hundred yards. The two men left the bus at the terminus and were last seen talking together outside the Bridge Hotel. I am satisfied that there were two men and so shall make further inquiries along the

river. I think that A left him and arranged to meet him later at the Bridge Hotel, that B mounted the bus and talked with him outside the hotel, and that A then turned up and entered the hotel with Lomas.

"E. DAWES. Sergeant."

Knollis laughed. "Enlightenment seems to have come to all of us at the same time. Probably the night work dulled our wits during the early part of the day. Mr. Lomas was not—still, Desborough! Get a car round, Bates."

They met with some delay when trying to interview Lawrence Lomas. He was occupied in his surgery and refused to emerge before he had finished the operation upon his patient. Knollis realised that he was quite justified in so refusing and settled himself down with the current issue of *Punch*.

Lawrence Lomas was grave when at last he appeared. He nodded to the sergeant, and asked Knollis if he had brought news of his father's death.

Knollis shook his head. "I'm afraid not, Mr. Lomas. We are in search of information again. Where were you between four o'clock yesterday afternoon and ten o'clock last night?"

Lawrence Lomas stared indignantly. "I beg your pardon!"

The Inspector quietly repeated the question.

"I'll answer that in my own way," snapped Lomas. He strode to the doorway and called down the passage. "Dick!"

His white-coated mechanic came through a doorway at the other end of the passage and joined them, an inquiring expression on his face.

"Where was I at four o'clock yesterday afternoon?"

"Why, in the surgery," the mechanic answered. "Four o'clock? You were fitting Mrs. Richardson's dentures."

"And after she left us?"

"Extractions until a quarter past five."

Lomas turned to Knollis with a twisted smile.

"Well, Inspector? There is your answer. Satisfied?"

"You have a record of these visits?" asked Knollis. He was by no means satisfied.

Lawrence Lomas clicked his tongue. "Fetch the engagement book, Dick!"

Knollis examined the book when it was handed to him and then closed it with an air of finality.

"Quite satisfactory—so far. You were in Burnham last evening, Mr. Lomas?"

"I was," Lawrence Lomas said flatly. "I got there just before six, had a couple of drinks with my father in the Golden Angel, then drove back to Desborough."

"And yet," Knollis pointed out, "when you were interviewed at the station you told us that you hadn't seen him since last Wednesday. Why?"

Lomas looked astonished.

"I said that? Then I don't know what the deuce I was thinking about. Good lord, I must have been vacant!"

"Probably upset by the tragedy," Knollis suggested. "It's a common form of shock—a sort of mental numbness."

Lawrence Lomas nodded thankfully.

"Yes, that must have been it, Inspector. I did see him of course. It was about half-past six when I left the hotel with him. We parted outside and I never saw him again. I'm sorry I misled you."

"That's all right," said Knollis. "You didn't go on to the Commerce Club with him then?"

"No, I returned to Desborough, as I have said."

"So you did," murmured Knollis. "You knew that he was going on to the Commerce Club?"

"Oh yes," Lawrence Lomas said frankly. "He was due to meet Ericson there—Ericson was to buy the business if they could agree on the purchase price. In my opinion my father was underselling, and I tried to persuade him to hot up the price. I think he agreed with me when I pointed out the pros and cons of the matter."

"Did you come back to your home after leaving Burnham?"

"No. I went to my fiancée's home. We had a run into the country, returning about ten o'clock."

Lomas glanced slyly at the Inspector.

"Her name is Miss Nora Gretton, and she lives at Briar Cottage, Grove Road."

"Thanks for the information. You anticipate my actions."

"I know that you will want her to corroborate my story, you see, Inspector," Lomas smiled amiably. "And now I should like to know the reason for all these inquiries."

Knollis was pleased to oblige him.

"It's quite simple. When you were in the Golden Angel you were wearing a suit of heather tweeds, a grey trilby, and yellow gloves."

"That's correct, Inspector. But what—"

"So was the man who accompanied your father to the Commerce Club, and the Bridge Hotel and then followed him along the towpath."

"Ericson!"

"Not necessarily," said Knollis. "In fact there is a distinct possibility that there were two men—and that is why I wanted a list of your movements."

"And the other man—or two men—were dressed as I was? That's a peculiar coincidence—or wasn't it a coincidence?"

"That," said Knollis, "is the point we are considering."

"I bought that suit in the early spring," Lomas muttered reflectively. "My tailor is Jenkins, of the High Street."

"We'll have to check that, you know," Knollis warned him, "so don't be alarmed if you hear that we've been to see him. We can't afford to have a confused trail." Lomas gave a grim laugh. "I'm beginning to understand your thoroughness, Inspector. See him by all means. I hope you will. You know, at first, I thought you were accusing me of being responsible for my father's death!"

"Do you know Ericson's address?" asked the Inspector.

"Ericson's? Oh yes! He was staying at The Ferryman."

Knollis jumped. "What? The Ferryman? You are sure?"

"I'm dead certain. He advertised for a prosperous general business and my father wrote to the box number provided. I understood him to say that Ericson called three days later and gave the inn as his temporary address."

"Thanks," murmured Knollis. "Thanks a lot for that! Now; another question. John Steadfall has been your father's friend for many years?"

"Old John? Yes, they were very good friends. There was a year or two between them, but they had been friends from boyhood. They both courted my mother, you know," he said with a smile. "Old John always insisted that she loved them both equally, but married my father because he was the elder of the two and she considered him the more capable of making his way in the world. Old John was always easy going, bless his old heart!"

"He is married now?"

"Yes," he replied slowly; "he's married now, but there are no children of the marriage. I'm afraid his wife turned shrewish, probably because she discovered that she didn't hold his whole heart. I'm particularly fond of him. I don't think he has too happy a time of it at home—he wouldn't spend so much time at the club if he was happy. And a damned shame it is. He's one of the best. There isn't a ha'porth of malice in him."

"There was never any bitterness between him and your father, Mr. Lomas?"

"Good heavens, no! Old John is incapable of resentment. Don't go suspecting him of killing my father even if he is a chemist," he added dryly.

"Such a suspicion would be too obvious," said Knollis. "By the way, have you met Ericson?"

"No; I wouldn't know the man if I saw him, Inspector."

Knollis appeared to be suffering intense embarrassment as he asked his next question.

"Er—you hinted last night that your home life was not too happy. Was your father—that is, did he ever lay hands on your mother?"

Lawrence Lomas took a deep breath. His lips compressed themselves into a straight line. He looked at Knollis with blazing eyes.

"Yes, he did—the swine. And he kept it up until I was old enough to take him by the scruff of the neck and threaten him with the same treatment. The only reason I interfered with the sale of the business was because Gertrude would have suffered as a result of his stupidity. It would have meant a loss of several hundred pounds to her. He wouldn't have lost anything really because he hadn't many more years of life left in his body anyway. You want the truth, and you shall have it. He killed my mother by his treatment of her as surely as if he had thrashed her to death or strangled her. And I'll tell you why! Because he always thought that she really loved old John!"

He paused, and added: "Do you know that until I was seventeen I never had a ha'penny spending money from him? My mother used to squeeze odd sixpences from her housekeeping allowance, and pray to God that she would never be found out. That, Inspector Knollis, is the kind of man my father was. It was a shock to hear that he had died violently, but that was the only shock I suffered. The rest was pure relief. It meant that Gertrude's future was assured. And there'll be the usual guff in the papers about a fine citizen and a kindly father and all the rest of it. Convention is a strong restraining force, and I tried to keep my feelings penned for that reason, but there are limits to human endurance, and, well, you have the truth now, Inspector."

Knollis nodded his satisfaction. "The information you have so freely given me will be invaluable, Mr. Lomas. I cannot thank you enough. I'm sorry it has been necessary to question you so closely, but it was essential that we should get a clear idea of your father's character. Mr. Steadfall was strictly loyal to your father and that view was in no way satisfactory to us inasmuch as a man must have at least one enemy or he would never be murdered."

He and Bates went on to interview Lomas's fiancée. She was a fresh-looking girl of about twenty-eight, with clear blue eyes. She appeared at the door dressed in a colourful jumper and navy slacks. When Knollis introduced himself and Bates she invited them into the cosy cottage and waited expectantly for the Inspector to state his business.

"Mr. Lawrence Lomas tells me that you can confirm a statement he has made with regard to his movements during the course of last evening," he began.

A flash of fire appeared in her eyes, but before she could express it verbally Knollis hastily added:

"I should explain that someone apparently attempted to impersonate him and so it has been necessary to take account of his whereabouts. I understand that he was with you from half-past five until ten o'clock?"

She glanced up suspiciously, retorting: "I was in my bath at half-past five! It was half-past six when Mr. Lomas arrived. He took me for a run in the car, into the country, returning about ten o'clock. He took supper with me and then drove home."

Knollis fell back on one of his favourite devices for gaining time in which to think out the next move. He consulted his notebook.

"Half-past six of course! I take it that you live alone here, Miss Gretton?"

"I fail to see the relevancy of the question," she replied, "but the answer is yes. I live here alone and unprotected and I have never yet found it necessary to ask for a police guard!"

"That's a pity from one point of view," said Knollis with an arch smile. "Strictly officially, I hope you never have to do so. Well, thanks a lot for your assistance."

"And that is all?" she asked with astonished eyes. "I thought you like to question people for hours and hours!"

"Suspicious people, yes," said Knollis. "It was nothing more than a confirmation we needed in your case, and we can go home now. You are not a suspicious person, you know."

"How reassuring!" she exclaimed mockingly as she rose to show them out.

They drove to the High Street, there to make known their requirements to Lawrence Lomas's tailor. He was an owlish little man with a pre-occupied air. He looked at them over his spectacles and scratched his head with a heart-shaped sliver of chalk. "Mr. Lomas's spring suiting? Ay now, I seem to remember that we made three suits of that length. Where's the book? Lomas ... Lomas ... Lomas ... Ay yes, I've got it now. Asher, the hosier, had the second suit, and a Mr. Steadfall the other—"

"Steadfall?" Knollis exclaimed.

"Yes, that's right. He gave his address as Desborough Road, Burnham."

"You sent the suit or the bill to that address?"

The tailor lifted his head so that he could look squarely through the lenses. Knollis could see his tonsils.

"No! Oh no! He called for both fittings and also for the finished garments. He paid before he left. I had no occasion to use his address."

"Can you describe him?" asked the Inspector as patiently as he could. The little tailor's abstraction was annoying him intensely.

"Well, yes and no. An inch less on the chest, and half an inch on the trouser leg, but otherwise very very similar in build."

"To who?" Knollis hooted ungrammatically.

"Mr. Lawrence Lomas, of course. Not at all unlike him, although I didn't realise it at the time. Same heavy face, thick neck, and general build. Remarkable coincidence, isn't it?"

"Coincidence be—Come on, Bates," said Knollis. "I don't believe in 'em. They aren't natural beasts. I'd as soon believe in a phoenix."

"Where are we going?" murmured Bates as they left the tailor open-mouthed in his doorway.

"The Ferryman. We must find this Ericson fellow."

CHAPTER V
THE PROBLEM OF MR. LOMAS

The Ferryman was doing good business when Knollis swung the car round the corner into the parking ground. Every newspaper reporter and every morbid sightseer in the country seemed to be there, and although it was nearly four o'clock and the bar had been closed for an hour a fine trade in teas, jugs of tea, and snacks was helping to swell the profits of the landlord and landlady. The latter was really both.

The Ferryman was a long, narrow, whitewashed house with a blue slate roof. There was nothing remarkable about it at all unless one considered the signboard, and that was only notable because an illiterate signwriter had credited 'proprietor' with three 'p's' and taken a 'c' out of tobacco to balance matters. The same signwriter had limned an adjacent notice for a taxi-owner in which vehicles 'of every discription" were offered for hire. Knollis noted these attempts at simplified English with amusement and pushed his way through the throng, Bates following in his wake.

"You'll have to go outside and wait your turn," called a stout little woman who met them in the passage. She tried to shoo them away. "Pulled out of the place we are. Never known anything like it in all my days."

Knollis smiled at her. "You are the landlady?"

"That I am."

"I'm Inspector Knollis of the Burnham C.I.D., ma'am. I'd like you to spare a few minutes if at all possible."

"Detectives, eh?" she asked with new interest. "That's different."

She pushed a door open.

"Come in here. Now we can talk and I'll have an excuse for a rest. Phew! What a day. And to think he should have caused all this, a quiet little man like him. I always did say he was a bit queer and was one of them still waters that run deep, but I never thought he'd have dived off the deep end and had me rushed out of the place like this."

"Who?" Knollis asked naively.

"Mr. Lomas of course. We don't get this crowd every day, you know!"

"No?" Knollis murmured. He was highly amused.

"Once before we did, and that was when Jackson's paddle-boat turned upside down. They was all wet of course, and a tidy mess they made me. Jackson should have had more sense than to bring a thing like that down here. Fourteen years come August Bank Holiday Monday it was. We'd only been in eleven months and if we'd have expected that we'd have knocked twenty pounds off the valuation. And now all this through him! What do you want to know about him, Inspector?"

She sat back with the air of one being interviewed for a lurid life-story for publication by one of the more sensational Sunday newspapers.

"I'm not interested in Mr. Lomas for the moment," Knollis said gently. "You have a Mr. Ericson staying with you?"

"Mr. Ericson?" she exclaimed. "What's he got to do with it? He can't have had anyway, because he left me over a week ago. He was a fortnight in advance with his board money, but he went, bag and baggage, and never asked for a penny back. Proper gentleman, he was."

"So I should imagine," said Knollis. "What was he by profession? Perhaps you can tell me that?"

"Mr. Ericson? Why, he was a writer gentleman, Inspector. Used to sit for hours on the bank, writing and scratching out. Told me that you couldn't be too particular. He was an artist as well, although I must say that I never saw any of his pictures. He isn't mixed up in this Mr. Lomas business, is he?" she asked anxiously.

"I can't say that he is," the Inspector replied with a great deal of ambiguity. "What is his home address?"

"That I can't say, sir. He came one afternoon and had tea. After tea—which he complimented me on—he went for a walk, and when he came back he said he had fallen in love with Willow Lock, and it was just the place he had been looking for. He asked me if I could put him up for a few weeks, and I did."

"Very interesting, ma'am. Is your husband about?"

"He's knocking around somewhere, but I can tell you anything you want to know."

"I'm sure of that," said Knollis. "About Mr. Lomas; was he a regular visitor to the house?"

"Not this past few years, Inspector. He used to fish with the club in his earlier days, but I think he got past that. It's a good way from the city and he seemed to have enough to do with looking after his own business."

"Understandable," murmured Knollis. "Were you about when he came shortly before his death?"

"I'm always about. I only leave the house once a week, and that's on Wednesday for the market."

"Did Mr. Lomas appear to be in good spirits?"

"Well, he was and he wasn't," she answered. "He'd had too much to drink somewhere, but he wasn't offensive with it; just muzzy in the head. I don't think he quite knew where he was."

"What patrons were in at the same time?"

"Only the regulars. Hopkin, the lock-keeper, two cowmen from the farm, and folk like that. Nobody as would want to poison him."

"There were no strangers about?" asked Knollis.

"Well, I did notice a car along the towpath. A courting couple most likely. I see them so often that I don't take any notice. Let 'em love, I say. It don't do nobody much harm and it's good for trade—they usually call in here, you know!"

"And did they?" Knollis asked with a smile.

"No-o, they didn't, now I come to think. It was a quiet night on the bank. Never sold a Guinness or an Advocaat all night."

"Was the car a large one?"

"Two-seater, a grey one. Just the behind of it was sticking from the bushes. As I tell you, I didn't take no particular notice. Just said to myself, 'They'll be in here later,' and left it at that."

"Has such a car been in here before—in the parking ground or on the towpath?"

"Well, plenty of cars like that one have been here," the landlady replied flatly. "That's no sort of a question to ask, Inspector. Mr. Ericson's car was something like that now you come to mention it, but so are lots of others."

"Was Mr. Ericson a married man?"

The landlady pondered the question, her finger-tips in her mouth. "I should imagine so. He never had no letters come. If he'd been courting he'd have had some every day or so. Young women like to know that their men are not moving about so much. I know. I've been one myself."

Knollis was satisfied with the results of his inquiry, and next went to see the lock-keeper. He asked if any craft other than the police launch had been on the river prior to the recovery of Mr. Lomas's body.

"Two barges," he was told. "Going through to the Humber with gravel. I let them through the lock about five past ten."

"Five past ten?" Knollis repeated. "That's interesting. You would know the barge-masters, of course?"

"Know them? I've known 'em for years, Inspector. Both barges belonged to Barky Burgess. He was skippering one, and his son the other."

"Horse-drawn?" Knollis asked laconically.

"Motor. Barky is up-to-date."

"What is their home address?"

"Barky lives down River Lane, topside of the Sea- Scouts' place. Young Bert lives by Barnard's Wharf. They'll be back through here on the return journey y'know."

"Thanks," said Knollis. "I must see them."

He and Bates moved to Rose Cottage. Here they were faced by a bow-legged man who invited them to enter with a deal of fuss and false servility. Knollis suspected him on sight.

"I saw Mr. Lomas pass by here about ten minutes to nine," he said in reply to the Inspector's first question. "He was walking with his head down, and his feet weren't too steady. I'd half a mind to ask him in for a few minutes to save him walking into the water, but I thought I'd better mind my own business."

Knollis looked hard at Dodson as he gave the callous reply. He had deep-seated, crafty eyes, and the Inspector instinctively felt suspicious of him, although he was as yet unable to relate his feelings to any definite subject.

"You knew that he was Mr. Lomas?" he queried, as he sought for a way of drawing the man.

"Only by the description and photo in the paper," replied Dodson quickly. "I didn't know who he was until then. Mind you, I've seen him down this way one time or another. He used to fish with the Willow Lock club, and I'd seen him then, without knowing who he was. You do see folk when you're up and down the river all day. I used to be in charge of the boats, pleasure boats, for Waflesby down at the bridge—hiring skiffs and punts, you know. Used to do a bit of coaching, but I'm getting on a bit now and not so fond of hard work. I still do painting and repairing for him although I don't go on the river much."

Knollis nodded toward a green silk dress that hung behind the door. "I see you have a daughter!"

Dodson jerked his head as if he had been taken unawares.

"Daughter? Ay, that's Marjory. She's got a job in town, an office job; what they call sec-re-tarial. Ay, that's Marjory's. A good daughter, she is."

"And that is all you can tell us about Lomas?" said Knollis. "You didn't see a tall man with a grey trilby following him?"

Dodson gaped.

"A—a tall man with a grey trilby . . . ?"

"That is what I said, Mr. Dodson. You seem to be upset. Perhaps you did see such a person?"

Dodson stared into the fire and shook his head. "No, I never saw anybody like that. I didn't see nobody. Y'see," he said eagerly, "I came in after Mr. Lomas went by and so I wouldn't know whether anybody followed him or not, would I now? Eh?"

"That's obvious," said Knollis. "And if you didn't, you didn't, and you can do no more for us."

When they were outside the Inspector said: "What's wrong with the man, Bates? He's afraid of something. The remark about his daughter knocked him clean off his balance. And so did our queries about Ericson—if it was Ericson. Very queer. Now I think we'll go on to the Bridge Hotel and see if the manager has more to tell us. He may know something of Ericson."

But the manager denied all knowledge of him. Even the name was strange, and he could not help them.

Similar results were obtained at the Commerce Club and at the Golden Angel, so Knollis went to Lomas's shop and again interviewed the girl, asking her if she knew of a Mr. Ericson.

No, he had never mentioned the name to her, but she had seen a note left on the sitting-room table. It just said 'Ericson' and 'six-thirty' and no more.

"So that Mr. Ericson probably came round one evening after you had left the shop?"

The girl refused to imagine the probability.

A thought occurred to the Inspector. "You knew that Mr. Lomas was contemplating the sale of the business?"

"Oh yes, sir. He said he would see that I was kept on. He said I should be useful to the new owner because I knew where everything was to be found."

"Did Mr. Lomas say where he would live after selling the business?"

"Well no, Inspector, but he once told me that he would like a cottage by the river when he retired."

"How long ago was this?"

"A long time ago. Perhaps three months. I'm not at all sure, sir."

Knollis wagged his finger. "I am going to ask you a question and I want you to think hard before attempting to answer it. Have you, at any time within the last four weeks, had as a customer, or a visitor to Mr. Lomas, a girlish-looking young man? He was slim and willowy, had brown pointed shoes, a green suit, blue eyes, and delicate hands."

The girl had no need to hesitate this time. She answered straight away.

"Why yes! It was a month ago. I was cleaning the windows and saw him coming along the road—"

"From the direction of, say, Mr. Steadfall's shop, or from the other direction?"

"From the direction of Mr. Steadfall's shop—from the city end of the road. He raised his hat to me and went in the shop. I heard him talking to Mr. Lomas, and then they went through to the house. I think they did," she added, "because I didn't hear their voices again. He came out just as I was finishing the windows."

"How long does it take you to clean them?"

"Over twenty minutes. There are so many little panes."

"And how long had you been working on them when he arrived? Long?"

"I'd only just started, Inspector."

"Thank you," said Knollis. He touched Bates on the arm and they left the shop.

"What do you make of it all?" Bates asked heavily.

"A conspiracy, and an involved one at that, Bates. But as to guessing what is behind it—well, I'm still in a fog. Patience, and more patience will unravel it eventually. It always has done so."

The Inspector found Dr. Whitelaw's report waiting for him when he returned to his office. As he did not wish to lose any time by going home he had a light tea sent in and over it read the report, together with the added statement to the effect that the Coroner had ordered a post-mortem examination to be held on the remains and was calling an inquest for the following afternoon, mainly for the purpose of identifying the deceased. It would not be necessary for Knollis to attend this as the two river police and the men from Willow Lock could give all the evidence that was necessary at this stage of the proceedings.

He felt a little more satisfied with life when he had disposed of the meal. After a deal of thought he went to the typewriter and set to work to collate the facts and information which had been gathered to date. His first list detailed the *dramatis personae*:

Ezekiah Lomas
The deceased. Rather a mystery. Motive for death not established. Neither is the method for that matter.

Lawrence Lomas, son of above.
Not quite straight. Inclined to contradict himself and withhold information, when he expresses surprise in a naive manner. Watch him closely.

Gertrude Lomas, daughter of deceased.
Told that she is queer as a result of a dud love affair. Didn't like the old man but doesn't look as if she is capable of either doping him or pushing him in the river.

John Steadfall.
Has a good motive as the losing suitor who never forgot, especially as Lomas seems to have given Jennifer hell all through their married life. And yet I don't think he bumped Lomas—and don't know that I should blame him if he had. Worth keeping an eye on for all that.

? Ericson.
Far too little known about him at present, being a shadowy figure who seems to be involved in some way. To be traced at all costs.

Nora Gretton.
Lawrence Lomas's fiancée. She's a little liar and I won't change my opinion until the reverse is proved up to the hilt. Note: who was the man with whom she drove into Burnham? Ericson?

The Inspector's second list concerned facts definitely established about the dead man:

He had exhibited, and reported, symptoms of poisoning. Said symptoms indicated cocaine as the lethal agent. He was found in the river, very dead.

He had been crudely shaved, apparently after death. He was full of whisky.

Light bruise on back of head reported by Whitelaw. He left ten thousand pounds. (How amassed?)

His son does not benefit financially.

There is no evidence of an insurance policy.

He was afraid of dying, as proved by his visit to Sir W.

At this point Sir Wilfred Burrows and Bates entered and looked over Knollis's shoulder.

"Made any sense of it yet?" the Chief Constable asked.

Knollis shrugged and half-turned. "I'm only just getting down to it. Up to now I've been a fact-collecting machine. You can't beat facts. Watch this!"

He slipped a new sheet in the typewriter.

QUERIES:

1. At a quarter past four Lawrence Lomas and Gretton were seen leaving Desborough by the Burnham Road. Lomas and his mechanic state that Lomas was engaged

in his surgery at that time. Gretton's own statement supports the latter statement. Which party is right?

2. Manager of Bridge Hotel states that Lomas's companion, presumably Ericson, left after nine. Newsboy states he left at five minutes to nine. Which is right?

3. If both are right, it suggests that Lomas and Ericson were both in the vicinity of the Bridge Hotel at nine o'clock. The statements of Lomas and Gretton infer that they were out in the country until ten o'clock and had spent the evening there. Where were Lomas and Gretton?

4. Steadfall states that after leaving the Commerce Club he went straight home, and stayed there. Is this true?

5. Steadfall states then an attempt to obtain cocaine illegally was made a month ago; bicarbonate of soda has been substituted for his stock of cocaine. Is he aware of this? Is his original story true?

"Whitelaw tells me that the prescription made up by Steadfall has no cocaine in it," said Sir Wilfred. "Bicarbonate of soda, as you suspected."

"And Dawes and Slater got an idea about Steadfall and are satisfied that he really was at home after leaving the Commerce Club," Bates added in his turn.

"They've been to the house?" asked Knollis.

"No, I don't think they did that."

"Steadfall is interesting," Knollis murmured, more to himself than his audience. "There is a vague motive to be imputed to him. He was a rival for Jennifer's hand in the long ago. Lawrence admitted that his father treated her cruelly and also that Steadfall was not happy in his married life. From those facts it is possible to infer that Steadfall was not in love with his wife, still hankered after Jennifer, and could have planned Lomas's death with vengeance as his motive. The only fact that makes me shy away from the possibility is that cocaine—or any poison—is too obvious for a chemist to use. It inclines me to believe that it was administered by some person unaccustomed to handling it—and that is helped by the lavishness of the treatment. I think we'll have to cut Steadfall out of the picture, although he will still be useful as a means of providing us with an authentic description of the background of the Lomas home."

"You are raising doubts about Lawrence Lomas even though he does not benefit by the old chap's will," the Chief Constable pointed out as he read through Knollis's lists.

Knollis grew evasive.

"His interest in his sister's welfare could have been his motive," he said without conviction.

"In spite of the fact that he only saw his father once a week you think he managed to pump him full of cocaine?"

Knollis looked up with gently-smiling eyes.

"It does sound silly, doesn't it, Sir Wilfred?"

"And this Ericson? What motive could he have for the killing of Lomas?"

"That depends whether we can trace a connection between them," said Knollis. "At the moment it isn't so much a matter of motives as a matter of finding who was there, or near Lomas, when he met his death. I've included Ericson because all the reports to hand from the Angel and the Commerce Club point to a business meeting with someone who was interested in buying the shop and stock. Unless there was a second prospective purchaser we have to consider that it was Ericson who was with him in the Commerce Club.

"Lomas, you see, did not advertise his business; he answered an advertisement inserted by Ericson. Ericson was the one who would have to interview several people—prospective sellers, and not Lomas who was interviewing prospective buyers. As far as we know, Lawrence and Ericson were the only two people who knew of his intention to sell, and the only people directly interested who saw him last night. We know that Ericson was in the district, and we think we know that Steadfall, his friend, was at home when he died. We know that Lawrence saw his father during the evening, but three people, including himself, say that he was not in Burnham after half-past six."

"Very complicated," murmured the Chief Constable. "In spite of that evidence," Knollis continued, "we hear of two people dressed in a similar manner to Lawrence being seen in the vicinity of the Bridge Hotel. That is the weak spot in the defence, and the point from which we must work. If we can get round that, and discover the identity of the lady-like man who called on Steadfall, and at least once on Lomas, we can soon unwind the tangle. And I'm willing to wager a shilling that when Dawes and Slater have done with the Stadium inquiry we'll find the first genuine coincidence in the case! We'll find that our fop was in no way connected with dog racing. And whenever we find Lomas's killer we shall find that the motive was a simple one, that the method was a simple one, and entangled circumstances are the only complicating factor!"

"I'd like to say something," said Bates importantly. "Three things are puzzling me. Dodson at Rose Cottage was the last person to see Lomas go away from Burnham. The barman was the last person to see Lomas leave The Ferryman and go back toward Burnham. Now Dr. Whitelaw said that Lomas died between ten and half-past. At five past ten Hopkin let Barky's barges through the lock. Dodson was uneasy about something, and we didn't know what it was. You think, Inspector, that either Lawrence Lomas or Ericson hold the key to the solution. I can't agree with you. I think either Dodson or Barky hold it. I'm so sure of it that I'd like permission to spend a few hours on those angles."

Knollis gazed reflectively at his lieutenant.

"Do you know, Bates, I think you've got something there. Take that end up and see what you can make of it."

"One point seems to have been overlooked by both of you," said Sir Wilfred. "You, Knollis, say that Lawrence had nothing to gain by his father's death. You also appear to have taken in his story that it was he who persuaded his father to cut him out of his will. I suggest that the matter was never discussed between them, but that Lawrence came into possession of the information and planned to kill his father before the new will was signed—not knowing that it was already valid!"

Knollis narrowed his eyes. A light smile hovered round his lips.

"The most obvious solution, Sir Wilfred, and that's why I am not considering it. There's one point in your favour; it makes Lawrence a liar whichever way you look at it. On the face of it he has a good alibi. Ericson, as yet, has none. I'm bound to agree with Bates that the mystery lies between Dodson's cottage and The Ferryman. It would be foolish to ignore the obvious. So you go ahead, Bates, and Dawes and Slater can follow the greyhound end of it, and also try to trace our effeminate gentleman. I'm going to have a shot at knocking Lawrence's alibi to pieces—and if I do that it means that Nora Gretton is in it up to her chin. She's a riddle."

"And what is my share of the work?" the Chief Constable murmured dryly.

"Get the B.B.C. to broadcast an appeal for Ericson to come forward," said Knollis. He glanced at the clock. "It should be possible to get it out on the nine o'clock news bulletin. It would also be useful, sir, if you could get further information from Caine and the bank manager. Oh yes, and one more thing! You'll find a batch of In Memoriam cuttings in the top drawer in my desk. You know the editors of the Courier and the Echo better than I do. Ask 'em to find out through their advertising departments whether all were inserted and paid for by Lomas, and if not, by whom."

"They were nice thoughts," said Bates stubbornly.

Sir Wilfred raised his eyebrows. "You haven't given Steadfall up completely then?"

"I've no intention of giving anybody up yet," said Knollis.

Sir Wilfred stared at the wall for a moment, and then said: "Knollis!"

"Well, sir?"

"This Emsworth—I keep getting him almost in focus, and then he slips again. I'm sure I've heard of him somewhere or other."

"That's very likely," said Knollis. He buried his face in his handkerchief.

CHAPTER VI
THE ALIBI OF LAWRENCE LOMAS

Knollis set out for Desborough shortly after tea. He called at Lawrence Lomas's home and was told that he had gone out with the car. Knollis went on to Grove Road, and allowed himself a smile of satisfaction as he saw the car standing outside Briar Cottage. Neither Lomas nor his fiancée were overjoyed to see him, and Lomas went out of his way to express his feelings.

"We were going out for a run," he said bluntly. Nora Gretton elbowed him aside, and took charge of the proceedings. "If the Inspector has business with you, Lawry, then you must attend to that first. You will sit down, Inspector Knollis?"

Knollis accepted the invitation and paid more attention to her than he had done on the occasion of his previous visit. She was, he estimated, about twenty-eight years of age. She was confident in manner, self-possessed, and it was highly probable that she knew her way round. That she knew how to handle Lomas was evident from the way she had crowded his objections from the picture. As far as looks were concerned Knollis had to give her full marks. She was bright-eyed and fresh. Her hair was dark, and wavy—although the Inspector was unable to guess whether the waves were natural or induced. She was again wearing slacks, and a cream blouse that showed most of her arms and rather too much chest, too much, that is, for a married man of Knollis's taste. He was all for the demure, modest woman.

She gave him a twisted, mocking smile. "Now that you've taken stock, and provided yourself with a description for your records, Inspector, perhaps we can get down to the business of the meeting," she surprised him by saying.

Knollis started, and shook his head free of thoughts of her for the moment.

"Yes, of course, Miss Gretton. Well, I took a statement from you, Mr. Lomas, and one from you, Miss Gretton. While I, personally, am prepared to accept those statements, it has become necessary to check them. Evidence given by other witnesses would seem to contradict them."

Lomas raised his eyebrows. "Oh? How? In what way?"

Knollis affected a reluctant attitude.

"Well, we have your statement with regard to the time you went into Burnham, and your mechanic has, of course, corroborated it, but now I'd like to know where Miss Gretton was at the same time—between a quarter past four and, say, half-past five."

Nora Gretton made a great show of astonishment which Knollis was prepared to doubt or accept with equal alacrity. Lawrence Lomas was immediately indignant.

"Is this necessary?" he demanded.

"I'm afraid it is," said Knollis. "A matter of routine, and no more. We have to clear every doubtful point as we go along. Progress is impossible without such care."

"I seem to have heard that from you before," Lomas replied with a cynical twist on his lip.

"There's nothing to be afraid of in such a question," Nora Gretton interrupted soothingly. "I was at home. I stayed here until Lawrence called for me." She turned to Lomas. "Didn't I, Lawry?"

"Naturally," Lomas said shortly. "Where else could she be? I don't see the point of your question, Inspector."

Knollis smiled. "You are hardly in a position to verify Miss Gretton's statement," he pointed out. "If you were not here you could not be aware of her movements. Not that it matters. I naturally accept Miss Gretton's statement."

Lomas was somewhat mollified by Knollis's manner. "Oh well, that alters everything. I thought you were doubting Miss Gretton's word."

"You weren't here at the time in question?" Knollis murmured quietly.

"My mechanic settled that point, Inspector."

"And you, Miss Gretton, were not at the surgery?"

"I've already told you that I was here."

"Quite so," said Knollis. "The point I am making is that Mr. Lomas is completely unable to substantiate your statement to the effect that you were, in fact, at home between a quarter past four and half-past five."

Lomas stared wonderingly. "I thought you were investigating my father's death, and not Miss Gretton's movements!"

"That's right," confirmed Knollis.

"But he died at ten o'clock, and in any case what can Nora's movements have to do with it?"

"Miss Gretton is concerned inasmuch as she verified your statement. You'll agree there?"

"Why yes."

"Then I repeat, in spite of your cynical attitude, that this is purely a matter of routine. It is my plain duty to make sure that Miss Gretton was able to verify your statement. You see," Knollis added in a more conciliatory tone, "in a homicide case we take statements from everybody who is even remotely concerned in the case—as is Miss Gretton, for instance. Among all the statements we take, one at least is bound to be false. You see that?"

"Yes, I see your point," Lomas nodded reluctantly.

"And so it is absolutely essential that we go into each statement thoroughly. Until we find those statements that can stand up to examination we cannot deal with those that don't, and it is always these that bring a case to a successful conclusion. In this present instance we find that Miss Gretton cannot prove that she was at home at the stated time. It may be of no importance at all. Indeed, I don't think it is, but I have to go through the same performance with it just the same. If Miss Gretton has no guilty conscience she has no need to fear my questioning—although it may prove irritating."

"Yes, I see now," said Lomas.

Nora Gretton made no remark. She sat with her hands clasped, staring past Knollis, and apparently paying no heed to his explanations, long-winded as they were by deliberate design. He had to keep Lomas in ignorance of Nora Gretton's trip in his car while scaring her to the utmost.

"Your car now," Knollis said directly to Lomas. "Where was that between a quarter past four and half-past five?"

Nora Gretton shot a quick glance at Lomas, and then composed her features.

"My car?" Lomas asked with astonishment tinging his voice. "It was garaged of course."

"Where?"

"Well, normally it is garaged behind the house, but I had taken it into the High Street garage to have the spare wheel repaired. There was a puncture."

"Who owns the garage?"

"Empton. His place is nearly at the end of the street, the northernmost end. You will be making inquiries there?"

"Not necessarily," said Knollis.

Nora Gretton gave a deep sigh. It may have been one of relief, but she covered it by yawning and stretching her round arms.

"This doesn't seem to be getting anybody anywhere," she said. "Suppose you tell us where it will all lead, Inspector."

Knollis recognised the pert challenge, and hesitated. He was satisfied that the mobile patrol had made no mistake in identifying Gretton. He was equally satisfied that Lomas was not with her in the car. It appeared that she had made an unauthorised trip and that Lomas was unaware of it. It was no part of his, Knollis's, job to make Lawrence Lomas suspicious of his fiancée at this stage. Not yet. Her queer behaviour may have had no connection with the death of Lomas Senior, but Knollis's main rule was: Suspect everybody, including the corpse. He had met corpses who were as deceptive as the living elements in a case, and so he had no intention of side-slipping that rule for anybody on earth.

"Suppose you tell us where it will all lead, Inspector," he heard Nora Gretton say again.

"I've told you," said Knollis. "It is sheer routine. We should be asses, you know, if we accepted all statements at their face value. And as we have to test some of them, well, we go the whole hog and test them all without fear or favour."

"We shall soon know that," Lomas said bitingly.

"You should do," Knollis retorted. "I've tried to hammer the idea home, but the material seems to be wooden."

He reached for his hat, and smoothed the brim.

"I think I've covered all the vital points now, but there is one item you could clear up for me. You told me that you went for a country run. Which way did you go?" Lomas looked up sharply, and licked his lips.

Nora Gretton blinked and said hurriedly: "Why, we went out to the river. Not Willow Lock way, but out to White Horse Ferry."

Knollis considered the reply. Desborough lay roughly north of Burnham, and White Horse Ferry lay to the east of Desborough, about five miles out. From there . . . "You stayed there all the evening?"

Lomas looked across at his fiancée. "We-ell, we left the car and walked in the woods for an hour or so."

"Left the car at the White Horse?"

"Well no, not exactly. We drove up river for about a mile and left the car there, just off the towpath."

"You're sure you didn't go to Willow Lock?" Knollis asked, and then added: "Your presence in the locality would not necessarily indicate that you were in any way connected with your father's death."

"I should hope not!" Lomas replied indignantly. He set his jaw and demanded in a truculent voice: "Look here, Inspector! You've said that there is no suspicion attached to either of us. Then why this persistent questioning?"

"It would be possible for you to have seen the person who did kill your father—if you had been at Willow Lock," Knollis replied naively.

"Then you don't think I had anything to do with my father's death, Inspector?"

"Good lord, no!" Knollis replied. "That would be the last thing you would ever do."

To himself, he said: "Or almost the last."

"What facts *have* come to light with regard to his death?"

Knollis laid his hat aside and ticked the items off on his fingers.

"He was found in the river. He was apparently drowned. He was exhibiting the symptoms of cocaine poisoning. He had been shaved. He left ten thousand pounds—"

"What?"

"He really left all that?"

Lomas and Gretton jumped from their seats.

"Ten thousand pounds," Knollis repeated softly, as if that sum was quite a normal one to mention.

"You—you are sure, Inspector?"

Knollis shrugged his shoulders. "I have only the evidence of the bank and your father's solicitors."

"But where the hell did he get it from? The business never made more than ten to fifteen pounds clear profit in any one week when I lived at home, and it has gone down rather than up of late."

"Investments, probably," Knollis suggested. "He was a thrifty man, of your own evidence, and if he saved every penny of his profits he would make—what? Five hundred a year? It is possible, you know! Five hundred a year for twenty years would do it."

"But my father wasn't a thrifty man after my mother's death. He drank like a fish."

"Which suggests that the business was making nearer fifteen than ten."

Nora Gretton stared hard at her fiancé. "You were an ass!"

Lomas stared back. As if in self-justification he said: "But I never thought he would leave more than two or three thousand. I was prepared to sacrifice that."

"Otherwise you would not have persuaded him to alter his will?" Knollis suggested. "Is that it?"

"Well, ten thousand," Lomas said gloomily. "There's enough for both of us. Gertrude will be on velvet."

"And you regret that?"

Lomas shifted uneasily. "Not exactly. But ten thousand! Good lord! Where did he get it from? He must have had another business somewhere under another name. The dark old horse. A case of still waters . . ."

"Your father was in the habit of inserting In Memoriam notices in the local papers," said Knollis. "Have you ever done anything in that line?"

Lomas shook his head. "No, I hate parading my sentiments," he said. Then he looked up at Knollis with a half-smile on his lips. "You don't miss much, do you?"

"The complete set of cuttings were found in his bureau," he explained.

"Anything else of interest, Inspector?"

"Several family photographs."

"I can have those, I suppose?"

"Later," said Knollis. "I'm finding them of extreme interest at present."

"Oh? How? I don't quite understand."

Knollis ignored the question, and lifted his hat again. This time he rose, too, and sauntered slowly to the door.

"It's a stock question, Mr. Lomas, and the answer is always the same, but I feel impelled to ask it in case the answer should be different. Had your father any enemies?"

"Who would want to kill him? Who could bring themselves to kill him?" Lomas asked blandly.

"That," said Knollis, "is exactly what Sir Wilfred Burrows asked your father at that fateful interview."

"And what did my father reply?"

"He was cynical, and bitter," Knollis replied. "He, too, asked Sir Wilfred in turn who would want to kill him, a poor old man with one foot in the grave. Heigh ho, but it's a queer world! The allotted span of a man's life is three score years and ten, and there are people who simply can't bear to see others live even that short span to its terminal point. Well, we shall find our man, Mr. Lomas, and then all this questioning will be over and done with, and Teddy Jessop will earn another fiver."

"Teddy Jessop?" murmured Nora Gretton.

"The—the hangman," quavered Lomas.

"The hangman, executioner, or call him what you will," said Knollis pleasantly. He half-closed his eyes. "Queer when you come to think of it! We are a Christian nation, but we follow the old Mosaic law. We take an eye for an eye and a life for a life, whereas the Christian law bids us to ignore all evil and let the Lord repay. *'Vengeance is mine,' saith the Lord*. But we are not satisfied with letting the mills of God grind slowly. We demand vengeance and call it deterrent action. Three agonising weeks in the condemned cell—the utter refinement of mental torture—and then the nine o'clock walk . . ."

"The nine o'clock walk," Nora Gretton said bleakly.

"Not a very long one," said Knollis as he opened the door, "but rather startling and shocking. I saw Cartwright hanged three years ago. Ten feet from the gallows was the door of his cell, and he had to walk that ten feet. His feet were like lead. He couldn't pick 'em up. They half-carried him. They even had to hold him upright on the scaffold while Teddy fixed the noose." He paused for a moment, and then went on: "Awful? Yes, it was, but it was soon over. He hadn't to live with his conscience for another thirty years—his conscience and the ghost of the woman he killed."

He broke off again, sighed, and said in conclusion: "Oh well, thanks for your assistance. I'll let you know how we progress. Good evening, Miss Gretton. Good evening, Mr. Lomas."

He drove away from the house, ran the car into a side street, and then walked back down Grove Road and waited in a doorway. A few minutes later Lomas and Nora Gretton came from the house, scuffled into Lomas's car, and disappeared in a cloud of dust. Knollis went back to his own car and patted the bonnet affectionately. "There's a short cut to White Horse Ferry, old lass. It will be rough on you, but I think we'll take it. We may find Lomas and his girl arranging an alibi."

He got to White Horse Ferry ten minutes before his people, mainly by taking a cross-country route and keeping his foot well down. He left his car some distance from the hotel and hurried along the tow-path. As he walked he reflected on his next move. He could catch Lomas in the act of trying to arrange an alibi—as he was sure to do since it was so evident that both he and Gretton had been lying—or he could go in first and question the landlord. The latter was the most straightforward course, and would have the added virtue of throwing Lomas and his companion into confusion if they found him there.

The landlord, whom he knew by sight, was in the lounge. Knollis sent his card in by a waiter and, being human, was secretly pleased by the way it brought the man rushing to meet him.

"Inspector Knollis?"

"Yes, I'm Knollis. You are Samuel Holmes?"

"Nothing wrong, is there? Nobody been complaining about the house? I'm most particular, you know!"

"No complaints at all," Knollis assured him. "Er—can we talk somewhere more private? It's rather public here."

"Come through into the house, into the sitting-room, Inspector. Now, perhaps you will have a drink with me? A beer, or perhaps a whisky?"

"Nothing for me while I'm on business, thanks," said Knollis. "You've heard about Lomas's death at Willow Lock?"

"Of course, Inspector. It's the only topic of conversation among our customers—and everybody else if it comes to that."

"Well, you know how it is when one of these cases comes up," Knollis said confidentially. "We have to ask a thousand and one questions that prove to have no bearing on the case. Rumours here, and rumours there, and they all have to be investigated. You know!"

"Oh yes, I understand, Inspector. Anything I can do to help I'll do willingly. You can be sure of that."

"Well," Knollis went on, "all this is in the strictest confidence. It seems evident that our man went out of his way to impersonate the dead man's son—Mr. Lawrence Lomas. Perhaps you know him?"

"Quite well. He's one of our best customers. He often brings his lady along in the evenings."

"Was he here between half-past six and ten o'clock last night?"

"Last night?"

"Last night!"

The landlord stuck a reflective tongue in the side of his cheek. Then he shook his head. "Not last night, he wasn't. I can swear to that."

"You know Miss Gretton—Lomas's fiancée?"

"Yes, I know her."

"Did she show in yesterday, at any time during the day?"

"Oh no, Inspector. She hasn't been since Sunday night, when she came with Mr. Lomas. There's nothing against Mr. Lomas, is there?" he asked anxiously.

"Not a thing," said Knollis. "Only the trails of himself and his impersonator have become confused and I'm trying to sort them out."

At that moment the door opened and Nora Gretton, with Lawrence Lomas behind her, burst into the room. She fixed her eyes on Knollis, almost fearfully, halted, and glanced back at Lomas. She made a hurried effort to gain control of herself, and forced a laugh.

"We do seem to be running into each other, Inspector!"

The landlord seemed to sense the atmosphere and in trying to make Knollis's presence appear normal he did exactly the opposite.

"Then I'm not likely to hear any more about it, Inspector?" he asked in a too highly pitched voice.

Knollis grinned. "You aren't, but somebody else is. Thanks for the information. It was all I was expecting."

Lomas roughly swung Nora Gretton out of the way and faced Knollis angrily.

"I'm getting a bit sick of this, Inspector. Of course," he said with heavy sarcasm, "you haven't been asking questions about Miss Gretton and myself!"

"Only testing your alibi," Knollis said grimly. "I thought it wasn't very solid when you produced it in Grove Road, and it is positively paper thin at the White Horse Hotel. Anyway, you'll be pleased to hear that I am asking no more questions."

He bowed, and walked from the hotel. In his car he sat back with a lighted cigarette to do some highly necessary thinking. It did seem that no possible motive could be imputed to Lawrence

Lomas, because he had lost everything in persuading his father to alter his will. And yet it was certain that he and Nora Gretton had been up to some queer business that would not bear investigation—from their point of view.

Some minutes later he heard voices, and recognising them as belonging to Lomas and Gretton he slid to the floor of the car, fumbling with the wires behind the panel in case they should chance to look in.

"That's Knollis's car," Nora Gretton exclaimed as they drew near. Knollis kept low. The car was twelve feet from the towpath and they might pass it by without making a closer inspection.

"He's too quick on the scent," Lomas said in a worried voice. "I only hope he doesn't get on to Dodson."

"Be quiet, you fool," Nora Gretton hissed. "He may be within earshot."

"Not him," Lomas laughed bitterly. "He'll be further up river, making inquiries about our movements last night. He'd third-degree his own grandmother for fourpence."

They passed along the towpath, arm in arm. Knollis waited a few minutes and then regained his seat. He nodded grimly. So Bates was right. There was something fishy at Rose Cottage. Dodson knew something—but what? Dodson had seen Lomas Senior pass toward The Ferryman. And he had not seen him return—or had he? There was the matter of Lomas's ten thousand pounds, too. Where had that come from? Another visit to the bank was indicated, and this time he would attend to it himself. Sir Wilfred was the Chief Constable, but as an investigator he was but an amateur, a dilettante. Bates, in spite of his stodginess, was better than six Sir Wilfreds. With the aid of Bates, Dawes, and Slater, he could put this case in the bag in record time. It just needed penetrative insight and patience, chiefly patience. Knollis had a theory about character that had solved many cases and would eventually solve this. In the main it revolved round the idea that it was desirable to let your man underestimate your abilities. His natural vanity, a vital flaw in the criminal mind, became inflated when the culprit thought he was pulling your leg, and as a consequence he eased the tightness of his lips.

And talking of character, there were certain things he wanted to know about Gertrude Lomas. She interested him.

He glanced at the clock on the panel. It was eight now. He would have ample time. When he had interviewed her he intended to spend the night in bed. He needed the sleep, and was not afraid of his man bolting. He was still not at all sure whether Lomas, Steadfall, or Ericson was responsible for the murder but he was quite sure that his man would stay put. It was a pity really, because once that panicky dash was made the task of proving guilt became easier.

He drove north for ten miles and then turned down a tree-lined avenue. A further half-mile and he came to the lodge gates leading to Fountains, the home of Captain and Mrs. Geoffrey Gregory. The production of his warrant card got him past the gate-house, and he drove up to the magnificent grey stone mansion before which three great fountains played. He put his hand in his pocket for his card-case, and then changed his mind.

"Will you please inform Miss Lomas that Mr. Gordon Knollis wishes to speak with her," he said to the liveried and liverish flunkey who received him.

A few moments later he was shown into a small reception room and here he had to wait for a considerable time. At last Gertrude Lomas entered the room and Knollis rose.

"I thought it would be you, Inspector," she greeted him. "You will have brought news of my father. Do be seated, please, and tell me all you can."

Knollis eyed her with professional interest. She was oval-faced, and pale, and when she smiled it was only with her lips. Her grey eyes were pre-occupied with some matter other than the immediate one of Knollis's visit. "This is an unofficial visit," said Knollis.

She made an effort to appear interested. "Oh yes?"

"You are aware, of course, that your father's will makes you his sole legatee, apart from two minor bequests of twenty-five pounds each?"

"Oh?" she murmured with mild surprise. Then, as the significance of the fact penetrated her mind, she said: "But surely Lawrence benefits?"

"Lawrence doesn't get a cent," Knollis replied flatly.

"But his will—" she broke off, and stared.

"You were saying . . ." prompted Knollis.

"Well, he made a will long before my mother died. He left his money in trust for Lawrence and myself, my mother to have. But I believe this was all mentioned earlier, as was the possibility of a new will. I suppose it is to the new will that you refer?"

"A new will, yes. He left twenty-five pounds to the Willow Lock Angling Club, and twenty-five pounds to John Steadfall as a token of esteem and respect—"

"I'm glad of that," she said softly. "Dear old John! The amount is not much, but it does prove that he really valued his friendship."

"And the remainder to you, Miss Lomas. A matter of ten thousand pounds."

Gertrude Lomas leaned toward him. "I beg your pardon!"

"Ten thousand pounds."

"My father?"

"Your father!"

She gazed dreamily at the ceiling, and a happy smile wreathed her lips. Then an expression of doubt came over her eyes, clouding them. "You are sure, Inspector?"

"That is the amount stated by his solicitors and his bank, Miss Lomas. There is no mistake."

She interlaced her fingers and pressed her hands to her breast. "At last! At last!"

"This means the realisation of your dreams?"

She nodded. "Yes, all of them! Egypt, Africa, the South Seas, moonlight evenings in Hawaii, the Grand Canyon, the Rockies—everything, everything I've ever wanted to see; every place I've ever wished to visit. I can do it now!"

She turned towards him happily.

"Mother always wanted to do that, and I've dreamed of them ever since I was a girl. Mother used to take me on her knee and work her way through the geography book. There was romance, and happiness, and sunshine, and colour in it. And then my father came upon us one day, and burned the book, and—and—"

"Struck your mother for what he called her foolishness," said Knollis quietly.

"Yes," she replied with a sudden movement of her head. "How did you know?"

"Your mother and Old John as you call him were lovers once, were they not?"

"Yes. Mother made a great mistake. She mistook father's hardness for experience of the world. Poor old John was a gentle soul. He never wanted money, but only to help his fellow men. He could not afford to be a doctor, and so he did the next best thing and became a chemist. Mother told me that she saw her mistake when it was too late, but she forced herself to be faithful to my father, even in thought. Father saw from the first that mother was impressed by Old John's gentler qualities. He himself revelled in making money and he would periodically throw his bank book down on the table and tell her to look at it. 'You've married a business man, not a lily-livered monk!' he would tell her. Mother seldom remarked on his treatment of her, but on one occasion she asked him what good the money was doing while it was lying in the bank. My father replied that one day she would be glad of it, and in turn she replied that she would like a few flowers while she was living and not stuck in a vase over her grave when it was too late for her to appreciate them.

"My father's original motive in making money may have been to impress her, but it faded, leaving him with nothing but an insatiable urge to collect it—for that was all it was. I know he worked hard, but how he collected ten thousand pounds is beyond my comprehension. You don't think that he—he did anything dishonest, Inspector?"

"I have no means of knowing that," Knollis replied.

"It was a good business," she went on absently, "but I cannot see it making ten thousand pounds."

She had been staring through the window at the slowly darkening sky. Now she turned on him again. "You must think I am horribly disloyal to my father! I am disloyal, and it is shocking bad taste, and yet, somehow, I have never regarded my father as a parent. My mother was both parents in one; he, the man who ill-treated her and yet provided the bread and butter. If you had been brought up with us I think you would understand, Inspector. Still . . ."

"I take it that you have met Miss Gretton?"

Gertrude Lomas looked up sharply. "Gretton? That woman? Yes, I've met her. I'm surprised that Lawrence cannot see through her. She is a common little gold-digger—or is she? Perhaps there is more behind it than that. I don't trust her, anyway. You know, Lawrence will expect me to share my little fortune with him, but I have no intention of doing so. I have been a fool in the past, and treated him as a spoiled young brother. All that is over now. I realise the power of money at last. In some ways my father was right, and in others very, very wrong. His idea regarding money was sound when regarded without the distortion which he brought to it. Money does talk! It is power! It gives confidence!"

Knollis stared at the carpet. "I wonder if you would accept what I consider to be sound advice, Miss Lomas?"

"Anything," she said firmly. "At this moment you are a messenger from the gods, bringing me news of my release!"

"Then just at present I wouldn't tell your brother anything of your intention to keep all your legacy." An unbelieving horror slowly crept over her pale face. "Not that, Inspector! Not that!"

"It's merely a suggestion," the Inspector said heavily. She nodded her head. "It may be good advice, very good advice, Inspector. I accept it."

CHAPTER VII
THE MYSTERIOUS MR. ERICSON

THE INSPECTOR was thoughtful as he left Fountains. Gertrude Lomas was a woman, and women were something of a perplexity to him. He could not understand the feminine viewpoint, nor their method of shifting the ground. He puzzled over it as he drove towards Desborough, and there dismissed it while he paid a visit to Empton, the garage proprietor. The man was in the act of locking up for the night.

"Sorry to butt in just now," said Knollis, "but I'm thinking of buying a second-hand car."

That much was true, and so was his next statement. It was only when the two were taken as connected parts of a whole that any objection could be taken to their accuracy. Knollis mentally crossed his fingers and allowed a suitable pause before continuing: "I'm interested in a car at present owned by a dentist of the name of Lomas. Perhaps you know it? I understand that you do all the running repairs. Is the car in good condition?"

Empton eyed him steadily. He was a thin man with a slight squint and more oil about him than seemed consistent with good workmanship.

"Mr. Lomas's car? Ay, it's a good 'un all right. I'm surprised to hear that he wants to part with it."

"I heard that it was out of commission," said Knollis. "Got it here?"

He peered past the garage owner into the darkened building, as if looking for the car.

"He's running it now," said Empton. "The car's all right in every respect."

"He did bring it in on Sunday night though," Knollis persisted. "If you've been working on it ever since it must have something radically wrong with it."

"Working on it ever since, my foot," exclaimed Empton. "He'd got muck in the carburettor feed. It was no sort of a job. Why, that young woman of his took it out for a trial run yesterday at tea-time. How much is he asking for it?"

"Well, we haven't got to that point yet," said Knollis. "I'm not too sure that he'll want to part with it when it gets to talking cash, but this one of mine is getting cranky and I'll need to think about a change very soon."

"Ay well, if you get Lomas's you'll not do so bad, and I'll get the order for his new one."

"You do his cleaning and greasing as well?" Knollis murmured conversationally, and then added naively: "Anyway, cleaning won't give you a deal of trouble. These professional gentlemen are faddy people, and when a car sticks to the main road it doesn't get more than a good layer of dust on it. A hose and some body cream, and there you are!"

Empton was not inclined to agree with the Inspector, and the Inspector did not seem displeased by the opposition to his ideas.

"He gives me some tidy jobs to do," said Empton. "Where the 'ell he takes it I don't know, but he can lard that car up like nobody on earth. Monday night, for instance, it was filthy. He brought it in for filling-up and cleaning. What a bleeding job! And he wanted it out early. As it happened it wasn't wanted that night because the police fetched him to see about his father and used a police car, but he'd said he wanted it out early and as the lad doesn't get here until half-past eight I had to sam into it myself."

"He must have been out very early," murmured Knollis.

"Before half-past eight. Still, here we are, gossiping like two old washerwomen and the time knocking up to ten o'clock. Glad to have been of assistance to you."

He walked into the garage, pulled the roller shutter down, and two bolts clanged into position. Knollis returned to the car, smiling.

Bates was waiting for him at the office. After one short glance at his lieutenant Knollis knew that things were going well. "Cough it up," he said shortly.

"Dodson's done a guy—if his name really is Dodson," Bates replied. He sat back to enjoy the expression on Knollis's face.

The Inspector refused to express surprise, or indeed any other emotion. "Let's hear the rest of it," he said.

"I started at Walesby's place, and soon learned that Dodson left the district eighteen months ago. He wasn't bow-legged, and he never lived at Rose Cottage. Rose Cottage belongs to Walesby, and he rented it to our Dodson three months ago. He told Walesby that he was the original Dodson's second cousin and had been recommended by him. He said he was a retired stable-boy from Newmarket, and wanted to live the rest of his life out by the river. Walesby let him have the place at six bob a week, rates inclusive. He is understood to have occupied the place spasmodically, and the girl Marjory did the same. Dodson seems to have spent the time dodging about racecourses.

"I went to the cottage, and it looks as if Dodson has scarpered. I found the key under a stone by the back door, and I let myself in. There was a note on the table, addressed to 'M'—whoever she might be. It just said 'The gate's up' and that was all."

"The starting gate, I should imagine," commented Knollis. "And that would indicate Dodson's belief that the race was on. An easy code message for somebody. Carry on."

"I—er—well, I searched the cottage . . ."

"Without a warrant?" Knollis asked with a smile. Bates affected a coy attitude. "I was not searching it really, Inspector. You see, I found the cottage abandoned, and thinking that some harm may have come to the owner I looked round the place in search of him. That is what I meant when I said I had searched the place."

"You looked in drawers, and wardrobes, and cupboards for him?" Knollis suggested.

"And under the beds," said Bates. "There was nobody to be found at all, at all! But, while looking for Dodson, I found a suit of clothes, and a shirt, and everything necessary but a human being to fill 'em to correspond with, or to,—I never could remember which was right—"

"It doesn't matter a hang," said Knollis. "You found the girlish young man who went to see Steadfall, found all but the body! That right?"

"That is what I was trying to say," chuckled Bates, flicking his ghost of a moustache.

"And so the believed-to-be sissy is—"

"Our Marjory, for a guess."

"Anything else?"

Bates nodded, and his smile broadened.

"A cut-throat razor. You should see the edge. Just like a saw. It might have been used to give somebody a dry shave. And there were grizzled hairs mixed up in the hinge and in the handle."

"What have you done with it?" Knollis asked sharply. "Left it upstairs with the keen-eyed microscope boys. They were very interested. Almost kissed me for providing an interesting subject."

"Find anything else?"

"The fire had been banked with coal slack as if in readiness for someone who would come in later. That, I think, was Marjory."

Knollis slapped one fist into the palm of his other hand. "By the Lord Harry, you've done well, Bates. Who did you leave to watch the place?"

"Forster, our new man. He's as keen as mustard. I parked him across the river with a pair of night-glasses, a flask, and some sandwiches."

"Can the cottage be reached from the rear, Bates?"

"I thought of that," Bates grinned. "It can, although not by a recognised footpath. There are four fields between the cottage garden and the lane leading parallel with the towpath. I found footprints down the side of the fields, and the barbed wire fence at the rear of the cottage was strained in one corner, as if the top strand had been forced up to allow somebody to pass underneath."

"Put anybody there?"

"It wasn't necessary," Bates pointed out. "Anybody coming to the cottage would automatically poke the fire into a blaze. I told Forster to keep an eye on the chimney."

"Yes, that should be all right," said Knollis. "Now I'll tell you how I fared."

He plunged into a detailed account of his investigations. When he was through he made a suggestion.

"Suppose that Marjory and Nora Gretton are one and the same person, Bates? We know that Lomas had an appointment with Ericson. We know, in spite of her denials, that Nora Gretton brought a man, mistaken for Lawrence Lomas, into Burnham at teatime on Monday, and I know from her demeanour that she does not want Lawrence to know that. If she is Marjory, then she is connected with the events that have taken place in this cottage, and we can hazard a guess from the razor that Dodson was connected with the shaving of Lomas. Now then, what can we make of that?"

"A conspiracy, as you said before, Inspector."

"We also have to consider Lomas's ten thousand. His son was certainly not aware that the old man was worth so much, and, what was more, couldn't think how he amassed it. Neither was Gertrude aware of it. She was likewise puzzled about the method of acquisition. Now I have an idea, Bates. It is not entirely disconnected with the distribution of snow. You'll remember the girl in Lomas's shop saying that he took no end of callers through to the living-room? Ask yourself why. It is hardly usual, surely, to entertain all the travellers and bagmen as if they were personal friends. My idea—and it is nothing more—is this; that Lomas was not supplying snow to individuals in Burnham, but to the trade as it were. He was a main distributor. I want you to put a police guard on the Desborough Road premises to-night. If I remember my Burnham correctly there is a ten-feet way running behind that side of the Desborough Road. See that it is watched. It's a complicated mess at present, is this case, but we are seeing light, and we'll pull it clear."

"Sir Wilfred managed to get the message re Ericson over the air," said Bates. "The usual guff about wanting to interview him in connection with the death of Lomas, and all that. I wonder whether he'll turn up? Oh, and I have knocked out a description of Dodson for circulation. Also got the Newmarket people on the phone, but they don't know of him."

Knollis considered the point. "Well," he said eventually, "if you really think he is a horsey man, get in touch with the other racecourses. He may have favourites."

Sergeant Dawes and Detective Officer Slater entered the office, both heavy-eyed and yawning.

"What a do!" complained Dawes. "All our trouble for nothing. We've wasted a hell of a lot of time."

"A dead-end job," added Slater. "We are the Kids."

"All phoney?" Knollis asked quietly.

"So far, yes," Dawes explained. "There was trouble over the Star dog, but it worked the opposite way round. It really did win unexpectedly, and the chap who owns it dragged a heap of winnings, but they hadn't doped it to win. They left it untrained, so that it lost race after race and got a long mark. Then they kept it off the tracks and trained it to the last inch. They knew all along that she was a good girl, and it did the trick on this particular evening. The track officials got suspicious and made inquiries."

"But Steadfall said he had watched the papers and the dog had not won a race since," protested Knollis. "That doesn't sound as if it was a first-rate track dog!"

"The officials clamped down on the dog's owner," said Dawes. "They insisted that the dog be kept at the Stadium and be trained there—and then made training as difficult as possible. All very much under cover, of course, but Slater and I ferreted the truth from its burrow. We went to see a chap named Blunt who lives up east. He didn't want to talk until I showed my warrant card, and then he uncorked himself and spilled everything. It seems that he got in touch with a fellow by the name of Dodson who knew a lot of horse-racing—"

Knollis and Bates exchanged glances.

"—and this Dodson put them up to the game. He said he knew just how long to hold back, and if they'd cut him in at the game he would guarantee a ripe harvest. They did, and they did! There was a row, as stated after the race, and Dodson never showed up again." Knollis turned to Bates. "I wonder if the thing was wangled in some way so that it fitted with the call on Steadfall, or was the whole thing really coincidental?"

"Well, I'm slowly catching your ideas about coincidences," replied Bates heavily. "All we've met with so far have proved to be apparent only."

"True enough," Knollis said thoughtfully. "There's a link between Lomas, Ericson, and Steadfall if only we can find it. Where is it, and what is it? The obvious answer is Ezekiah Lomas."

The telephone bell sounded, and Knollis lifted the handpiece mechanically. "Inspector Gordon Knollis; Burnham City Police."

He waited, and then blinked.

"Who? Roger Ericson? Yes, I presume you are the gentleman we are looking for—if, that is, you are the one who was considering the purchase of Lomas's business. Certainly I'll be pleased to make that arrangement. Where are you speaking from? Edinburgh! Well, you won't be here for some hours. Certainly, sir. Most gratified. Pardon? Well yes, on the face of it. Some bright fellow apparently tried to impersonate you. If we can satisfy ourselves that the evidence in our hands does relate to you we can probably lay the same hands on the right merchant. Thank you, sir. Good night."

Knollis winked, waited a moment, and then lifted the receiver again.

"Inspector Knollis speaking. Hello, Exchange. Can you tell me where that call came from? Cambridge? Thanks!" He smiled as he relaxed in his chair.

"Gentlemen, you may go to bed if you have beds to go to. I am doing the same. The third suspect will soon be in our hands. Sweet dreams!"

When they left he again spoke into the telephone, to the police authorities at Cambridge. On his way from the building he called in the charge room.

"A fellow by the name of Ericson will ask for me some time before morning, Sergeant. Keep him until I come. If he wants to go, arrest him."

"And charge him with what, might I ask, Inspector?" the station sergeant asked acidly.

"Oh, withholding information, dope peddling, homicide—anything you like, because you can't go far wrong."

The Inspector whistled gaily as he walked across the pavement to his car. He flouted the law twice by sounding his hooter although it was well past eleven, and drove home in a happy state of mind.

He slept well, and took his time about getting to the office next morning. He arrived long after Ericson, and even so he kept his visitor waiting. A long wait, in Knollis's opinion, knocked all the previously-prepared self-assurance of a witness or a suspect skywards, and as he privately regarded all persons concerned in a case as potential suspects he treated all alike as far as possible.

So that Ericson was inclined to be irritable when he was at last shown into Knollis's office. He was wearing the suit which had been described by the witnesses at the Commerce Club and the Bridge Hotel, and it was looking a little the worse for wear, a fact that the Inspector noted even as Ericson was upbraiding him for his lack of interest.

"I travel through the night to place myself at your disposal," he complained, "and I'm kept waiting in a most uncomfortable room—probably the worst in the building!"

Knollis shook his head. "You're wrong there, Mr. Ericson. We have nine more uncomfortable rooms, rooms with hard beds, barred doors, and high windows. However, as much as I regret the inconvenience to which you have been put, I have to remind you that there are a great many other tasks which need my attention. I have been attending to one all night." Ericson made a muttered apology and waited expectantly for Knollis to launch his questions.

"You said, Inspector, that an attempt to impersonate me was suspected. In what way could that affect me?"

"How did you come to meet Mr. Lomas?" Knollis asked.

"I advertised for a business, and Lomas was one of the many who wrote to me. Years ago I knew Burnham slightly. I liked the city, and so I came over to see him. I liked the shop, and I knew that I could modernise it and build a first-class business. I should have clinched the deal straight away, there and then, but for one thing . . ."

"And that was?"

"He was asking too little for it."

"Oh?" Knollis murmured with well-simulated surprise. "Too little? That is a surprising twist."

"So I thought. He seemed almost too willing to get rid of it at any price. I naturally wondered if there was a catch in it. I looked through the books and they seemed to be in order. I was still suspicious, and so I took a room at an inn by the river and stayed there for about a week, making inquiries. Lomas knew the spot, and visited it frequently in the past, so I was able to learn quite a lot about him. I went home and gave the matter further thought. Then, on Monday evening, I met Lomas again, and we agreed to instruct our respective solicitors to go ahead with the transaction. It was not until noon yesterday that I learned of the old gentleman's tragic end."

"Where did you meet Lomas on Monday evening?" asked the Inspector casually.

"Outside the Council House. We went to his club, and from there to the Bridge Hotel."

"How did you get from the club to the hotel?"

"By bus."

"You travelled the whole way with him, I presume?"

"Oh no," said Ericson. "Lomas had a further appointment. We walked from the club to the market square, and parted there. I turned into the Saracen's Head for a drink, after arranging to meet him again at half-past eight. This was about ten minutes to eight. I went to the Bridge Hotel later and met him as he was entering the building. We had a friendly chat, discussed a few more details, and shook hands on the projected deal. I am of the opinion that he had talked it over with someone since I last saw him. He excused himself again and hurried away. I stayed on until about ten minutes past nine and then made my way to the station."

"Your home is—?"

"Cambridge."

"You came from there to-night? Last night, that is?"

"Cambridge? Edinburgh."

"At what time did you arrive in Burnham on Monday?"

Ericson thought that one out, and took his time over it.

"Why, it would be about five o'clock, probably a little earlier. I did a spot of window gazing, and then had a light tea in a café. I met Lomas about quarter to seven and we went straight to his club—the Commerce Club in Devonport Street."

Knollis regarded his man thoughtfully for some moments, and then asked in a slow voice: "That suit you are wearing, Mr. Ericson; would you mind telling me where it was made? And how long ago you bought it? Yes, I know it is a peculiar question, but I have a sound reason for asking it."

Ericson stared, and then gave an uncertain laugh. He rose, removed his jacket, and threw it into the Inspector's lap. Knollis read the name on the tailor's tab, and nodded his satisfaction.

"Made in Cambridge, eh?"

"Late March, I should say," Ericson informed him. "You would not object if I was to get in touch with this firm in order to verify your statement, Mr. Ericson?" Ericson shook his head, and grinned.

"The thing is paid for, Inspector. I have no objection at all. If you have any doubts at all I'd prefer you to do as you suggest."

"Do you happen to know Lomas's son?" Knollis asked.

"No, I cannot say that I do. I do not remember meeting him, although I may have done without knowing who he was."

"Or a Miss Gretton?"

Knollis could not be certain, but he thought he detected a momentary hesitation before Ericson said that he had no knowledge of such a person.

"Did Lomas give any reason for the projected disposal of his business?"

"Only the one that might have been expected. He was getting on in years, had made a certain amount of money, and intended to retire and enjoy it."

"Did he say anything about the state of his health?"

"Never, Inspector."

"I see," Knollis murmured. "You visited his home, of course? We can take that for granted."

"Oh yes, I went there to inspect his books."

"Did he take you through to the living-room?"

"A fusty room with one window?" queried Ericson. "He did. I promised myself that I would knock another window in the wall and have both open day and night for months—and probably have the room fumigated."

"You intend returning to your home on leaving here?"

"Unless you wish me to stay in Burnham. I can do that, you know. There is no reason why I should return home. After all,

I suppose I was one of the last people to see Lomas alive—or was I?"

"He went along to The Ferryman after he left the Bridge Hotel," said Knollis. "He stayed there until shortly before ten. It is estimated that he met his death during the next twenty minutes, as he was walking home, and before he reached—but we'll leave that for the time being."

"The morning papers said that he was shaved of his beard," said Ericson. "Surely that is a strange feature of the case?"

"The whole case is strange, Mr. Ericson," Knollis said as he watched Ericson's features. "Lomas even knew that his death was at hand."

"He—he what?"

"He knew that he was to be murdered. He reported the fact to us on the morning of his death and placed valuable information in our hands."

"Oh!" said Ericson. "Oh!"

He stared at the carpet and then raised his head. "I'm itching to ask the questions which I am not supposed to ask and which you are not likely to answer."

"Such as?" murmured Knollis.

"How was he killed?"

"Well, he was found in the river, you know!"

"Yes, I read that in the papers, but that does not necessarily imply that he was drowned. I'm sorry if I'm too curious, Inspector!"

"Curiosity is a human instinct, Mr. Ericson," said Knollis. "I can satisfy you so far. Lomas was poisoned. Then his beard, moustache, and eyebrows were shaved off, and he was put in the water. The current carried him down to the lock and he was found wedged against the gates."

"It's so bizarre," Ericson muttered thoughtfully. Knollis smiled his appreciation of the point.

"That does seem to be the most apt description. I had not thought of it. It is the only word for it."

"What could be the motive for the murder?" persisted Ericson. "He seemed to be such a mild little man."

"Now you have a question I cannot answer," said Knollis. "The usual monetary motive cannot be applied since the daughter receives all his worldly wealth. Vengeance, you will suggest? He never made an enemy in his life—or so all his friends and relatives hasten to assure me. Passionate motives? At sixty-five we expect him to be past that—unless indeed he was experiencing an Indian summer. No, at the moment we are stuck. We have to rely on your evidence, and the evidence of a few others, Mr. Ericson. Perhaps we shall be able to fit the unconnected pieces together and produce a picture of the whole thing. By the way, you are an independent gentleman?"

"I was a chemist in an East Anglian town," Ericson informed him readily. "I built a good business and sold out to a large firm. I got fed up with idleness and intended buying Lomas's business to give me a new interest in life."

He smiled.

"You are a very suspicious man, Inspector Knollis!"

Knollis nodded his head in agreement. "I have that reputation, Mr. Ericson. I have to be suspicious. It is all part of my job."

He regarded Ericson warily for a time and then asked:

"What can you, as an ex-chemist, tell me about cocaine?"

"Cocaine?" Ericson asked with surprised eyes. "Well, very little actually. It is a commodity that chemists seldom use. An occasional prescription, and that is about all. I know very little about it."

"Queer that you should have been a chemist," murmured Knollis. "So is the man who was Lomas's best friend. Name of Steadfall. I don't suppose you know of him?"

"No, I can't say that I do. I have noticed the name over a shop in the Desborough Road, but I know nothing of the man."

"The remarkable thing about this case is the number of coincidences we've encountered," Knollis said slowly. "They come up one after the other—by the way, you say that you lived at The Ferryman for a week. Did you ever see the people at Rose Cottage?"

"A little bow-legged man named Dodson?" asked Ericson. "Yes, I saw him on the towpath a few times. I dabble with a brush sometimes, and I made a few sketches down by the river. This Dodson used to toddle along and watch over my shoulder. A dry little fellow with a fund of comical racing stories. A bit of a card, I should say."

"That's the man," said Knollis. "Ever meet the girl, his daughter. Marjory, I think her name is."

"Daughter?" Ericson stared. "I didn't know he had one. In fact I'm sure he hasn't, mainly because he told me that he had never married."

"Did he now!" murmured Knollis.

"I take it that we are about at the end of the interview," said Ericson as he reached for his hat.

"Almost, yes. Tell me, Mr. Ericson; in what papers did you advertise for a business?"

For the first time during the morning Ericson was flustered by a question.

"Er—why, in the *Courier* only."

"Then you particularly wanted a business in Burnham?"

"Well, yes and no. I like Burnham, and always have done. If there was a suitable business in the district I intended buying it. If not, then I should have advertised in another area. I was not at all worried where it was."

Knollis rose, and extended his hand.

"I owe you a lot, Mr. Ericson. Thanks for coming along, and thanks for your patience. You have borne up well under my pestilential questioning. I take it that you will stay in town for a few days?"

"I'll go back to the Ferryman. They owe me a week."

"You'd be safer at the Bridge," Knollis said ominously.

"Safer?"

"Safer!"

Ericson shook himself. "Oh well, in that case, the Bridge it is!"

As soon as the door closed behind him Knollis pressed a bell-push twice, and was thus assured that Ericson would be shadowed from the doorstep and never deserted during day or night. Then he reached for the telephone and asked River Station to oblige by duplicating the job of watching Ericson. "Keep him tailed, wherever he goes, until I give the all-clear. Either he or young Lomas killed the old man."

CHAPTER VIII
THE LADY OF THE NIGHT

SIR WILFRED BURROWS rang for Knollis shortly after Ericson's departure. The Inspector collected his notes and tramped upstairs.

The Chief Constable was in a boisterous mood and wished Knollis a good morning. Knollis looked out through the window and then smiled.

"I suppose it is, although I haven't had time to look at it. Ericson left the building a few minutes ago. He can tell a very convincing story. He wanted to go back to The Ferryman, but I persuaded him to stay in town. Easier to keep an eye on him."

"And how's the mental picture forming?" the Chief Constable boomed.

"I'm getting it into something like focus at last," Knollis said with intense satisfaction. "This is how I see the events of Monday evening—although I have to admit that I still have to connect Gretton and Ericson satisfactorily. All that end is still vague. For the rest, well, Ericson was in Desborough, or came into Desborough, during the afternoon and there met Gretton. She drove him into Burnham in Lomas's car, and then got back without being seen by Lomas—Lawrence Lomas I mean. Lawrence Lomas came into town at half-past five, fetched his father from the shop, and they went to the Golden Angel. They parted then, and Lawrence is supposed to have gone home to Gretton and taken her for a country run, but their alibi was flat. Lomas Senior then met Ericson and took him to the Commerce Club. After a chat they parted, for Lomas had an appointment. We have heard of a man who answers to Ericson's description leaving the old man at the bus stop and then getting on the same bus further along. Lomas obviously saw Lawrence again—probably to report progress—and it was Ericson who mounted the bus and eventually turned into the Bridge Hotel with Ezekiah Lomas. It was Lawrence, or a mythical third man, who followed Lomas down the embankment. Ericson stayed in the Bridge Hotel until five past nine and then, according to his own story, caught a train home to Cambridge.

"Dodson, at Rose Cottage, certainly saw Lomas making for The Ferryman. It is here that the picture is hazy. Lomas, as we know, left the inn at ten to ten, and must have made his way back to Burnham—or started to do so. If he had taken the other direction his body would have been found nearer to the White Horse Hotel than The Ferryman. We have good reason to suspect that he was shaved either in Rose Cottage or with a razor found in the cottage—which brings this Dodson into the picture.

"The ladylike man who called on Steadfall was the girl at Dodson's cottage. Forster has been making observation at the cottage all night, and his report should be available any time now, if he has anything to report. What I am wondering now is if there were two plots against Lomas's life, and if they managed to collide on Monday evening. There can be but one explanation of the shaving; somebody wanted to delay identification and hold up the inquiry. The move came from the cottage, from Dodson and the girl Marjory. If we can prove that Ericson is connected we'll have done a substantial part of the work. Then we have to discover why Gretton is the link between Ericson and Lomas Junior.

"As soon as the men come in I'm taking Bates with me and we'll go through Lomas's premises with a small tooth comb. He didn't make ten thousand by selling papers and thick twist, and the answer to our problem must be in the house or the shop—"

Sir Wilfred halted him with a wave of the hand. "Just a moment, Knollis. I think you should know that some of the reports are to hand from the laboratory. The Turkish Delight was coated with cocaine."

Knollis rubbed his hands together. "Good! Go on!"

"I went to the *Courier* office and the *Echo* office. The In Memoriam notice which attracted your suspicious attentions was the result of a countermanded order. Ezekiah sent it in, and the next day it was changed as the result of a telephone call. He didn't change it himself. Steadfall did so in his name.

"The bottles of medicine were all in order. They contained nothing but what they were supposed to contain. On the other hand, the bottle of carbonate of soda and the two tins of health salts contained adulterated cocaine. The place was filled with snow. Now is that suggestive or not?"

Knollis narrowed his eyes and watched a pigeon curvetting past the window.

"Yes," he said, "there is a lot suggested by that information. I think I'll get down to the shop and have a look round."

Forster was waiting for him in his office, together with Bates, Dawes, and Slater. He was the newest addition to the staff, a keen young fellow eager for promotion via the royal road of achievement.

"She came, Inspector!" he said with bright eyes.

"At what time, Forster?"

Knollis could not be stimulated into an excited state. He was far too old a hand at the game.

"One o'clock. I saw the headlights of the car swing round at the bridge, and then she switched them off and coasted down to the cottage. She left the car on the towpath and went into the cottage. She used a torch in the cottage. I scudded along the bank and over the bridge. She was still in the house when I got there. Twenty minutes later she emerged. She was dressed in a male outfit; trousers, pullover, and sports jacket, with a trilby hat. She drove away in the car. I tried the door, and it was not locked, so I went in. Her own clothes were lying on a chair by the fire. They were initialled 'M.E.' and the—er—er—well, anyway, the same initials were embroidered on the legs."

Dawes gave a deep chuckle, and Forster flushed. "Embroidered french knickers by the sound of things," Dawes said wickedly. "Forster wouldn't know, of course!"

"I—er—think you are right, Sergeant," said Forster. "Never mind the type of garment," Knollis said gravely. "The initials are even more suggestive than Dawes' humour. M.E. sounds like

Marjory Ericson. D'y'know, I'm beginning to see more than a little daylight. Did you follow her, Forster?"

"No, Inspector. My instructions were to watch the cottage to the exclusion of all else. She came back shortly after two o'clock, changed, and—"

"How do you know that?" Dawes asked bluntly.

"Well, she came out in her own clothes!" Forster almost shouted in reply.

"And drove away?" asked the Inspector.

"Yes, sir, the same way that she came."

"Quiet now," warned Knollis, seeing that Dawes was about to pass a facetious remark. He reached for the telephone and asked for the uniformed department on the ground floor.

"Knollis speaking. Any report come in from the men who were holding Lomas's premises during the night? Yes? Is the man still on duty? Making his report out? Please send him along, will you? Thanks."

He was silent until a knock sounded on the door and a burly constable entered.

"Ah, it's you, Johnson! What have you for us?"

The constable straightened his back, clutched his notebook, and gravely recited:

"At thirty-five minutes past one, while on duty at the premises of Ezekiah Lomas, deceased, at Desborough Road, a car drew up. A young man stepped from it and asked for Inspector Knollis. He said that he arranged to meet you at this time and place. I told him that I knew nothing of it and that Inspector Knollis was not present. He then produced a large envelope and pushed it under the shop door before I was able to stop him. He said I was to report that he had supplied the evidence as arranged and that he would call on you at a later date. He re-entered the car, turned it round in the roadway, and drove back in the direction of the city centre. I duly made a note of the time."

"Why the devil didn't you detain him?" stormed Knollis.

The constable recoiled.

"I was told to watch the premises and see that no one attempted to enter same during the night, Inspector Knollis. The young man made no attempt to enter the premises, and so I consider that I carried out my instructions."

"Oh get to hell out of it," snapped Knollis. Then he relaxed. "My apologies, Johnson! Your orders were too vague. You were right in acting as you did. Thanks for the report."

"A constable," said Dawes as the door closed, "should be a man of intelligence, capable of exercising his discretion in difficult circumstances. God save the King."

"I've a rotten job for you and Slater," said Knollis. "Ericson is supposed to have come to town by train on Monday afternoon shortly after five. He is further supposed to have left the Bridge Inn at five past nine. Test those times and find what he did before, and after—particularly after. Trace him back to Cambridge if necessary and draw exes."

He then turned to Forster.

"I'm giving you an important job. Go to Cambridge and dig into Ericson's past history. At one time he had a business in an East Anglian town. He was a chemist. I don't want to alarm him at the moment by asking further questions, and so you must do the work. I also want to know whether he was ever acquainted with Steadfall, in what year he retired from business, and what he has done and where he has been since. And I want you back by to-morrow night! See the treasurer and take one of the police cars. It will be necessary in Lincolnshire and Norfolk! Travelling by rail is a slow and painful business, as I know from experience, and if you aren't careful you'll find yourself stranded on March station, surrounded by frozen rabbits and nine veg. That's all, my lad! Now scram."

Forster's eyes gleamed. "Watch me, sir!"

"A good lad," murmured Bates as Forster disappeared.

"Get a car round, Bates," said Knollis.

They drove to Lawrence Lomas's house and caught him preparing for lunch. His manner was as surly as ever. "What is it this time?" he grunted.

"You have a speedometer and mileometer on your car?"

"Why yes, of course. Why the devil do you ask?"

"Can you remember the figure on the total mileage check?"

"I can. Yes, I think I can, but I'm darned if I see why you are interested. I'm rather proud of the old bus, and I keep an eye on the mileage. She's done eighteen thousand since she was last decoked."

"What was the figure when you put the car away last night?" asked Knollis.

"It was 32446."

"Been to the car this morning, Mr. Lomas?"

"No; I've had no occasion to do so."

"I'd like to see it," said Knollis.

"Okay, Sherlock. Follow me. Perhaps you'll relax sufficiently later to do a little explaining like your famous prototype—or will you?"

He led the way to the garage, opened the doors, and waved towards the car. "There you are. The figure is 32446. I can't remember the tenths."

"They don't matter," said Knollis. He bent over the car door and inspected the mileometer. He was smiling as he turned to Lomas. "Read that!"

Lomas flashed him a curious glance and studied the figures. "That's funny! It reads 32467. There must be some mistake—and yet I'll swear it stood at forty-six when I put the car away."

"In which bedroom do you sleep?" asked Knollis.

"The side one, at the other end of the house."

"Care to try an experiment? I suggest that you go to your bedroom, stay there two minutes, and then return."

Lomas hesitated, and then turned and walked away. Knollis consulted his watch. After a minute he gave Bates the signal to start the engine. After a further minute he ordered him to switch off. When Lomas returned he asked him: "Care to say whether I've had the engine running?"

"You haven't," said Lomas.

"But I have, Mr. Lomas, and that proves that it is possible to take the car out at night without you hearing it. Now, you have a dipstick? Then try it in the petrol tank. But wait a minute! Did you fill up before taking Miss Gretton out last night?"

"I did," said Lomas. "There was a gallon in the tank when I left here. I called and got Empton to put two gallons in. My trip last night should have taken about three-quarters of a gallon. We only went to the Ferry—and you know that yourself!" he added grimly. "Now try the dipstick."

Lomas obeyed without question. His face told its own story as he withdrew the stick. He leaned on the door of the car, his lips tight.

"Look here, Inspector! What is happening?"

Knollis raised his shoulders. "That is what I am asking you. All I can say is that we have good reason to believe that a young man was driving your car about Burnham in the middle of the night. He called at your father's shop and pushed a large envelope under the door. Care to come with us while we investigate the matter?"

Lomas nodded without speaking. He climbed into Knollis's car and slammed the door. They were halfway to Burnham when he broke his silence.

"I'm getting weary of this affair. My father is even more trouble dead than he was when alive, and God only knows that he scattered enough misery when he was alive."

He again fell silent. A mile further on he said: "Ten thousand pounds! The bloody old miser!" Knollis nudged Bates just as he was about to remark on Lomas's outburst. He was hoping that Lomas would continue his tirade, but he did not. He was still staring angrily ahead when the car drew up outside his late father's shop.

The constable on duty stepped forward and saluted as he opened the car door for the Inspector. "Anybody called?" Knollis asked.

"Only the girl, the shop assistant. I sent her home again—and hope I did right, sir."

"Quite in order," said Knollis. He unlocked the door and pushed it open, then bent to collect the large manilla envelope that lay at his feet. He took it to the counter, noted that it was addressed to him, and carefully slit the flap. A number of packets scattered on the counter. No message accompanied them.

"What the deuce are they?" Lawrence Lomas inquired.

"I have my suspicions," Knollis replied, "but we'll open one before saying more."

He slid the point of his penknife under the red seal and a trickle of white powder fell into his palm. He dipped the point of a finger in it and applied it to his tongue. Then he smiled at Lomas.

"Care to try it?"

Lomas accepted the challenge. A look of surprise came into his eyes. "Is it cocaine?"

"You know the stuff?" the Inspector countered.

"I think so. I took chemistry years ago. Where has it come from?"

Knollis fixed him with keen eyes.

"Do you know of any secret hiding-place in this house? Some place in which similar packets could be stored?"

Lomas hesitated.

"Well yes," he said reluctantly, "if you remove the top drawer of the bureau and feel at the back. . . . The old man used to keep his money there when he was—when I was a kid, that is."

"The most obvious of all hiding-places!" exclaimed the Inspector. "What an ass I am!"

He strode into the inner room and lifted the drawer to the table. He then plunged his arm to the back of the cavity and drew forth a number of packets similar to those found in the envelope.

"Now we can ask more questions," he murmured.

"It's—it's pretty rotten," said Lomas. "It looks—but isn't it possible that this stuff was planted?"

"Quite possible," Knollis hastened to agree. "But who was likely to know of the hiding-place?"

"Nobody but my father, my sister, and myself," Lomas admitted. "It's rather mysterious, isn't it?"

"We can hardly drag your sister into this," Knollis said flatly. He hoped Lomas would grasp the inference.

"No, I suppose not, Inspector. It begins to look rotten for the old man."

"As if he was a dope distributor?" suggested Knollis. Lomas did not answer.

"Who was your father's doctor?"

"Doctor? Well, he hadn't one. Teesdale used to attend to us when we were kids, and he attended mother during the last few months of her life . . ."

"All right," said Knollis. "I think that is all for now. Bates will run you home again if you wish."

"I'm staying in town, Inspector. I don't feel much like work after this. I'll have a meal and a good think. There are one or two matters which need my attention, too, and I may as well do them now as later. I hope to heaven that we soon get it all cleared up. It's nerve-racking! I'm—oh lord, I'll clear off, Inspector."

Knollis made an almost imperceptible signal, and as soon as Lomas was clear of the premises Bates followed him.

Left alone, Knollis made a thorough search of the house and the shop, hoping to find some record of the transactions which he now believed Ezekiah Lomas to have conducted over a period of years. But no such record was to be found. Either Lomas was a wary old bird, or someone else had removed the evidence which would connect them with the case. The Inspector perched himself on the postal library box and made a few notes. Then he went to interview Dr. Teesdale.

The doctor had long retired from practice and welcomed the Inspector as a break in a quiet day. "A police officer is the last person I expected to see," he remarked as he led the Inspector to his study. "I—er—can hardly assume that your visit is not connected with your official duties?"

"I am seeking past history," said Knollis. "You attended Mrs. Jennifer Lomas in her last illness?" The benevolent old doctor nodded and became reminiscent.

"A sweet lady. Most patient, and far too resigned. She let herself slip away. Simply relaxed her hold on life and so there was nothing I could do to save her."

"What was the nature of her illness?" asked Knollis.

"Acute nervous exhaustion, with tachycardia—that is irregularity of the heart, you know."

"Interesting," murmured the Inspector. "Tell me; did she suffer acute bouts of depression by any chance?"

"Why yes. That was symptomatic, Inspector," the doctor replied. "Why do you ask?"

"And periods of intense excitation?" persisted the insatiable Knollis.

The doctor chuckled. "You seem to know a little about such matters, Inspector, although I expect it is merely a layman's smattering, eh?"

"Well," Knollis admitted, "I know just as much as comes within the range of forensics, and not too much at that."

"Then you don't think you've missed your vocation?"

"I don't think so," Knollis replied. "It's every man to his own trade. If I'd a knowledge of medicine I shouldn't have come to you to-day."

"And why have you come to me to-day, Inspector?"

"Because I am interested in the death of Jennifer Lomas's husband—and in the death of Jennifer Lomas herself."

"Of course! Of course! I grow dense with age, Inspector. A shocking end—and yet strangely appropriate, if I may say so without prejudice. I never did like him. A most disagreeable fellow, and he never paid his bills until the last moment. I understand that he intended to retire and enjoy the fruits of his scraping and scratching! It is a judgment on him. Indeed it is!"

"We are satisfied that he died of cocaine poisoning," Knollis said quietly.

"So I understand," the doctor nodded. "I was talking to Whitelaw yesterday. A shocking affair."

"What symptoms would you expect to find in such a case, sir?" Knollis asked in a tone intended to lull any suspicion the doctor might harbour as a result of his visit.

Dr. Teesdale unhooked his spectacles and tapped them on his hand. "Symptoms, eh? Well now, if I am to be truthful I must say at once that I cannot remember having a case of cocaine poisoning, and so my answer must be entirely technical—dear me, I mean theoretical! Theoretical! I do remember my toxicology however. Well now, you would expect irritability, and a leaning toward alcohol, and occasional periods of excitation. The drug acts as a stimulant, you know, Inspector, and then lets the victim down suddenly and with terrible results. Suicide often follows the—"

He broke off, and resumed his spectacles, to look over the top of them quizzically.

"You are pulling my leg, Inspector Knollis! You are suggesting, without saying as much, that Mrs. Lomas was a victim of cocaine poisoning! Are you not? Are you not?"

"I was not suggesting it," replied Knollis, "but I was wondering. I have no tangible physical evidence, Dr. Teesdale, but I am convinced that Lomas poisoned his own wife and got away with it."

"But, good gracious, that is a shocking insinuation, Inspector! Why should he do so? What motive would he have for such a vile crime?"

"He suspected her of being in love with another man."

"Preposterous!" exclaimed the doctor. "She was too old for such nonsense—and she was a loyal soul. I can assure you of that. She thought of her husband's comfort and welfare right to the end. And again, Inspector; who was this imagined other man?"

"His old rival. They had both wooed Jennifer, and she chose Lomas because he was the elder. She realised her mistake when it was too late. She remained faithful to Lomas, he realised the truth, and being the man he was he could not believe that it was possible for her to remain faithful to him even in thought. He renewed the old friendship. The one-time friend was invited to the house, and Lomas was able to watch their behaviour while in each other's company. They were devoted friends, but no more. Both respected the marriage vows that had parted them. As Lomas grew older he grew more cantankerous and suspicious. He always ruled his children with an iron hand—"

"That is too true," interpolated the doctor.

"And Jennifer always acted as the buffer between father and children—"

"That also is true."

"He refused to spend a single unnecessary penny on the daughter's education, but spent a pretty penny on Lawrence. Lawrence was his one extravagance, and he only spent money on him because he wanted to bask in the reflected glory when Lawrence became successful.

"Now Gertrude also favoured her brother. He was the kid brother, the hero, and I have good reason to believe that she spent her few spare pounds on Lawrence even in her state of comparative poverty. Until quite recently, when she suddenly realised that he was nothing more than a sponger, he was the apple of her eye. All in all, he was spoiled. When he tackled his father for money and was refused he turned to his mother and sister and found that they were prepared to make any sacrifice for him. Slowly, you see, we are defining Lawrence's character.

"Now then; we can revert to the old man. He was developing a lust for money, and in some way still not very clear to us he became a cog in the cocaine racket. He left ten thousand pounds, all of it to Gertrude. Lawrence asserts that he persuaded his father to do this, and then he appears shocked when told the extent of his father's estate. This, on the face of it, suggests that Lawrence had no motive or interest—and yet, unless I am very wrong indeed, I think it displays a particularly deep motive. From childhood Gertrude had shared with her brother, even when he did not share with her. Lawrence Lomas, as I see it, got his father to alter his will, knowing full well that Gertrude's affection and high sense of duty would compel her to hand over a half-share of the legacy. Later he would be able to wangle even more of the money into his own possession. I am still unable to say definitely that Lawrence did murder his father, but I think it highly probable. You see that I am being perfectly frank with you, Dr. Teesdale."

The doctor gazed wonderingly at Knollis. He removed his spectacles again and slowly polished them on a silk handkerchief.

"I never did like Lawrence," he said reflectively. "Even as a child he was a nasty piece of work, as the moderns put it. Speaking strictly in confidence, I am inclined to agree with you. I am inclined to believe that he is capable of murder, even such a shocking murder as this, the murder of his own father, but I must ask if you are sure of the motive, Inspector. He may have avenged his mother. Really, you know, you fill me with apprehension when you mention Jennifer Lomas. You are indirectly suggesting that I wrongly diagnosed her case. It is incredible that I should do any such thing—and yet, yes, it is possible! Who would suspect poisoning?"

He drew a deep breath.

"And now there will be an exhumation, and a public inquiry, and—oh, Inspector, if only we could see into the future as we act for the present!"

"I have no intention of exhuming Jennifer Lomas," said Knollis. "I'm no sentimentalist, but I think the poor lady suffered enough without being unearthed and subjected to dissection. Even if we proved a case against Ezekiah we couldn't hang him, and it will be best to let the dead deal with the dead. As far as Lawrence is concerned, well, if he was responsible for his father's death, then his motive was a mercenary one. I came to you to-day merely to get your private opinions of the Lomas family—for my own satisfaction. I badly needed the background. And I wanted to ask you whether you are inclined to agree that Jennifer might have been poisoned by Ezekiah."

The old doctor again polished his glasses needlessly, and stared into the empty grate. He was greatly perturbed by Knollis's news and seemed at a loss for an answer to the questions.

"I have known the family since the first child arrived," he said sadly, "and while I knew it was an unhappy household I never thought for a single moment . . . Inspector, I have given you my frank opinions about the Lomases. The rest, including your suspicions, can be regarded as no more than conjecture. It is five years since Jennifer Lomas died, and after this lapse of years even an exhumation is not bound to prove your theory. Strictly in confidence I am bound to say that I believe you have good grounds for your belief. Further than that I cannot go."

Back at headquarters the Inspector made his way to the Chief Constable's office, and a discussion on the case followed.

He placed all his facts before Sir Wilfred, in duty bound, and propounded his theories.

"I'm convinced by now," he said, "that we are up against two entirely different lines of action. Lomas Junior was working for his father's money. The other side, probably represented by Ericson, was in some way concerned with the cocaine racket. It looks like coincidence again, and again I am suspicious. I'm convinced that we shall find a connecting link somewhere. Where? I'm blessed if I know. My experience of complicated cases has taught me that complication is an illusion. The alphabet may look complicated when the letters are jumbled—just as does a cipher—but the whole thing is simple when once you've arranged the letters in their proper sequence. That is the only thing wrong with this case. We haven't got the logical sequence. When we do—then somebody can look out!"

Sir Wilfred was slow in commenting. He withdrew his gaze from the window and frowned.

"When do you think this thing really started, Knollis?"

"When Jennifer married Lomas," Knollis said readily. "That was the indispensable incident. Everything comes from that point. Lomas was responsible for his own death."

"How the deuce do you arrive at that remarkable conclusion?" the Chief Constable asked, not too brightly.

"Steadfall and Lomas were in love with the same girl. Lomas won her. Steadfall remained a firm friend of the family. Both he and Jennifer knew that a mistake had been made, but Steadfall was a gentleman, and Jennifer was a real lady. Lomas, on the other hand, was a cad. He couldn't believe in a disinterested friendship. He set to work to make pots of money in order to prove to Jennifer that he was the better man. He developed a mania for making money. He got a chance to join the cocaine business and pushed his conscience in the cupboard. On the other hand—and this is pure guesswork—he kept Steadfall as a friend, probably revelling in the misery both Steadfall and Jennifer suffered by this constant companionship. In time he found that he could not do without Steadfall's friendship, although his attitude to Jennifer remained constant. I think he came to hate

Jennifer after a time. When she died he found himself alone in the world. Lawrence had left him. Gertrude had left him. He had lost his love for Jennifer, but had come to regard her as an essential part of his background—just as was the furniture. A blank was left when she died, and so he held on to Old John and soon came to regard him as the sole prop in a barren world.

"And now we begin to see light. He was obviously thinking of retirement, or he would not have answered Ericson's advertisement. For Lomas to sell the business meant a dislocation of the cocaine traffic. Suppose that Ericson was in it also, and that he laid a trap for Lomas? Suppose Lomas did not know of Ericson's connection and that Ericson did not want him to know? Suppose that Ericson wanted Lomas and no one else to answer that advertisement? Lomas would know that there would be trouble when his shop, as a cocaine market, closed down; that would explain his readiness to sell at a low figure. Lomas was as anxious to sell as Ericson was to buy. Now where do we stand?"

"I don't know where you stand," said the Chief Constable, "but I'm still trying to decide why this Marjory tried to buy Steadfall's cocaine. Dawes and Slater have proved that it was not, and could not have been used on the racing dog. Then why was it needed? If Ericson was in the racket as you suggest, he should have been in a position to obtain as much as he needed. I'm certain in my own mind that the affair between Dodson and the owner of the dog was a set-up to make Marjory's tale, as told to Steadfall, convincing—to hide the real need for the dope."

Knollis was suddenly alert.

"I think I've got it. It has been proved that the cocaine was taken from Steadfall's poison cupboard, hasn't it?"

"According to you and Whitelaw, yes."

"And the amount found in the envelope which was pushed under Lomas's door would be about right—equal, I mean, to the amount taken from Steadfall! It was taken so that it could be planted there. It's obvious."

"But it was taken before Lomas's death," Sir Wilfred protested.

Knollis fell back in his chair, crestfallen.

"Yes, that's so. But why should Nora Gretton, who is engaged to marry Lawrence Lomas, push packets of dope under his father's door?"

"Eh? What's that?" demanded the Chief Constable. "Nora Gretton, do you say? But it was this Marjory girl!"

"Yes," Knollis replied in a matter-of-fact manner. "She and Marjory and the sissy young man are one and the same person. She's Ericson's sister. That's as clear as daylight! As Nora Gretton she took Lawrence's car from the garage and drove to Rose Cottage. As Marjory she changed into male attire and drove to Lomas's shop. Then she came back, reassumed her nom-de-guerre, and drove back to Desborough and Briar Cottage. A soft streak in the girl's mental makeup and we get a clue. Women often do similar tricks."

"Such as what, Knollis? I don't follow you."

"Briar Cottage by the river. Rose Cottage in Desborough. I'll bet a quid that she took the Desborough cottage because of the name."

Sir Wilfred brightened considerably.

"Then the Ericson family were conspiring against the whole Lomas family? We've got a feud!"

Knollis shook his head.

"I don't think so. There's an alternative suggestion somewhere, but I haven't found it yet. Perhaps I will when I've interviewed Steadfall again, and Lomas's assistant, and had another long talk with Ericson. Yes, I think I see the way, Sir Wilfred."

CHAPTER IX
THE EXAMINATION OF TWO CHEMISTS

Detective Forster was pleased with himself when he reported to Knollis an hour before lunch the next day. He beamed sunnily, and the Inspector knew that he must have been lucky as well as industrious.

"Take a pew and get the works off your chest," said Knollis.

"Roger Ericson lives at White House, on a heath beyond Cambridge," said Forster. "He is a bachelor, forty-two years of age. Until six years ago he was in business as a chemist in Norwich. He then sold out to a multiple firm. Six months ago he began to travel for a firm of manufacturing chemists, a London firm. He still does so. Our friend Dodson was his Man Friday, but left Cambridge several months ago. Ericson was away each week from Monday morning until Friday evening, and Dodson looked after the house."

"So he is stringing us, eh?" Knollis murmured. He narrowed his eyes. "We'll let him play his game out without telling him what we know."

He looked across at Forster. "Steadfall and Ericson? Traced any connection between them?"

"No, I was unable to do that," said Forster, "and I did not pursue the angle after learning that Ericson was in the travelling line. It seems obvious that he calls on Steadfall in the normal course of business."

"Learn anything about Ericson's financial position?"

"He is well off. All the people I questioned were of the opinion that he was a rich man, comparatively. The house is a beauty, and he runs two cars."

"His movements on the night?"

"He was not seen to leave Burnham, and I proved conclusively that he did not arrive in Cambridge and was not seen at his home. I tried all the hotels at which he might have stayed, and they knew nothing of him. I believe he stayed in Burnham, or Desborough."

"Follow that line," said Knollis. "Question the people around Gretton's cottage, and make further inquiries about Rose Cottage. He must have stayed either at Rose Cottage or with Gretton. You're doing well, Forster. Now do even better. I'm pleased with your work."

Forster blushed at Knollis's praise, and left the office. Knollis went to Steadfall's shop and once more coralled the aging chemist in his dispensary. Steadfall was apprehensive as Knollis began the inquisition.

"I'm a tiresome man," Knollis said without humour, "but I must be endured."

Steadfall displayed the ghost of a smile. "I understand that, Inspector. I take it that the case is progressing satisfactorily? That you have a suspect?"

"Quite satisfactorily," Knollis assured him. "Do you know a Roger Ericson? The question is important."

"Ericson?" the chemist repeated slowly. "Why yes. He travels for Medal Chemical Manufacturers. Why do you ask about him, Inspector?"

"Did Lomas know him?"

"Not to my knowledge, Inspector!"

"Then you were not aware that it was Ericson who was contemplating the purchase of Lomas's business?" Steadfall gaped. "Ericson! Surely you are mistaken! Ericson has no experience of such a business as Ezekiah's—"

"I can assure you that there is no mistake. Now, another question. Would you say that Ericson resembled Lawrence Lomas in any way—physically, I mean."

Steadfall pondered the question, finally answering: "There may be a slight superficial resemblance now you draw my attention to it, but I had never thought about it before. What *are* you getting at, Inspector?"

"The murderer of Ezekiah Lomas," replied Knollis.

The chemist wiped his hand over his forehead. "I don't see the drift of your remarks and questions."

"You aren't intended to do so," Knollis said bluntly. "And now, without beating about the bush any longer, I want to know the full extent of your relations with Lomas, and Jennifer Lomas."

Steadfall winced.

"I also require an account of your movements on Monday evening," added Knollis.

Steadfall gave the Inspector a glance of reproach.

"This is unwarrantable! It is definitely accusative!"

"I'm sorry if you think so," said Knollis. "I understand that you and Lomas were rivals for the hand of the lady who afterwards became his wife?"

"I fail to see—" the chemist began.

Knollis cut his protest short. "It is seldom that I run out of patience, Mr. Steadfall, but I am on the point of doing that—not only with you but with everybody concerned in the case. Did Lomas and yourself remain friendly after his marriage?"

"No," Steadfall replied slowly and reluctantly. "I was a young man then, and I am afraid that I sulked. Lomas was cockahoop because he had won the battle, and he was inclined to be patronising towards me. I resented that, and for some months we were on cold terms. Then he asked me round to the house, and I went, mainly because I was anxious to see whether Jennifer was happy."

"And was she?"

"No. She was most unhappy."

"But you repeatedly visited the house?"

"Oh yes. I was keeping an eye on Jennifer and was prepared to interfere if Ezekiah went too far."

"But you married some time later?"

"I—look here, Inspector," the chemist pleaded, "how can all this have any bearing on his death? I protest most emphatically! It is unfair, raking up the past in such a way. I did not kill him, and I know nothing about his death."

"What bearing can it have?" Knollis asked. "That is what I am trying to find out. I am not accusing you of causing his death, but I am convinced that Lomas was doomed from the moment he married Jennifer. That was the circumstance that started the ball rolling. You must trust my motives, Mr. Steadfall, and answer my questions."

Steadfall flushed. His fists slowly closed. "From the moment he married Jennifer? Then you are suggesting that I planned his death!"

Knollis shook his head.

"No, I am not suggesting that. I have told you so. I am suggesting that you were the unwitting cause of it. If she had married you instead of Lomas she would have been happy?"

Tears flooded into the chemist's eyes. "Dear God, I could have made her supremely happy. I swear I could."

"You would never have money-grubbed as Lomas did in order to show her that you were the better man?"

"I'd have worked my fingers to the bone for her," said Steadfall sincerely, "but she would never have known what it was to lack."

"And I take it that you would not have entered the dope traffic in order to swell your bank account?" Steadfall stared in a bewildered manner.

"You mean that Lomas did that?" he gasped.

"I can't say that he did," replied Knollis, "but there's enough cocaine in the house across the road to—well, there's too much, anyway," he said, lost for words.

"Ezekiah Lomas!"

"Why did you marry if you were so attached to Jennifer Lomas?" Knollis asked quickly, taking advantage of the chemist's state of mind.

"I—well, I wanted a home of my own, and comfort, and I realised that I was making Jennifer unhappy by staying single. She was chastening herself, believing that she had ruined my life as well as her own—which, of course, she had. It was the least I could do for her. Caroline, my wife, was ready to marry me, and we, well, we married."

"And your friendship with Lomas continued?"

"It was more of an acquaintanceship than a friendship at that time, Inspector," Steadfall said reminiscently. "It was not until after Jennifer's death that we resumed our friendship. He seemed pitifully alone in the world, and then again he was my only link with Jennifer . . ."

"If not the rose, to be near the rose," Knollis muttered under his breath.

"I beg your pardon, Inspector?"

"Skip it," Knollis said shortly. "Now, for the night of Lomas's death. Exactly what did you do, and where did you go after closing the shop?"

"I was under the impression that you had already made inquiries about my movements," was the petulant reply.

"Perhaps I have," said Knollis. "I want your own story."

"Well, if it comes to that, I did no more than I usually do. After locking the shop I went to the Angel, waited a while for Ezekiah, and then walked round to the Commerce Club. I was told that he had been and gone, and so I went home. This was shortly after half-past eight. I got home before nine, and did not go out again."

Knollis waved a hand toward the poison cupboard.

"The cocaine is still there?"

"Oh, yes."

"Used any of it?"

"A small amount. A prescription came in yesterday—I think it was yesterday." The chemist smiled. "It was one of Dr. Whitelaw's, and so I was justly suspicious of it. I still am suspicious."

"That's how it should be," said Knollis, "and yet I can tell you that there wasn't a fraction of a grain of cocaine in the stuff you mixed up."

"Oh yes, there was!" said Steadfall. "Look, I can show you the prescription!"

He took a sheaf of them from a drawer and found the one that Dr. Whitelaw had prepared.

"You misunderstand me, Mr. Steadfall. I didn't say that there was no cocaine in the prescription. I said there was none in your mixture, in your version of the prescription."

Steadfall gave a grunt of impatience and unlocked the poison cupboard. He handed the bottle to the Inspector.

"That is it!"

Knollis removed the stopper, dipped his finger, and touched it on his tongue. "Just as it was the other day when I called, Mr. Steadfall. Bicarbonate of soda. And I'm no chemist."

Steadfall snatched the bottle and tested the contents. Then he looked at Knollis, his features grim.

"Bicarbonate! You're right, Inspector. Then that young man did get into the cupboard!"

"You will remember that I asked if you left him alone in here? You said that you served a small boy, I believe?"

Steadfall climbed on the stool and clasped his hands between his knees. "So that's it! And Whitelaw's prescription was a trap! And if the analysts had found cocaine in that mixture . . ."

"I should have arrested you," said Knollis.

"Lord!" exclaimed the chemist. "Lord!"

"You were with Lomas every week-night?"

"Eh? Oh yes, except for the occasions when he went to Desborough for his extractions."

"Your wife must have been flattered by your continual absence from home."

Steadfall flushed.

"My wife has her own amusements, Inspector, and I'll thank you to leave my domestic life out of this. I'm trying to help you, even if I cannot see where you are going, but I must insist on that exclusion. It is irrelevant."

"Then we'll consider the interview at an end," smiled Knollis. "I know I'm an awful nuisance, but I mean getting to the bottom of the mystery by hook or by crook. And if I don't get results soon I'll have the Chief Constable asking for Yard assistance, and that would hardly redound to the credit of the city, would it? Oh well, I'll probably run into Sergeant Luck, or Inspector Chance, and they'll help me."

"I didn't know there were such officers in the city force," Steadfall said absently.

"I've never met 'em yet," the Inspector replied. He went on to the home of Lomas's assistant and put a few questions to her.

"You've been very helpful up to now," he said. "Now I wonder if you can improve on previous efforts? We know that Mr. Lomas had lunch and tea at the shop, and that he went to the Golden Angel after closing the shop in the evenings. What I want to know is this; did he never leave the shop during the day?"

"Every day after tea, unless it was raining. He used to walk up the road in the direction of Desborough, just as far as the cemetery and back."

"And did Mr. Steadfall ever call in to see him during that time?"

"Once or twice, sir. He'd wait in the sitting-room. Usually he'd take a magazine from the shop with him."

"How many times did this happen during the past three months? Four times? Five? Or more?"

She could not remember, and frankly admitted as much. She could not even hazard a guess and refused to commit herself.

"But you'll agree that he did actually visit the shop during the tea-hour, and within the last few months?"

"Certainly, sir."

Knollis then boarded a corporation bus and went to Steadfall's home in Flamborough Avenue. He assumed a winning smile which was only a surface one, and knocked on the door. A trim maid took his card and showed him into the Steadfall drawing-room, where he awaited the arrival of Mrs. Steadfall.

She was a handsome woman with an arrogant manner. Knollis sketched her mentally as being all cheek, bosom, and behind. Her dress was stylish, if flamboyant, and she was made-up excessively. The Inspector gave a sigh for Honest John and knew at once why he spent so much of his spare time at the Angel and the Commerce Club.

"I have just called on your husband," he began diplomatically. "As he was a close friend of the late Mr. Lomas he was able to give us a deal of information about him which will doubtless prove useful. He tells us that he did not see Lomas on the night of his death, and that he was at home by nine o'clock. The point is," he went on loquaciously, "that the waiter at the Commerce Club appears to have mixed his times. He says that Lomas went out but a few minutes before your husband came in search of him, and that your husband left at *half-past nine*. If we can verify your husband's observations we can tax the waiter at the club—"

The lady gazed thoughtfully at the Inspector.

"You are wondering if it was possible for John to have murdered that horrible old man? Is that it?" Knollis blinked, but recovered in time to avoid the full count of ten.

"Good gracious, no! What an idea!"

"My husband told you that he arrived home before nine, you say?" she demanded in a belligerent tone.

"Yes, that is correct, ma'am."

"Then he did arrive home before nine. He may have his faults, but he is no liar, Mr. Inspector! I cannot verify his statement because I was not at home. And if John told you about his movements he must have told you that I was out. You are either trying to trap me into letting my husband down or trying to prove collusion. There is none of the latter, and absolutely nothing over which I could let him down." She gave her dress a sailor-like hitch.

Knollis passed a concealing hand over his mouth. His features were grave as he faced her again.

"Then here is a question I did not ask your husband. Did Lomas ever visit you?"

Mrs. Steadfall took a deep breath that filled her dress. She rumbled angrily. "That horrible old man? In my house? I'd have thrown him out, feeble woman though I am!"

Knollis doubted her description of herself as a feeble woman, preferring to regard her as an over-decorated old battle-axe.

"Did Mrs. Lomas ever visit you?" he next asked. He bowed his head for the coming storm.

"Mrs. Lomas! How much has my husband told you about himself and his connections with the Lomas family, Inspector? Not much, I'll be bound!"

"Oh, quite a lot, I suppose," Knollis murmured, hoping that a soft answer would turn away at least some of her wrath.

"Then you should know enough to—but I think I have answered the question which you came to ask, Inspector. John may have been home by nine. I am unable to say. But I am prepared to accept his word. You may consider that he was here at the time he gave you. My maid will show you out."

Knollis stood on the pavement for a time, a wry smile on his lips, and a number of thoughts in his mind. Eventually he went back to Desborough Road and asked yet one more question of John Steadfall.

"Why did you change the In Memoriam notice that Lomas had asked to be inserted in the local paper?" The chemist grinned guiltily.

"So you unearthed that as well? I must congratulate you on your thoroughness, Inspector. I can see that the murderer of my old friend has little chance of escaping you, and I am thankful that I am not the culprit."

"He hasn't a chance in the world, Mr. Steadfall. The pace may be slow, but we shall wear him down. Now, you will please answer my question."

Steadfall looked so weary that the Inspector wished it was possible to spare him, but he had to do his job and he meant doing it, no matter what the cost.

"There are times," said the chemist, "and there have been many of them during the past few days, when I cannot understand myself. At the bottom I hated Lomas, really hated him, and yet I professed to be his friend. That notice? Well, I knew he would have sent one in, and I knew the mealy-mouthed sort of thing it would be. I thought of it, and I suppose I became indignant. At all events, I telephoned to the office and asked them to substitute a more suitable one. You saw it, of course?"

"'Safe at last,'" quoted Knollis.

"Yes, that was it, Inspector. Lomas and I had a row over it. It was the first time that I had come into the open and told him what I thought of his behaviour during her life-time."

Knollis stared at the floor and wondered if he dare ask a certain question of Steadfall. Then he made up his mind.

"Are you satisfied that Jennifer Lomas died a natural death, Mr. Steadfall?"

The chemist blenched. His jaw trembled.

"So you know!" he whispered.

"I suspected, and so did you!" Knollis accused. "That was why you befriended Lomas after her death. You were hoping to find evidence that could prove his guilt, enable you to expose him, and bring him to the gallows. That is the truth, isn't it, Mr. Steadfall? Up to now you have played a part, and acted it very well if I may pay you such a left-handed compliment. You deceived me for a while. It was only when I tried to decide why you should befriend the man who robbed you of your happiness, and made miserable the life of the girl you loved, that I saw the truth of the matter. For five years you spied on Lomas, searched his house while he was absent—his tea-hour walk—and looked in every cranny and corner for the evidence you desired." Steadfall buried his face in his hands. Tears trickled between his fingers.

"May God judge me, but it is the truth, Inspector. I suspected the truth as she lay dying. I tried to hint as much to Teesdale, but he was not the kind of man to understand anything but a blunt accusation. I tried to get Lomas to allow me to prepare the medicines that Teesdale prescribed, but he sent them elsewhere. And so Jennifer died. I could have done something, you see. I was with her, and Lomas was down in that shop of his, drawing money across the counter like the unfeeling miser he was. If only I could have proved it! I would have strangled him! I've lain awake in the night, feeling my thumbs pressed into his throat. And then I would have come to you and confessed my crime. I should have been guilty, and you would have hanged me . . ."

He gave a deep sigh.

". . . and then I would have been with Jennifer, loving her, cherishing her, devoting myself to her for all eternity. But I never proved his guilt, Inspector Knollis, and someone else has avenged her for me. Robbed me of my one remaining ambition—to crush the life from his miserable body with my own hands."

"So that it really was a shock when you heard of his death on Tuesday morning?"

"And a disappointment," Steadfall murmured. "I had planned it in my mind, rehearsed it month by month. I should have gone to his house in the evening—it was just before seven o'clock that Jennifer died. I should have confronted him with the proof of his crime, and then—you know what would have followed."

"My ideas on religion may be all wrong," Knollis said gently, "but I am told that murderers and victims do not go to the same place. You got it all wrong, old fellow. Lomas and Jennifer would have been together, and you would have been far removed from her. You should thank God for saving you from that!" Steadfall regarded Knollis thoughtfully.

"Ye-es, I think you are right. I never thought of it in that way. And I have been prevented from doing the wrong thing? Strange, very strange, the way in which things work out for the best . . ."

Knollis left him staring through his cobwebbed window, out over the dismal backyard that was crammed with crates, broken packing-cases, and wicker-covered carboys; seeing none of them.

The Inspector looked up at the summer sun and grinned like an embarrassed schoolboy.

"My theology may be all pots and pans," he muttered, "but I think it has saved the old chap many a bad night."

He shook himself and went into the nearest kiosk. Automatic exchanges were not then installed in Burnham and he waited patiently while the operator connected him to his office.

"Tell Bates to take charge for twelve hours. I'm on my way to London. Back late to-morrow unless I decide to go to the Windmill."

He spent the two and a quarter hours in the train with a notebook and pen. Time and time again he looked up at the speeding landscape. He felt detached; detached from the train and the English countryside, and the familiar things of his daily life; detached from the earth itself, as if he was floating in space and able to take in the whole of life in one fleeting glance. He concentrated his vision on the southern part of the county in which he worked, on the area surrounding Burnham and Desborough, with the limelight of his attention focused strongly on the towpath that led in great sweeping curves from the famous bridge, beyond Rose Cottage, and on to The Ferryman at Willow Lock.

He turned back the hands of the clock and saw Ezekiah Lomas stumbling from the Bridge Hotel, down the ramp to the embankment, past the police station that housed the river patrol, past Rose Cottage with Dodson leaning over the gate, along the narrow tow-path until he staggered into the inn. He thrust forward the hands once more, and saw him leave the inn and set out for home. There were two barges chugging downstream to Willow Lock and thence to the Humber. In the willows beyond the towpath lurked a figure, watching. The barges went by, heading for the lock. Lomas came to the end of his strength and sank down on the bank. . . .

Knollis turned the beam on Desborough. Lawrence Lomas was calling at Empton's garage for his car, but Empton told him nothing of Gretton's trip, probably he saw nothing out of the way in the incident. He went to Grove Road, and Briar Cottage. Gretton was waiting for him. Together they left the house, entered the car, and drove off into the country. The country, yes, but in which direction? They had told him White Horse Ferry, and that was a lie. Knollis cursed himself for his carelessness. He had proved their alibi to be false, and had done nothing to trace their real movements. He must telephone through to headquarters when he arrived in London.

His picture of Lomas had faded when he saw him sink down on the bank of the river. His picture of Lawrence Lomas and Nora Gretton faded when they drove away from Briar Cottage. His picture of Ericson faded when he saw him leaving the Bridge Hotel at five minutes past nine. Ericson said he went back toward the city centre—and there was only his own word to support it.

He turned the beam of his attention on Steadfall. He saw him pottering about the shop, cashing up, locking the door, releasing the cords that lowered the green blinds in his windows; saw him open the safe and put the takings in—or did he take them home each night? He saw Steadfall leave for the Golden Angel, and here he came to another mental halt. There was no evidence, as yet, to prove that Steadfall had ever gone to the Angel on Monday. He had gone to the Commerce Club, and later than usual, because he said he had been waiting for Lomas at the Angel. He saw him next in the Commerce Club, asking for Lomas; saw him totter out with a queer pin-toed gait. Again the picture faded. Steadfall may have gone home, but there was no proof of that. Even his wife could not corroborate his statement.

Knollis made a few scribbled notes. They read:

Find Dodson.
Interview Barky Burgess.
Ask Empton if Gretton desired silence.
Trace the movements of Lawrence and Gretton.
Trace Ericson—after London interview.
Steadfall at Angel.

On arrival in London the Inspector took the Underground to Chancery Lane. In a cobbled court in Gray's Inn he examined the brass plates until he found one that informed him that Medal Chemical Manufacturers had offices on the second floor. He strode up the hollowed stone stairs and into the outer office. He was met by a petite girl dressed in green. To her he handed his professional card. While she stared at it wonderingly he asked: "The road staff work from here? The travellers?"

She was bewildered by the suddenness of his appearance, and nodded vaguely.

"I would like to see the manager—immediately."

"You—you have an appointment?"

"I have not, and I do not need one," Knollis answered humorously. "Please take my card in."

She turned on her heel and hurried through a baize-lined door. A few moments later she reappeared. "Mr. Lambert will see you at once."

Knollis found himself facing a plump man of forty or so. He was clean-shaven and as keen-eyed as the Inspector himself. A pair of horn-rimmed glasses swung between his fingers as he rose.

"I'm Lambert, the sales manager. I'm—well, taken aback. This is the first time that the police have called on me."

He laughed uneasily.

"Nothing wrong, is there?"

Knollis smiled comfortingly. He was in no way perturbed by Lambert's manner. He often found that the most innocent people were embarrassed when faced by the police. The guilty, on the other hand, managed to put a bold face on matters and appear naively innocent.

"I'm merely making routine inquiries about one of your travellers who looks like being a witness in a murder case. You've read of the Willow Lock murder, of course?"

Lambert's lids fell over his eyes like veils. He did not answer at once, and when he did it was but a bare admission that he mouthed. "Why yes. It is in the papers."

Then he remembered his duties as host and invited Knollis to be seated. He pushed a box of cigarettes across the table.

"What is Ericson's position in the firm?" asked Knollis.

"Roger Ericson? He is one of the road men."

"And what else?"

"What else?" Lambert echoed. "Why, what else could he be? I don't understand, Inspector."

"An independent gentleman, living on an unearned income," said Knollis. "I take it that Medal Chemicals are in business for reasons other than the good of their health?"

Lambert wriggled uneasily.

"It is a business, of course," he admitted lamely.

"And your main object is to keep chemists stocked with Medal preparations, if that is the right word?"

"Why, naturally!"

"I should imagine that every member of your road staff has a certain area to cover?"

"Yes, yes."

"And that this area has to be covered once every month, shall we say, Mr. Lambert?"

"That is the period," the manager replied. "Each agent covers his district once every month."

"And if a representative was to miss part of his round it would cause a dislocation of your office routine, and generally upset the plan of work?"

Lambert nodded, and kept his eyes turned on the surface of the desk. His hands toyed nervously with a paper-knife.

"Is there an extra man on Ericson's round?"

Lambert looked up. "What are you getting at, Inspector?"

"Simply this," said Knollis. "Ericson has spent a lot of time in the neighbourhood of Burnham of late, and I was wondering if the Medal people's sales were suffering as a result."

"I—I don't understand," the manager stammered.

"Oh yes, you do," Knollis said with a grim laugh. "Now I suggest that you come into the open. What is Ericson's real job?"

"He is our representative for the Burnham area."

Knollis nodded towards the large coloured map of England that hung on the wall. "Those the sales areas?"

"Yes."

"I'm not much of a hand at estimating," said Knollis, "but I'll make a guess that Ericson's square is about fifty miles each way—two hundred and fifty square miles of territory to cover every month. He can't afford to spend a week or more in Burnham if he is to cover the rest in the stipulated time. That being so I'm further guessing that Medal preparations must be getting rare in that area."

Knollis paused, and then said in a wooing tone: "Mr. Ericson wouldn't be acting as a private investigator for the Medal people, would he, Mr. Lambert?"

Lambert's head came up with a jerk. "Investigating what, might I ask, Inspector?"

"The illegal distribution of cocaine, snow, dope."

Lambert sagged as quickly as he had jerked into attention.

"So you're on to it! We were trying to keep it quiet. How do you come to know anything about it at all? Has Ericson blabbed?"

"I've been trying to explain for the last fifteen minutes, but you wouldn't take a hint," said Knollis. "It is very obvious that he can't be travelling for you. You'd have sacked him months ago for neglecting his job."

Lambert shrugged his shoulders as if in resignation.

He opened a deep drawer and produced whisky, a siphon, and glasses. "Say when. I need this."

It was against Knollis's principles to drink while on duty, but as he considered that the acceptance might mean the loosening of Lambert's tongue he said when at three fingers and a half.

"All the best, Inspector!"

"Good health, Mr. Lambert."

Lambert licked his lips and grinned.

"Knocked the stuffing out of me, you know. It wasn't as if I was prepared for anything of the kind. We were hoping to walk into the Yard, lay a complete dossier of evidence on the table, and then swank. The publicity value would have been worth thousands of pounds. The firm that protects the British Public! You know the idea!"

"You still have the chance," Knollis said glibly.

"You mean—"

"I'm investigating the death of Ezekiah Lomas."

"I see," Lambert said slowly. "By jove. I get you now! I can see the whole thing in black and white! 'As a result of information provided by Medal Chemical Manufacturers the police were able . . .' You mean that we can co-operate?"

"I mean that we've got to co-operate," Knollis said in a firm tone. "I represent the Criminal Investigation Department of the Burnham City Police."

"Yes, I see the necessity," mumbled Lambert.

"Now, why did you employ Ericson?"

"We didn't employ him. Not, that is, in the sense of giving him an assignment. He came to us and asked to be allowed to represent us. He said that there was a dope-distributing centre in or near Burnham and he intended to investigate it in the interests of his late profession. He couldn't go quizzing chemists without possessing some form of professional status, and so he asked to be taken on the road staff. He produced enough evidence to convince us—"

"Such as?" Knollis interrupted.

"A friend of his was going down the hill as a result of taking cocaine. Ericson had made inquiries and had elicited the fact that this friend was receiving bulky envelopes from Burnham, Desborough, and the neighbouring towns. He managed to intercept one of these and on opening it found a flat packet containing cocaine, but the packet bore a bicarbonate of soda label and our trademark. That, of course, interested us. Ericson brought it with him as evidence. It seemed that the packet must have come from someone we had supplied."

"You jumped a long way," said Knollis. "I take it that chemists sell your preparations? Then it would have been possible for a member of the public to obtain a label."

"We did think of that, Inspector," said Lambert; "strange though it may seem to your scientific mind. If that had been the case we could logically have expected to find at least one tiny grain of bicarb in the packet. Our research department analysed the packet and were unable to find a trace of anything but cocaine. On the strength of their report we took Ericson on our staff and gave him *carte blanche*."

"The label could have been used, and not the original packet," commented Knollis, as suspicious as ever.

"We also thought of that, Inspector," Lambert replied pointedly. "If that had been the case it would have meant that the label had been torn off the original packet and re-gummed. Our research department reported that this was not the case."

"I like the sound of your research department," said Knollis, "but I'm still puzzled. What did the report imply or suggest?"

"That a chemist with a supply of our labels was acting as a distributing agent."

"You do supply labels in bulk?"

"Oh yes. Preparations may be supplied in bulk, but even so we expect a chemist to use our labels when he had taken an agency."

"I'm getting the idea now," said Knollis. "So Ericson intended looking among your customers for his man?"

"That is so, Inspector."

"You and Ericson appear to have missed a good few vital points, nevertheless," mused Knollis. "You naturally keep a check on the amount of dope supplied?"

"That is very evident, Inspector. I am surprised that you ask such a question."

"Then your books should have told you whether there was an increase of the amount of stuff ordered by any one chemist in that area!"

"There wasn't," Lambert snapped back impatiently. "That was the whole point. If the stuff was being sent out under our label, the business was exposed by anyone but ourselves, it would look as if we were responsible for the abnormal supply. That was why we accepted Ericson's suggestion."

"You investigated Ericson's story about his friend?"

"We did, and were satisfied that it was true."

"Who was he? I must have the name, you know."

"It was a lady," Lambert announced. "Her name is Nora Gretton. We had difficulty in seeing her, but from the report received there was no doubt at all that she was, and still is, a dope addict. The twitching nostrils, the eyes, the blueness—"

Knollis arose, grim-lipped, and stood over the manager with an expression of pitying anger.

Lambert faltered in his triumphant recital. "Why, what is the matter, Inspector?"

"What is the matter!" Knollis exclaimed. "What is the matter? I'll tell you. If you let Ericson know that you've as much as set eyes on me I'll run you in and close the business down into the bargain. You are the most gullible man I've ever met. Barnum said once that a sucker was born every minute, and by heck he was right!"

He slammed the door behind him, and the glass pane fell to the floor in fragments.

CHAPTER X
THE ALIBI OF MR. ERICSON

KNOLLIS'S NOTEBOOK contained a list of instructions which he had intended to phone through to Burnham, but he changed his mind and merely asked Bates to wait for him at the office, in spite of the fact that the earliest possible train could not get him back to Burnham before eleven o'clock that night. He went over the facts of the case again and again as the train sped northward, and there was a predatory gleam in his eye when he at last stepped from the carriage.

Sergeant Bates was dozing in Knollis's chair when the Inspector walked into the office, but by the time the story was told he was as wide-eyed as a midnight bat.

"So Ericson wangled the Medal people into helping him!" he exclaimed. "What a nerve!"

"That's how I see it, Bates," said Knollis. "I'm still not sure how it is being worked, but I do see several ways in which it *could* be worked, and that helps. The dope in Steadfall's dispensary was taken away before Nora-Marjory-Gretton-Ericson called! That visit was a pure stunt to turn suspicion away from Steadfall, and to turn Steadfall's eventual suspicions away from the suppliers. I'm not a betting man, but I am willing to bet fifty shillings to a ha'penny that every agent for Medal preparations has a cocaine bottle full of bicarbonate of soda. Care to take the bet?"

"Not on your blooming life," Bates replied stolidly. "I know your hunches too well! If you think that, then it's a thousand to one that you're right. But how are we going to prove it?"

"In the most straightforward way. Dawes and Slater can go the rounds to-morrow, collecting samples. It seems to me that supplies were diverted from the chemists and handed over to Lomas, and Lomas did the rest. The thing is simplifying itself, don't you think?"

"I suppose so," Bates said dubiously.

"What's the doubt?" asked the Inspector.

"Who killed Lomas?"

Knollis opened his notebook and threw it across. "Answer those questions and we shall know who killed Ezekiah Lomas. It's a simple matter of elimination."

Bates nodded slowly. "I see the idea. We lost Ericson when he left the Bridge, Lawrence and Nora when they left Briar Cottage, Ezekiah when he left The Ferryman, Steadfall before he

THE DEATH OF MR. LOMAS

got home, and Dodson when he knew that he was rumbled. Do y'know, Inspector; we are going to be busy."

Knollis smiled. "Feel like a night on the tiles?" Bates shook his head. "I don't, but I know what you mean. Where is it?"

"Barky Burgess's place. He should be home again by now unless he's pulled the barges all the way from Grimsby or wherever he goes. Get a car round, please." Barky Burgess lived in River Lane, and his son half a mile beyond, by Barnard's Wharf. They called on Barky first. He was a typical bargee, mufflered, and jerseyed. He poked a weather-tanned face round the door.

"Just goin' to bed, I was. But come in. Hopkin told me you'd be on my trail before long. Now what can I do for you, Inspector?"

"You were on the river on Monday evening?"

"That's right. Went through the lock about ten. My Bert was with me."

"Where were you when your craft passed Rose Cottage, Mr. Burgess?" asked Knollis.

The barge-master spat in the fire. "Barky's the name, sir. I were at the tiller."

"Did you see Dodson, the fellow who lives at the cottage?"

"Yes, I did. I've been thinking it over since Hopkin mentioned the business to me. This Lomas as is dead, he were lying on the bank about two hundred yard below The Ferryman. Lying on his back he was, with his 'at tipped over his face as if 'e were shielding it from the sun—not that there was any strong light left at that time of the day. Dodson, as you say 'is name was, he were walking away from the garden gate, coming down-stream, and it looked to me as if he were putting his key in his pocket. Lomas wasn't in the same place, of course, but I mentioned him as you might be interested, see?"

"Notice anything else?" asked Knollis, at the same time offering his cigarettes.

"Well no, unless you can take in a courting couple."

Burgess paused while he took a cigarette, doubled it up, and crammed it into his pipe, which he lit.

"Courting very strong as you might say. *Very* strong!"

"How strong?" asked Knollis. He scented a new lead.

Burgess appeared to be embarrassed by the question. He spat in the fire and pulled at his pipe reflectively.

"Like as if they might find trouble afore the night was out," he said at last. "They was lying side by side, in each other's arms, and their faces was hid."

"Notice a car thereabouts?"

"Ay, that were back in the willows. Couldn't make out no perticulars, but then I warn't taking no perticular notice. I saw 'em, and says to myself 'Silly young devils!' and left it at that."

"Where were they, Barky?"

"On the bank 'twixt the towpath and the willow beds."

"No, no! I mean their situation. Were they between Lomas and The Ferryman, or between Lomas and the cottage?"

"To'ard The Ferryman. So was the car."

"Have another cigarette," said Knollis anxiously. He would have given the moon away just then.

Burgess obliged and crammed it into his pocket against the time when his pipe needed refilling.

"Notice how they were dressed?" Knollis continued.

"The wench had short skirts—too short. They was up above her knees. Her legs and shoes was all I seen. The shoes was brown, but that's all I seen, as I says. The chap now . . . A brownish sort of suit he had. A grey trilby was lying aside of him. An' I reckon that's about all I can tell you, Inspector."

"Very useful, nevertheless," said Knollis. "You'll have a drink with me next time your way takes you near the inn?"

Burgess pushed the two half-crowns into the pocket with the cigarette. "Half for the chapel box and half for The Ferryman, and thank you, sir!"

Knollis and Bates went on to Barnard's Wharf, and in a low-roofed cottage interviewed Burgess's son. His wife opened the door to them, a fresh girl of twenty-two, full-bosomed, black-haired, rosy-cheeked. She took them to her husband in the living-room and then went upstairs, leaving them to talk privately.

"I've just interviewed your father, Mr. Burgess," began Knollis. "He told us what he saw, but we'd like your story as well if you don't mind."

Bert Burgess accepted a smoke, and haltingly opened his story.

"It was just before ten, and we was going down to the lock. A bearded gent was lying on the bank with his hat over the top half of his face. I seen his beard distinct."

"You passed Rose Cottage, of course?"

"Oh yes. The chap was closing the door. He made off downstream—same way as us."

"And you saw the courting couple?"

Bert Burgess sighed. "I seen 'em! Loving couple they was an' all. I reckon they thought a lot of each other. Loving each other proper, they was."

"Your father didn't approve of them," commented Knollis.

"Dad wouldn't. He's a bit on the stiff side. It's 'is chapel what does it. He can see trouble where there isn't none and smell sin out before it starts. It's just 'is way. I seen nothing to grumble at."

"Been married long?" asked the Inspector.

Burgess glanced affectionately toward the stairs. "Three month, Inspector. Best three month of my life. If I'd ha' known before what I do now I'd ha' bin married when I left school. A girl in a million is my 'Etty. She can make money go twice as far."

"And you saw this couple clearly?"

"Well, yes and no. When I says clearly I mean as I see him, and her legs. There warn't nowt else to see. She'd got as good a pair of understandings as—well, they was good limbs, if you take my meaning!"

"And you didn't see their faces?"

"I reckon that nobody but each other did that."

"Where were they lying?"

"Further down-stream than the man with the beard; between him and the inn."

"Did you happen to see another man, walking on the path?"

"Not on the towpath, sir. He were walking down towards the cottage, but behind the beds. A tall gent with a grey trilby."

"Now wait a minute," said Knollis keenly. "Did you see a hat lying near that loving couple?"

"Why yes. It was a grey—" He broke off and stared. "Why, now I comes to think of it, them two gents might have been twins. Funny I didn't notice it before!"

"It was after sunset," Knollis reminded him.

"Ay, but it warn't dark by any manner of means, Inspector. It warn't proper dark all night if it comes to that. No, sir, I seen him clearly, and 'e might have been the other man's twin brother."

Knollis thanked him effusively and left. He led Bates down to the river, where they smoked and talked.

"The picture is becoming clearer, Bates. Ericson, young Lomas, and Gretton were all down by Willow Lock on Monday night. If only I could establish the relationship between them! Dodson is supposed to be Ericson's man, and yet last night I heard Lomas express the hope—to Gretton—that I should not get on to Dodson. All I can see for it at the moment is a conspiracy concerning three people, and one of them, Gretton, is double-crossing the others. And I still don't know who killed Ezekiah Lomas!"

"Gretton is definitely playing Lawrence for a sucker," Bates said heavily. "That is proved by the way she collared his car on Monday afternoon and brought Ericson into town, and then slunk back again. It looks to me as if Ericson, Gretton, and Dodson . . ."

He paused and pointed through the gloom. "What's that?"

Knollis followed his finger. "Where?"

"Under the far bank, Inspector. It looks like—"

"A body, Bates. By Jove, you've got a pair of sharp eyes. It is a body. Now I wonder—slip along to River Station for help while I keep an eye on it. The current may swirl it away."

Knollis went upstream and crossed the bridge. He returned along the opposite bank until he reached the spot where the dark form had been seen. Here he sat down and let himself slide down to water level. The body was beyond his reach, but he was able to identify it as a body of a man. When the motor craft chugged along with Bates as a passenger he called to the sergeant in charge, directing him to the spot. The sergeant grimaced as he saw the limp figure in the water. "Who is it this time, Inspector?"

"I may be wrong," Knollis called back softly, "but I believe it to be Dodson, from Rose Cottage."

Five minutes later Knollis stepped on board to examine the recovered corpse. "Dodson, all right," he commented. "Coshed behind the right ear. Straight back to the station, Sergeant."

As the craft drew alongside the miniature landing stage the Inspector ordered his men to take the body to the mortuary and notify Dr. Whitelaw and Sir Wilfred Burrows.

"And what are we going to do?" inquired Bates.

"Interview Ericson," the Inspector replied grimly, and strode toward the Bridge Hotel.

Ericson jerked into startled wakefulness as Knollis and Bates walked into his bedroom. The Inspector flicked the switch down.

"What on earth?" Ericson exclaimed. He sat up in bed, and blinked at them. "What the devil are you doing in my room!"

"You must excuse us," murmured Knollis. "We bring bad news, and bad news can never wait."

Ericson smoothed his hair back from his forehead.

"Bad news . . . ?"

"We've just pulled Dodson from the river."

Ericson gazed at the counterpane and then slowly turned his eyes on Knollis. "From the river!"

Knollis gave Bates a faint smile. He had succeeded in surprising Ericson into a betrayal of his knowledge of Dodson, which had been his intention.

"From the river," he repeated.

Ericson threw the bedclothes back and swung his legs to the floor. "Er—you'll pardon me if I ask? Who is this Dodson?"

"It's too late to ask that," said Knollis. "You've given the show away. You should have asked who he was as your first question, and then we should have thought that you didn't know him, but you were only surprised to hear that he was dragged from the river. No, Mr. Ericson, it won't do. I think the time is ripe when you should talk. Bates and I are good listeners, and we have the whole night at our disposal. You can either talk here, or come to the station. It's all one to us, but you are going to talk!"

Ericson reached for his dressing-gown and slid his arms into the sleeves. He fumbled for his slippers and crammed them over his heels. Then, still slowly, he folded the gown over his pyjamas and tied the cord just a little too carefully.

Knollis waited patiently. Ericson was trying to think, but he was at a distinct disadvantage.

"If it will help you in reaching a decision," he said, "I will inform you that I was in London this morning, with Lambert of the Medal Company!"

Ericson's head came up. "Oh!"

"So you see," the Inspector continued, "there is nothing to be gained by evading the issue. We can probably bring the case to a successful conclusion much quicker if we have your assistance, but we shall do so even if you don't feel inclined to co-operate. We have unrivalled sources of information."

"I've noticed as much," said Ericson. "You don't miss much, do you?"

"It wouldn't do," the Inspector smiled. "We don't miss anything—not for very long, anyway."

Ericson reached a cigarette from the bedside table and lit it. When the first puff of smoke was rising to the ceiling he asked: "What did Lambert tell you?"

"Everything," said Knollis.

"Then you know about Marjory?"

"Nora Gretton, you mean?" the Inspector murmured.

"Oh!" exclaimed Ericson. "Then you do know. All right, Inspector. I guess I'll have to talk."

He crossed his legs, and looked round the room.

"Suppose you find seats? It may be a long session." Knollis took the sole wicker chair, leaving Bates to dispose himself on the edge of the dressing-table with his notebook balanced on his knee.

"You will have realised that I was on old Lomas's trail?" began Ericson in a bland manner.

"From the word Go."

"It all began with Nora Gretton," said Ericson. "Your sister, you mean?"

"No, I mean the real Nora Gretton. She was Marjory's friend. We suspected that there was something wrong with her many months before her death. Marjory wheedled the truth out of her bit by bit. She had been tricked into taking cocaine until she found she couldn't do without it. She made fine attempts to beat the habit, but was unable to do so—you know how it is! Anyway, she went for a holiday on the Norfolk coast, and was pulled from the sea the same day that she arrived."

"Suicide?"

"We think so," said Ericson, "although the coroner gave her the benefit of the doubt and entered a verdict of death by misadventure. You can trace that in the files of the Norfolk papers if you wish to do so."

"We shall," said the Inspector, and Ericson winced. "Both Marjory and I were upset by her death. She was a fine girl until the damned dope ate into her will-power. I had time on my hands, and a sufficiency of money, and so we decided to trace her supplies to their source, and smash the game for good. I went to the Medal people and told my story. They were interested, naturally, because it was to their benefit, and to the benefit of the country as a whole, that the traffic be wiped out. I agreed to work for them to the best of my ability, quite apart from the investigation which was to be my cover."

"Why did you take that particular line?" queried Knollis. "You made a dead set at pharmacists and chemists."

"Nora told Marjory one fact that really mattered—that the stuff came from Burnham in the guise of bicarbonate of soda, and that the labels used were those of the Medal people. It seemed obvious from that that they were sent out by somebody connected with the profession."

"I see," said the Inspector. "Carry on, please."

"I realised after my second trip round the area that no chemist was responsible, and it looked as if I had failed. Marjory, looking through Nora's belongings, found one of Steadfall's labels—the usual bicarbonate one—and we set to work on Steadfall. Here again it soon became obvious that Steadfall was not in the act. By careful questioning I elicited the fact that his friend Lomas bought a deuce of a lot of bicarbonate of soda, and on the off-chance we turned our attentions to him. You know quite well that bicarb is used by traffickers. It looks like cocaine and is used for diluting the stuff. Here, it seemed, was a clue. Lomas bought plenty. He could use it as a diluting agent, and also use the Medal labels, and Steadfall's labels."

Knollis nodded. "I'm beginning to understand," he said. "Go on with your story."

"We had to get into personal touch with Lomas, and so Marjory took Nora's name and went to Desborough to contact Lawrence Lomas while I spent my time between Burnham and Fountains."

"Fountains? You mean Gertrude Lomas?"

Ericson smiled sheepishly.

"I'm going to marry her when this job is over." The Inspector took a deep breath. "But she never mentioned your name when I interviewed her!"

"Why should she?" Ericson demanded. "She was not likely to think it necessary. She has never connected me with her father, or so I hope."

"And you got into touch with Lomas through her?"

"No, I did not, but Marjory got in touch with him through Lawrence Lomas. Trust a woman!"

"Shades of night!" exclaimed Knollis. "No wonder I've been chasing my tail. So you and your sister are working with us?"

Ericson's jaw tightened. "No, we are not!"

"I beg your pardon?" murmured the Inspector. "You mean?"

"I mean that I am, but that my sister has ratted. She's head over heels in love with Lawrence Lomas—and if he didn't kill his own father you can call me a Polynesian!"

"Which means that your sister was an accessory, after the fact even if not before it?"

"My sister? What on earth do you mean?"

161 | THE DEATH OF MR. LOMAS

"You should know, Mr. Ericson," murmured Knollis. "You were on the river at the same time as they were, which means shortly after Lomas died."

Ericson stubbed his cigarette and lit another, which he puffed quickly. "Let's get this clear, Inspector. How much do you really know?"

"More than I am going to tell you," said Knollis. "But I will present you with an all-in picture of the river bank at ten o'clock on Monday night. Dodson was leaving his cottage and walking toward The Ferryman. Lomas was lying on the bank above the towpath, either dead or dying. Lawrence Lomas and your sister were engaged in hectic love-making between Lomas Senior and The Ferryman. *You* were strolling about behind the willow beds!"

"I was not!" Ericson exploded.

"Suppose I bring witnesses to prove it?" demanded the Inspector. "I can do that, you know!"

"Then they will be mistaken."

"So you are going to tell me that I have three people in this case who all wear grey trilbys, heather mixture tweed suits, and who carry yellow gloves."

"You are working on the alleged impersonation of myself on the night of Lomas's death?"

"What else?" said Knollis.

"I was in Lomas's house, searching it, just before ten o'clock, Inspector," said Ericson. "Marjory obtained a spare key a month ago. I watched Lomas, saw that he kept to a nightly routine—except for the evenings when he went to Desborough for dental treatment—and so after leaving the Bridge Hotel—this place—I went to the Desborough Road shop and searched the whole building."

"Find what you were looking for?"

"No, I didn't," Ericson said sulkily.

"You should have taken out the top drawer of the bureau, and then felt in the cavity at the back," said Knollis smilingly. "I found it—packets of it." Ericson gave vent to an oath.

"What a dam' fool I was not to think of that!"

"I wouldn't say so," the Inspector consoled him. "I had to seek Lawrence Lomas's assistance. It was one of the family hiding-places. Now, have you any means of proving that you were in Lomas's house?"

"Good heavens, no! It was an alibi I needed, not proof that I had broken into and entered premises. It was a criminal act, wasn't it?"

"I'll say it was," said the Inspector. "But what about Dodson? Where have you been during the evening?" Ericson grimaced. "Trying to connect me with his death, are you? Well, I don't know when he died, but I can tell you where I've been for the past few hours. It's well past one o'clock now and I came to bed shortly after ten. From a quarter to nine to ten I was in the smoke-room. From eight to a quarter to nine I was dining. From half-past seven to eight I was dressing for dinner. I don't mean in a monkey suit; just washing, shaving, changing my linen, and all that. From half-past six onwards I was generally mooching around the hotel."

"You mean that you didn't leave the building?"

"I hate walking with people on my tail," Ericson said smoothly, "and your stooges are not too good. They would not deceive a child of nine. Sorry, Inspector, you do seem to be asking for the truth—and those said stooges should be able to verify my statement."

"And Dodson?"

"Dodson? I'm afraid he skipped out for reasons of his own. He never was reliable."

"What part did he play in your investigations?"

"Liaison officer. I put him into Rose Cottage so that he could receive Marjory's reports and pass them on to me. I had no desire to be seen in her company until we had cleaned up Lomas and his associates."

The Inspector fixed Ericson with mild eyes.

"Why did you shave Lomas after you found him dead on the bank? To delay identification, I suppose?"

THE DEATH OF MR. LOMAS

"I don't fall for your little tricks, Inspector," laughed Ericson. "Dodson was solely responsible for that complicating factor, although I didn't know until later."

"Having found the razor at Rose Cottage I was prepared to hear you say that," said Knollis. "I don't suppose you know why he did it?"

"Mainly because the man was a fool. He thought I'd bumped Lomas off, and he wanted to protect me. He thought it would give me time in which to arrange an alibi—and that fine idea was the result of mixing with race-course sharps. I often wonder why I employed him."

"However disastrous such action may appear to the police," the Inspector said dryly, "it should have appeared to you as a highly commendable action. I wouldn't shelter behind Dodson. His action also proves that he saw you beyond the willow beds, otherwise he would not have found it necessary to take what we might call stalling action."

"It must have been some other fellow," Ericson said in a dogged tone. "I have told you the truth."

"Who could it be then?"

"Now how the devil do I know that? It would seem that there was more than one person on Lomas's track. What about Lawrence Lomas? He had his eye on the old man's money! Marjory told me that early in the game."

"Did Dodson put Lomas in the water?"

"He said not. I taxed him with it. He said that he saw Lomas lying on the bank above the path, and thought he was asleep. Then he realised that he looked oddly limp and went nearer. When it dawned on him that Lomas was dead his queer little brain began to work in a way peculiar to himself. He knew that we were trying to collar Lomas because of Nora, and he decided that I had gone the whole hog and taken the law into my own hands. He had a razor in his pocket—which was just one of the unexplainable things so characteristic of him—and so he whipped Lomas's face fungus off! Those were his very words. He stuffed the resulting whiskers in his pocket and burned them when he got back to the cottage."

Knollis smiled broadly. "You know, all this is rather remarkable—or don't you think so?"

"Why? What do you mean?"

"Lawrence Lomas and your sister were lying but a few yards away, locked in each other's arms. It almost looks as if they and Dodson worked together, unless of course they were very much engrossed in each other."

Ericson shrugged his shoulders and lit another cigarette.

"You'd better ask her about that. I've told you all I know about the affair. I'm beginning to wish I'd never embarked on it. Try to do a good turn and I find myself implicated in a murder mystery. I'll learn to mind my own business after this. Ask Marjory! I'm fed up!"

"We'll do just that," said the Inspector.

On the way out he telephoned the exchange and asked them not to allow any calls to be put through to Briar Cottage, Grove Road, Desborough, for at least an hour.

CHAPTER XI
THE EVIDENCE OF MR. LESTER

NORA GRETTON OPENED the door to Knollis and Bates only when they had given ample evidence of identity. The Inspector handled her tactfully, assuring her that only a matter of the greatest importance could have induced him to disturb her during the small hours of the night. She showed them into the sitting-room, holding a colourful wrap tight against her slim body. She plunged a gas poker into the laid fire.

"Knowing you," she commented acidly, "I realise that the sitting is likely to be lengthy and it can get cold even on a summer's night."

"The length of the interview depends on yourself," Knollis retorted. "All I need is a corroboration of your brother's statement."

She remained on her knees before the fire, but turned hurriedly. "My brother's statement, Inspector? I don't understand what you mean."

"We have just left Roger Ericson in his bedroom at the Bridge Hotel. He told us the whole story, from the suicide of Nora Gretton to the night of Ezekiah Lomas's death."

The girl seated herself on the arm of a chair, reached cigarettes from the coffee table, and lit one. Knollis watched her movements closely. One of the statements he had made had surprised her. He wondered which it was.

"What do you want to know?" she asked.

"Did you see a motor barge go down toward Willow Lock while you were on the bank with Lawrence Lomas?"

"Oh! So you know that I was there?"

The Inspector nodded his reply.

"Then I may as well tell you all I know. There were two barges. But why do you ask that?"

"Because if you saw those two barges it means that you were within calling distance of Lomas when he died."

"I see," she said slowly, and gave a wry smile. "You laid a trap for me, Inspector."

"Something like that," Knollis admitted. "As you and Lawrence Lomas were on the bank you must have seen his father when he left The Ferryman."

"We did," she said in a low voice. "He was lying a few yards away, about two hundred yards from us. There were bushes between us, tall hawthorn bushes, almost trees, but it was possible to see beyond them by lying flat and peering below their bottom branches."

"So you saw the whole thing from start to finish?"

She frowned and tapped a silk-clad toe on the carpet. Then she cast a quizzical glance at the Inspector.

"Well?" he murmured.

"I think you should know something," she said softly. "I am not Marjory Ericson. I really am Nora Gretton. It was Marjory who killed herself. And it would seem that Roger cannot play straight even with me."

Knollis showed no surprise at her statement.

"So that is the way of it. You are Nora Gretton. Then why were clothes found in Rose Cottage marked with Marjory Ericson's initials? You can explain that?"

"Marjory bought clothes which she never wore. Roger gave them to me—and I now see why he did so! I am Marjory, am I? We'll see about that!"

"It was Marjory who was found in the sea?"

"Doesn't it sound more logical that way, Inspector?" she asked. "Marjory was Roger's sister, and my friend. If Roger's story was true, and it had been Nora who died, then why should he have taken an interest in her, to the extent that he was prepared to disrupt his whole life in order to avenge her?"

"I'll gladly concede the point, Miss Gretton," said Knollis. "I like logical argument."

Nora Gretton continued: "Marjory told me some of the truth before she left for that last holiday, and in duty bound I passed it on to Roger after her death. He told me what he intended to do, and asked if I would help. I had no financial means, and so he offered to pay me if I threw up my job. That idea stuck in my throat, but I had to live, and so I accepted the amount of my old salary, and not a penny more. Once Roger got on to Lomas I came down here to contact him through his son. Roger worked Gertrude Lomas, and we put Dodson, who was Roger's man-servant, into Rose Cottage to act as liaison officer. And Roger has ratted, and I know why!"

Knollis made the expected noises of inquiry, and waited.

"Roger knows that Gertrude inherits the old man's ill-gotten gains, and he intends to marry them—not her!"

"And the investigation into the drug traffic?"

"He will let that drop. He hinted at such action a few days ago. Gave me what amounts to a fortnight's notice. But that won't work! I'll get a job and finish the inquiry in my own time and in my own way."

"And Lawrence Lomas? Would it be correct to assume that you and he are interested in each other?" She hesitated a moment, and then said:

"Lawrence proposed to me the other night. I asked for time in which to decide. You see, Inspector, I have been fighting his family, and doing it under cover, using him as a tool. I'm not quite sure that I should be treating him rightly if I married him—although I'd spend the rest of my life making it up to him."

"How far did you progress in the investigation?"

"Lawrence's father definitely was the distributing agent, not to the consumer, but to the last line of suppliers. Who they were, and are, is another matter. I don't think anyone will find out. Lomas died too soon. Another month . . ."

"Let us turn to the night of his death," Knollis suggested. "You have admitted that you were on the bank with Lawrence Lomas."

"That is obvious, Inspector."

"Then suppose you tell us what you saw, imagining that we know nothing at all about the events of the evening."

"His father came from The Ferryman shortly before ten. He was staggering. He passed close by, but Lawrence kept his face in my shoulder and was not recognised, although I doubt if the old man was capable of recognising anybody. He went two hundred yards beyond and then sat down. After a few minutes he swayed and fell over. Lawrence hurried to his side, and when he came back he said that his father was breathing heavily, and was ill. He would have to fetch the car and take him home. The car was toward the inn. Lawrence drove it back along the towpath, but his father had disappeared. We drove some distance and then turned the car round. Just as we got near the spot where old Lomas had been we saw Dodson coming from the willow beds. We asked him about Lomas, but he said he had seen nothing of him. We came to the conclusion that he must have made a miraculous recovery and walked away through the beds to the track across the fields. So we drove on and Lawrence took me home. We were home by eleven. Lawry took supper here and left about a quarter to twelve. The police must have called on him just before he got to bed."

Knollis leaned forward. "Why was Ericson buying the business from Lomas? You know that?"

"It's rather obvious," she said with a light smile. "He was hoping to take it over as a going concern, keep it under Lomas's name, and discover the agents as they came in for supplies. In this way he would have rounded up the whole gang, and later would have sold the business. That was the plan he explained to me."

"Had Lawrence any knowledge of his father's illegal transactions before he went to the shop with me?"

"No," she said stoutly. "He had no idea. He was shocked when he learned the nature of his father's death. He seemed stunned, because he kept asking over and over again where he could have obtained the stuff. I think he suspected John Steadfall."

"Of supplying, or causing death?"

"Naturally, both."

"There is one more item that requires explanation." said Knollis. "Why did you make that trip in the night to Rose Cottage, and from there to Lomas's shop?"

"Oh!" she exclaimed. "So you know that!"

"I seldom sleep when a murder case is on the books," Knollis said grimly.

"I—well, I . . ."

She stared into the fire, now burning brightly.

"And the trip to Steadfall's shop as a would-be dog hocusser."

"Oh!" she again ejaculated.

"You seem to think that I know considerably less than half of the story," said Knollis. "If that is so, then you are wrong, I know, for instance, that you lifted Steadfall's supply of cocaine and substituted bicarbonate of soda."

Nora Gretton sagged visibly under the Inspector's attack.

"It was all Roger's idea," she said wearily. "He knew that Lomas would sell out to him, but he suspected that he would clear the shop of dope before handing over the business. It seemed a good idea to obtain supplies in case any of the agents came round, and so he deputed me to get hold of it. I knew that Dodson was mixed up with the more shady side of dog-racing and I asked him for the name of a dog that was likely to win during that week. He told me one and I changed into a suit and went round to see the old chemist. He wouldn't part by fair means, but I had arranged for him to be drawn into the shop; while he was there I effected the substitution. That dope was put up in small packets at Rose Cottage. I got the wind up after Lomas's death, and delivered it at Desborough Road to get it out of the way."

"And what happened to Dodson?"

"He vanished, Inspector. I think he got on the wrong side of the men he was working with and had to clear out."

"Do you know where he is now?" Knollis asked mildly.

"I haven't the faintest idea, Inspector."

"In the city mortuary."

Her hand flew to her throat. "Dodson!"

"Dragged from the river to-night, Miss Gretton. Coshed, if you happen to know the word. Then put in the water. Can you suggest how he got there?"

She shook her head from side to side, staring blankly. "Doddy!" she gasped.

"Any idea where Ericson has been to-night, Miss Gretton?"

"He—he—Ericson? He was in his hotel shortly before dinner. I rang him there. But Roger wouldn't do Doddy in! No, I'm sure of that! He didn't kill Doddy!"

"I'm not accusing Ericson of killing him," Knollis pointed out tartly. "There are too many tender con-sciences in this case. I merely want to know where *everybody* was at the time of Dodson's death. It makes my job so much easier, and God only knows I can do with a break. Lawrence Lomas, for instance; where was he? And yourself? I'm sure you can both satisfy me, but it will save extensive inquiries if you do. I can then give my full attention to the people who have no alibis."

Nora Gretton looked round the room, as if for an excuse.

"I—I, well, I've been here all the evening. And Lawrence has been with me. He came early, and stayed until ten o'clock. Yes, yes, he did, Inspector!"

"Dodson died about eleven o'clock," said Knollis. Nora Gretton had nothing to say to that. She clasped her hands and gazed into the flames.

"You are sure that Lomas's body was gone when you and Lawrence returned with the car?"

"I'm very sure, Inspector. I may have got a few facts in this affair muddled, but not that one. I can trust the evidence of my own eyes."

"You're lucky," grunted Knollis. "I can trust neither my own eyes nor my own ears—especially the latter. Now, you did not go with Lawrence when he went to examine his father?"

"No, he told me to stay put."

"So that the hawthorn hush was between yourself and Lawrence and his father?"

"Why yes; I've explained the position earlier."

"You were watching Lawrence?"

"No. The two barges were entering the lock and I was watching them."

She suddenly swung round with fear in her eyes. "What do you mean, Inspector? What do you insinuate?"

Knollis smashed her concern in a second by shrugging his shoulders carelessly and saying: "If you had been watching you would have known whether anyone else was watching Lawrence. We know that someone was in the willow beds, and we thought it was Ericson, but he asserts that he was searching Lomas's shop for packets of dope."

"So that is what he has told you," she said slowly. Then she buried her face in her hands, ejaculating: "Oh, how I wish the whole sorry business was over and done with."

"It is, nearly," said Knollis.

"You—you know!" she gasped.

Bates, from the corner of the room, emitted a shrill whistle, then smiled, and settled down to his notebook again.

The Inspector inclined his head.

"Yes, I know. What is more, this is no story-book case, and there will be no surprise ending. The most obvious person killed him, for the commonest and most obvious reason. That person went about it in the simplest possible way, and, paradoxically, it is the factor of simplicity that has proved the complication in the case."

He walked to the door, bidding Bates pack his note-book.

"You will stay in Desborough, Miss Gretton, and not leave the town without my permission. You will be well advised to forget my visit to-night and say nothing of it to a soul. That is all. Good night."

Bates was silent as they drove back to Burnham, silent until they had broached the suburbs of the town.

"So you've got the fellow," he sighed with deep satisfaction, and Knollis knew that the remark constituted an unasked question.

"Yes, we've got him, Bates. It only remains for us to prove the case against him."

"How?" asked Bates laconically.

"That is something I have to decide before morning. I'm dropping out at my house. Take a message to the station and then go off duty until ten in the morning. I'll meet you at my office."

"It's like that, eh, Inspector? And the message?"

"It's for River Station. They have marked the spot where Lomas slid down the bank into the water. Ask 'em to start dragging operations at dawn—with a small-tooth comb. No matter what they fetch up it is to be sent to me. I've been dense, Bates, remarkably dense. Now on our list of suspects we have Lawrence, Gertrude—yes, Gertrude, Ericson, Nora Gretton, Dodson, Steadfall, and one other who almost slipped out of the picture."

"Almost slipped out? Who on earth do you mean?" Bates asked in surprise.

"Lester! The man who helped to drag Lomas out of the river. It's quite likely that he put him in first."

Although Knollis went to bed when he got home he rose at an exceptionally early hour and made his way to The Ferryman. Here the men from River Station were waiting for him with a choice assortment of articles they had dragged from the river. Knollis ignored the boots, old cans, broken buckets, and suchlike, but purred with pleasure when they presented him with a hypodermic syringe. It was almost new, unmarked, and brought a rare smile to the Inspector's lips. "Whitelaw *will* be upset!" he murmured.

He put it in his pocket and went to interview the landlady. She showed a degree of antagonism when he asked for Lester.

"You don't go mixing him with no deaths," she said with ripe indignation. "He's a gentleman."

"I wouldn't dream of mixing him with deaths," smiled Knollis, "but you see he was on the river that night, and I think he can help me."

"Then he will help you, Inspector!"

"How long was he away from the inn during the week?" Knollis asked in a casual tone.

The landlady expressed her surprise. "He hasn't left. Why should he? He's been here all the time. On a fishing holiday, he is, and a good enough holiday he was having until this business started."

"And where is he now?"

"In his bedroom, of course. He hasn't come down for breakfast yet."

"Lucky man!" exclaimed Knollis. "I wish I could stay in bed until this time of the day." Then he glanced shrewdly at her. "Which room?"

"He's in Seven, but I hope you aren't bothering him now!"

"You are right every time," chuckled Knollis. "Now, are you going to forbid me to go upstairs, or do I go without your permission? I'd hate to use force."

"Then you'd better go, but don't put him off his breakfast with grisly details. He's my best guest." Knollis went upstairs and tapped lightly on the bedroom door. A cultured voice bade him enter. The Inspector took him at his word, although he knew that Lester would be expecting a member of the staff.

He was, and he gave vent to an exclamation of mingled surprise and annoyance as he saw Knollis. He assumed a truculent manner.

"I know you're Inspector Knollis, but what the deuce is the meaning of this intrusion?"

"Sorry to disturb you at this unearthly hour of the day," Knollis lied. "I should have waited until you landed downstairs. Perhaps I'd better do that?"

He made as if to withdraw, but Lester suddenly grinned and threw a tie round his collar. "You'd perhaps better stay here. I was taken aback when I saw you. I'm not accustomed to entertaining detectives in my bedroom. I know that nothing is wrong, because my conscience is clean."

Knollis closed the door and seated himself in a wicker chair, resting his hat on his knees.

"No, I wouldn't say that there was anything wrong as far as your own person is concerned, but it struck me that you may be able to help me with this Lomas business. It's the very devil of a case, and I'm hanged if I can find the evidence I so badly need."

"Sorry to hear that," Lester said unconvincingly. "How can I help? I don't see the point."

"Well, for a beginning, where were you round about ten o'clock on Monday night? Can you remember?"

"Ten? In the saloon bar, I believe. Monday? Yes, I can give you that as a positive fact."

"And how long had you been there?"

"About ten minutes I should say. I'd taken a walk downstream and developed a thirst. You know how it is?"

There was an airiness about Lester's manner that raised Knollis's suspicions. He tried to conceal them.

"Yes, I know how it is," he answered. "You are sure you didn't go up-stream—towards Burnham?"

"Positive. I distinctly remember that I was walking forwards, following my nose."

Knollis ignored the mockery. His time was coming, and he knew it.

"Then how long were you in the bar?"

"Oh, until about five past ten. I went outside then."

"You saw the barges go through the lock?"

"Of course I did, my dear Inspector. I was interested. Not because I hadn't watched them on previous occasions, but I like to listen to Burgess. He doesn't swear, but he does run a pretty line in invective. He puts so much into his comments that a dam' good swear would be more appropriate to his temper. He means the same thing. A humorous old bird, what?"

"Quite, quite," said Knollis. He was prepared to be patient. "Did you see Lomas before his death—or before he was dragged from the water?"

"See him? I cannoned into him in the passage. He was leaving as I entered. Tight as an owl."

"Lomas? Tight as an owl?"

"Lomas," said Lester with an impish grin. "Tight as the aforesaid owl. As a matter of fact he was carrying a glass in his hand, apparently half-full of whisky, and it was neat whisky if I know anything about spirits. I was in a hurry, because I hadn't made a start then and I felt envious of him. I apologised for bumping him, but I don't think he knew that anything untoward had happened. He blinked blearily—like that owl—and staggered on. I remember that I followed him to the door. He sank the whisky and let the glass fall in the herbaceous border. I carried it back to the bar with me later. For a moment I was wondering whether to follow him in case he slipped in the river, but I noticed a courting couple some yards away who would have one eye on him, and so I turned back and went into the saloon bar."

"Were the couple there when you went out at five past ten? Or had they gone?"

"They were walking slowly toward the inn."

"And Lomas? Was he in sight?"

"I did not notice him, Inspector."

"How long have you been at The Ferryman?"

"Well, I'm damned if I know what that has to do with you, but I've been here about a fortnight. I'm on holiday."

"Your home is . . . ?"

"Cambridge."

The Inspector's eyes narrowed.

"Cambridge? Then you may know Roger Ericson?"

Lester smiled. "Ericson was here for a time. I knew him at home as a casual acquaintance. We've met in our favourite local.

He recommended this place. Said that the beer, food, and fishing were good, so I decided to try 'em!"

"What do you know about Ericson?" The Inspector leaned forward, displaying great interest.

Lester passed a hand over his newly-shaven chin.

"Well, not a great deal actually. I believe he used to be a chemist in Norwich some years ago. Lately he has been on the road for a firm of chemical manufacturers. He had a spot of trouble some time ago. A girl in whom he was interested was drowned while bathing off the Norfolk coast. Knocked him back a bit, or so I understand."

"Anything else?"

"Not a thing, Inspector."

"Do you think you would recognise the courting couple if you saw them again? Did you know them?"

"No, I did not," said Lester. He paused, smiled in a superior way and added: "You people expect your witnesses to have fore-knowledge of a crime, and to have had eyes for nothing but the environment and the *dramatis personae*."

"If people were more observant and less self-absorbed it would be impossible for a crime to be permitted," Knollis retorted, throwing his restraint to the winds. "Criminals have a good ally in the thick-headedness of the average citizen."

"And another in the thick-headedness of the average constable," Lester added maliciously. "I'm not including the detective forces, simply because I don't know enough about 'em, but I will say that the average bobby is better at chasing small boys from the streets and grabbing hawkers for crying their wares than at catching real criminals."

"That is your opinion," Knollis said bluntly.

"That is what I said. That is my opinion, and I am entitled to it. The reports of the petty sessional courts are all the evidence that a clear-minded man needs to bring him to the same conclusion—plus, of course, the omnipresent lists of unsolved breakings and enterings, unsolved murders, and the mysterious drug traffic over which the League of Nations has sat for years. But as far as the bobby is concerned, well, petty is the operative word. Petty sessional courts, petty crime, and petty mind."

Knollis gritted his teeth as Lester laughed at him, and applied a rein to his rising temper. "You do know something about the dope racket then?" he murmured.

"I read the newspapers," Lester answered. "And Dame Rumour would have it that Mr. Lomas was not unacquainted with that dirty business."

"You seem to be interested in criminal matters," Knollis then said. "It would be entirely illogical for me to assume that you have connections?"

"It would, Inspector."

"Nevertheless," said Knollis, "we do seem to be getting away from the point. I wonder if you would care to enlighten a mere puzzled member of the detective force on just one point, Mr. Lester?"

"Fire away with the question," mocked Lester. "The answer may come within the range of my knowledge."

"Why didn't you come forward with your information about Lomas? You were probably the last innocent person to see him alive."

"So I am regarded as innocent, Inspector? I breathe again! As for your question, well, it is rather an awkward one, isn't it?"

"That, again, is your own opinion," remarked Knollis. "What is your occupation? May I ask that?"

"You may. I work for the Forsyth Insurance Company."

Knollis reached for his notebook. "I must check that. The Forsyth Insurance Company? I seem to remember that they operate mainly in East Anglia. Er—in what capacity are you employed? You wouldn't be another investigator by any chance? I like to have plenty of private detectives scattered round me. It makes for simplicity!"

Lester regarded the Inspector thoughtfully. He strode across the room and came to rest again before Knollis's chair. "You've been pulling my leg, Inspector. You know damned well what I am! We've been wasting time. Shall we pool our resources?"

"I wouldn't say that," Knollis muttered suavely, "but I do think you'd better come clean. You know too much, and you have said too little. Now then. Mr. Lester; what's the game? Or do we talk at headquarters?"

Lester's mocking airiness fell away from him as he answered: "I am investigating the death of Marjory Ericson."

Knollis forced himself to restrain an exclamation of surprise. "And the angle?"

Lester seated himself and handed his cigarette case across. When both cigarettes were lighted he stared reflectively through the smoke.

"We believe that she was murdered by her brother. She had lately come into a small fortune, a matter of five thousand pounds—which would be a fortune to her. She insured herself heavily, an endowment and death policy that would bring in three thousand in hard cash if she died within fifteen years of taking out the policy, and a goodly sum to herself if she survived the period. She left no other bequests, and the whole lot goes to her brother as next of kin. He was so eager to draw from us that we grew suspicious. I was sent down to look into the matter. I can't prove my suspicions as yet, but I think I know what happened. You want it?"

"Go on. I'm listening."

"Roger took her to Overstrand in his car—for reasons to be explained later. He stayed with her for an hour and then drove away. Half an hour later Marjory went out to bathe. She was then in exceptionally high spirits. Please note that!"

"I've noted it," said the Inspector.

"An hour later she was found drowned. Now it is a lonely part of the coast, as you may know. It was the end of the season, and there was only one other guest at the hotel, an old lady who spent her time on the terrace, knitting. She says that she saw a man bathing from a car about half a mile north of the hotel. Her sight is not reliable and we can't use her evidence. She saw the car move away twenty minutes after Marjory entered the water. All supposition you see."

"Ericson looped round, drowned his sister, and then beat it home to manufacture an alibi?"

"That is the theory, Inspector."

"Two cases in one, eh? I suspected that all along. We have Lawrence after his father's money, and Ericson after Lomas. Lawrence's connection with the dope almost looks like coincidence, and yet it was only because . . ."

"Yes, Inspector?" Lester prompted him.

Knollis smiled. "Never mind that just now. I'm getting this thing clearer and clearer. Lawrence and Gretton and—no, just the two of them were watching Lomas. Ericson in the willow beds watching them. Dodson closing in from the cottage. Lomas hadn't a chance on earth. Only one point remains to puzzle me; why the sudden decision to bump off Lomas Senior?"

"That puzzles me, too," Lester confessed. "Was it planned in detail, or was a sudden advantage taken of circumstances? If I could answer that I could answer a lot more questions that trouble me."

"One thing is certain," said Knollis. "If it wasn't done then, at that very moment, it would have been left over for another night. There were customers in this inn, and it was almost closing time. Lomas had to be finished off and dumped in the water before they turned out. There's another point, too. Why was Lomas at The Ferryman? When he left the Bridge Hotel he excused himself because he had another appointment. With whom?"

"With Ericson, probably," suggested Lester.

"But he was with Ericson!"

"Lawrence, then; to explain how the business with Ericson had gone. We know that the old man was thinking of selling out to him."

Knollis mused on the point. "Lawrence, you say? Then why didn't he go back to the Commerce Club or the Angel? Why tramp all this way? And if they wanted to meet here, surely Lawrence Lomas could have picked him up and brought him round for a drink and a chat?"

"Thought about John Steadfall?"

"Until I'm sick of his name," said Knollis. "He was nearly as old as Lomas, and I can't see him tramping all this way when he would have been more comfortable in the smoke-room at the club. No, I don't think it can have been Steadfall!"

"Then there must be someone who is still outside the case, or else some fact that has not yet come to light."

"He didn't come out to see you?" Knollis asked with a return of his suspicious manner.

Lester went to his suitcase and returned with a sheaf of documents. "My credentials, Inspector. You are a most suspicious man!"

"I've been told so," remarked Knollis. He looked through the papers and handed them back. "All right. I have to be careful. Well, thanks a lot for your help. I'll probably see you later in the day. Call in if you go to town."

Lester assured him that he would do so, and Knollis left. He stood before the inn for some minutes, thinking over all that Lester had told him. Then he looked up and gave vent to an oath. Lester had told him that he followed Lomas to the doorway and watched him take the towpath, and also that he saw a courting couple on the bank. But from this doorway it was impossible to see the spot. It was hidden by a row of heavy-foliaged willows.

The Inspector considered this surprising fact for a time and then strolled carelessly downstream. He kept to the path until he came to a narrow road leading to the left. He followed it for three hundred yards and at last reached a second-class road that ran almost parallel with the river. Here again he turned left and walked back in the direction of the inn. As he drew level with it the road swung sharply to the left, revealing a track through the willow beds.

The Inspector accepted the invitation and trod the squelchy path until he reached a point from where he had a clear view of the river, the towpath, and the intervening banks. A smile came to his lips. He gave a sigh of intense satisfaction and lit his pipe. Then he retraced his steps.

On his return to Burnham he sought out Sir Wilfred Burrows and told him all that he had learned. The Chief Constable beamed on him.

"The picture is complete, Knollis?"

"Complete, Sir Wilfred. I think Ericson told the truth when he said he was searching the Desborough Road premises at the time of Lomas's death. Working from left to right of my picture we have Dodson approaching Lomas from Rose Cottage; Lomas lying on the bank a long way from dead but very drunk—"

"Not dead, Knollis?" Sir Wilfred interrupted.

"Not dead—yet. Next we have Gretton and Lawrence apparently cuddling each other—"

"Why apparently?"

"That will make itself evident, sir," Knollis replied evasively. "Then, in the background, we have Lester, now revealed as a private investigator. In the foreground we have Barky Burgess and his son and two barges. That is the complete picture. I know which of them killed Lomas, but . . ."

"Well," demanded the Chief Constable; "what is it?"

"I know which of them killed him, and I know three ways in which it could have been done, but I'm darned if I know which way was used. The onus of proof lies with us, as the prosecution, of course. Proving it will be the very devil."

"You can do it, Knollis?" pleaded Sir Wilfred. "Surely you can do it? We mustn't slip up now. We can't afford to slip up now. The Watch Committee wanted to fetch the Yard in days ago and I said we could manage without them. You can do it!"

CHAPTER XII
THE CROSS-EXAMINATION OF TWO WITNESSES

At three o'clock that day the Inspector sent for Dawes, Slater, Bates and Forster. He invited them to be seated and then tapped a pile of documents on which he had been working for the past two hours.

"We're on the last lap. I've been looking up the subject of dope peddling and I see that at one time there was quite a boom in East Anglia. Strangely enough, it faded away about the same time that Ericson gave up business. Surprising, isn't it?" he murmured with a grin.

"Forster, you and Bates will go to Norwich and make inquiries there. I won't insult your intelligence by explaining further. On the way home, hop off at Cambridge. You'll probably find a search warrant waiting at police headquarters; you'll assist in the search of Ericson's home. And when I say search, I mean search, even if it means taking the roof to pieces or digging up the kitchen floor. Got it?"

Both men nodded, and Knollis dismissed them.

"Slater, I want you to trot round to all the chemists in the immediate district who stock Medal preparations and obtain samples of snow from them. Unless I'm very much mistaken we shall have enough bicarbonate of soda to keep the wind down for a twelvemonth. Off you go!"

"What's for me?" asked Dawes.

"You'll join me in a re-examination of all the people concerned in the case, starting with Gretton. Fill your pen to the top and get a new notebook."

Nora Gretton's attitude was undefinable as she once more invited them into the bungalow. She seated herself on a low stool, pulled her skirt well over her knees, and locked her fingers over them.

"You know why we've called, of course?" Knollis began in a conversational tone.

"I don't, Inspector. You are a man of surprises."

"It's just a formal visit."

"They always are," she countered.

"We want to run over the facts with which you have supplied us—to check them. Then perhaps you will oblige by signing the resulting statement as correct."

"I'm listening," she said flatly.

"We are referring to the day of Ezekiah Lomas's death," Knollis began. "You told me that you were in your bath at five-thirty that afternoon."

"That is correct."

"And that Lawrence Lomas arrived at six-thirty."

"That also is correct."

"That he drove you into the country and returned at ten-thirty?"

She nodded. "Yes."

"Now at first you asserted that you drove to White Horse Ferry Hotel, and later agreed that you were in the neighbourhood of Willow Lock. You still agree on the latter statement?"

"Yes; I have no choice, Inspector."

"And you were nowhere near White Horse Ferry?"

"Well," she said hesitantly, "we went out that way, and turned for Willow Lock."

"You also told me that you were at home at four-fifteen that same afternoon, Miss Gretton!"

"And so I was!" she retorted defiantly.

"Yet," Knoll is went on, "Empton says that you took Lawrence Lomas's car out, and members of the mobile patrol are prepared to swear that you and a man dressed in heather tweeds passed them at four-fifteen, driving Lawrence Lomas's car in the direction of Burnham."

Nora Gretton studied the question and then grudgingly admitted the truth.

"I drove Ericson back to Burnham. I denied it because I didn't want Lawry to know anything about him. He would have been jealous."

"So Ericson visited you?" Knollis queried.

"Yes; I told you that I was working with him. He came over to tell me that he thought he had got Lomas where he wanted him, and that Lomas was badly soaked in dope."

"That is interesting," commented Knollis. "Now we will move on to the same night, when you and Lawrence were lying on the bank. You have told me that you were between Lomas and The

Ferryman, and that hawthorn bushes were between yourselves and Lomas."

"I won't contradict that, Inspector."

"Can you tell me whether the doorway of The Ferryman is visible from the spot where you were lying?"

"I know it wasn't," she said quickly. "Why do you ask?"

"You'll learn later," said Knollis with quiet confidence. "There is one other point which is not clear to me. You admit that Lawrence and yourself saw his father stagger from The Ferryman, and that he passed you. Why did Lawrence not intercept him on his way from the inn and take him home in his car instead of waiting until he had collapsed?"

Nora Gretton looked up with troubled eyes. "I—I don't know, Inspector."

"And how long had Lomas been lying on the bank when Lawrence went to his side?"

"Several minutes, Inspector."

Nora Gretton sprang to her feet. "What is the purpose of all these questions? They are—they are intolerable!"

Knollis looked surprised in turn. "I'm trying to prove the guilt of Lomas's killer, of course! What other object should I have?"

"But Lawrence could not have been responsible for his father's death," she replied vehemently.

"I never suggested that he could," said Knollis. "If you care to sit down again and listen to me you may see light in a few minutes. I owe you that."

She obeyed sulkily, and suspiciously.

"You told me that on Lawrence's return you both went back for the car. You are certain that Lawrence did not go alone?"

"I'm positive, Inspector. You asked me that before."

Knollis waved his hands. "There you are then. One more question and you will see where I am driving. Did either of you, at any time while you were on the bank, see a man pass along the track in the willow beds?"

"A man?" she exclaimed. "Why, yes! A man wearing a grey trilby. It was just after Lawrence had examined his father. I told him, but he took no notice, being so much in a hurry to get back for the car."

"And when you returned with the car his father had disappeared? Is that the way of it?"

Nora Gretton's eyes brightened, and she gave a gasp of relief. "So that was it! It was while we were going for the car—"

"A grey two-seater?"

"Yes. Lawry's car."

"And it was nearer to the inn than to old Lomas?"

"Oh yes, a lot!"

"Were there other cars about?"

"I didn't see another, Inspector."

"And the man in the willow beds was not to be seen when you both returned with the car?"

"I can't remember seeing him."

"You think you would have seen him if you had continued in the direction of Burnham?"

"I think so, Inspector. Those bushes cannot be more than five feet high."

"Now for Marjory Ericson," said the Inspector. "You knew her well?"

"Oh yes! We were great friends."

"And her occupation?"

"A secondary-school teacher."

"And you had a secretarial situation?"

"Yes."

"How did you come to know her?"

"We met at dances. Roger was in business then and she was very much alone in the world. I had no friends either, and so we chummed together."

"And how did she come to be introduced to cocaine?"

"It was several months after the stuff had taken hold of her that she first told me of it," Nora Gretton said in a whisper. "She was so miserable that she had to confide in someone. I was studying for an examination in accountancy, and had not been out with her for some weeks. She went to several dances alone, and it was at one of these that she met some person who persuaded her to take a sniff. He told her that it would liven her. She did not know what it was, of course. She repeated the performance again and again and at last reached the stage where she could not manage without it. He gave her an address somewhere in this district from which further supplies could be obtained. I wanted her to expose him, but she would not agree—she daren't! She had confided in me in the hope that I could suggest a cure. If she exposed him she would be cutting off her own supplies—and she was afraid of insanity following that. So you see why she would never tell me the man's name."

"You told this to Ericson after her death?"

"Yes. He was livid. I have never seen a man so angry."

"And how did Marjory die?"

"Well," Nora Gretton said slowly, "I think she swam out to sea and—and just gave up swimming. She was terribly unhappy!"

"You are aware that Roger drove her to Overstrand?"

"Oh yes. I was at the inquest."

"Do you know whether Roger came straight back or not?"

"He did," she said, and then looked at Knollis with a startled expression on her pleasant features. "I think he did, anyway. What do you mean, Inspector?"

"I think I will tell you the truth," said Knollis. "Shortly after Ericson left she went down to the beach to bathe. There was only one other bather, a man. He was bathing from a car. He dressed and drove away twenty minutes after Marjory entered the water. Now don't jump to conclusions, Miss Gretton! But do bear in mind that Ericson *could* have driven northward, come back down the coast, and—well, you see the idea?"

"But he took me to a dance that same evening!" Nora Gretton protested.

"He did, eh?" murmured Knollis. "Was that the first time he had entertained you?"

"Oh yes! He suggested it several days before Marjory went away. He said that I should be lonely, and that he would, too."

"Nice. Very nice," said Knollis.

Dawes grunted, and nodded brightly.

"And Marjory never gave you a single hint about the identity of the man who first introduced her to snow?" Nora Gretton was puzzled. "Snow? Oh, cocaine! Well no, except once when she mentioned him. She said he came from Leicester."

"Not very helpful," Knollis said ruefully.

"Or perhaps it was Leicestershire."

"And as neither Burnham nor Desborough are in Leicestershire that isn't at all helpful."

Then Knollis's eyes glittered, and he looked Nora Gretton straight in the face. "It's years since I went dancing, Miss Gretton, and manners have changed. These dances to which you went with Marjory Ericson; were they starchy, or free and easy?"

"We-ell, more on the free and easy side, Inspector."

"Sponsored by money-making people, or club dances?"

"Oh, the latter, definitely. There was nothing of the palais de danse atmosphere about them. Perhaps that is a wee bit snobbish, but one must have a boundary!"

"Quite, quite!" Knollis said absently. "At these dances, if you met a man for the first time, would you go to the trouble to be introduced before dancing with him?"

"Good gracious, no! The odds are that you might never see him again."

"And you would hardly exchange names and addresses?"

"No," Nora Gretton stared. "You are asking queer questions, Inspector Knollis."

"I'm a queer man," Knollis retorted. "So we can assume that on the first occasion they met they would perhaps call each other by the Christian name? She may have known this man as Jim, from Leicester?"

"It's possible, Inspector, but of course she saw him many times after that."

"That is the point I am considering, Miss Gretton. They would learn the identity of each other when it was too late."

"Too late?" exclaimed Nora Gretton. "For what, pray?"

"Too late for Marjory to be allowed to live."

"I still don't understand you, Inspector!" she protested.

Dawes, by an expressive gesture, intimated that he was in a similar state of mind. Knollis enlightened him to some extent as they drove round to Lawrence Lomas's surgery.

"A most remarkable case of parallelism," he said. "I'm not a lover of long words, as you know, but I can't find a simpler one that means the same thing. We now know that Ericson did not kill his sister."

"Do we?" asked Dawes.

"The whole thing is resolving itself into a straight-forward case."

"I'm pleased to hear it," Dawes returned.

"I thought you would be," Knollis said gravely, and it never occurred to him that Dawes was unable to see into his mind. "This next interview should be just as interesting," he added gratuitously.

Dawes closed his eyes and smiled blandly. "How glad I am! How glad I am! How wonderful!"

Lawrence Lomas wished them a grudging good day as they broke in on him, and continued to sterilise his instruments, his back towards them. "I take it you are asking questions again, Inspector Knollis."

"Something like that," Knollis admitted. "That is my destiny. One of these days I'll go on the stage as a second Datas. Meanwhile we are checking statements. Miss Gretton has just obliged."

Lomas turned then, a scowl on his features. "Bothering her again, eh? Is all this necessary? She's only a girl, and the persistent heckling is getting on her nerves."

"I wouldn't say that from her demeanour this afternoon," said Knollis. "She appeared to be enjoying herself."

"What a girl feels, and what she shows, are two entirely different things," Lomas retorted.

"I wouldn't know that," said Knollis. "I'm not a psychologist. Anyway, she's a material witness. Actually, we haven't bothered her. She was quite willing to help us—and even to supplement her original statement."

Lomas was interested in this revelation. "In what way?"

"Oh, several ways," Knollis answered in an evasive tone. "But we must not detain you longer than is necessary. I realise that you are a busy man."

"Well, yes, I am," said Lomas, mollified by Knollis's remark. "What is it you want to know?"

Knollis made a pretence of examining his notes, although by now he knew every date and time of the case by heart.

"I see that you stated that on the day in question you were busy in your surgery until half-past five. I can take that as correct?"

"You asked that twice before. My mechanic corroborated the statement. There is no doubt about it?"

"Quite so, Mr. Lomas. And you went to Burnham to see your father, returning about half-past six?"

"Yes, that is all right."

Knollis gave a discreet cough.

"I think we can overlook your first statement with regard to your alleged trip to White Horse Ferry?"

Lomas looked away. "I was a fool in trying to mislead you. I must admit that, Inspector."

"I still don't know why you denied it in our first interview," Knollis murmured in an interrogatory manner.

"I—well, I suppose I got windy," said Lomas. "You see, I thought you were trying to connect me with my father's death, and as I had said a few harsh things about him at one time or another, well, you know how it is? All kinds of thoughts fly through your mind in times of stress. I really was an ass."

"That is a courageous admission," said Knollis, simulating an expression of admiration.

Lomas smiled, and straightened his tie.

"There is one other point which I cannot understand," said Knollis, taking full advantage of the flow of the tide. "You saw your father leave The Ferryman, and watched him walk past you to collapse on the bank. Why on earth didn't you go to him as he approached? You must have seen that he was far from normal in his behaviour."

"I've had to ask myself that same question," Lomas replied ruefully. "I find it impossible to analyse my motives with any degree of satisfaction. It's queer, Inspector, but all inhibitions seem to vanish when death knocks at the door so violently. I find now that I have no compunction at all in saying what I thought of my father. You see, I think I was partly ashamed and partly annoyed at seeing him in such a condition. Miss Gretton was with me, you will remember, and it was humiliating to be in the company of the girl I hope to marry and have my father walk in on the scene when he was drunk to the wide—I thought he was drunk, of course. I remember telling myself that it would serve the old reprobate right if he walked into the river and got a cold, sobering douche. It was not until he collapsed and had lain there for some minutes that I realised that he was seriously ill; that his condition was more serious than I had imagined."

"And you went to him? Miss Gretton tells us that." Lawrence Lomas nodded. "Yes, I went to him. I saw at once that he was seriously ill. I told Nora—Miss Gretton—and we hurried back for the car."

"Surely it would have been more humane to leave Miss Gretton with him while you went for the car?" suggested the Inspector softly.

"I—I suppose it would," Lomas stammered, "but you don't think of these things."

"We'll skip that then. He was gone when you returned?"

"Absolutely vanished."

"In a matter of three or four minutes?"

Lawrence Lomas was uneasy. "I suppose so," he said.

"Notice anyone else hanging around?"

"Miss Gretton did see a man on the path in the willow beds, but that was just before I went to my father, or just after I came back, and I'm not sure which. She said he was walking toward Burnham. It didn't seem to be of interest then, of course."

"You made a search for your father?" asked Knollis.

"No. No, I didn't," Lomas admitted. "I concluded that he had somehow pulled himself together and was on his way home. I was glad to be rid of him. That sounds callous, I know, but I'm being frank without trying to excuse my actions. I've upset matters previously by concealing my feelings towards him."

"Your habitual attitude toward your father would influence you unconsciously," said Knollis. "We must take that into account."

Lomas jumped at the face-saving explanation and seemed to regard the Inspector with more favour. "I only wish I was able to help you more," he said with a sad shake of his head.

"You can, Mr. Lomas!"

"Oh? How, Inspector?"

"Tell me how long ago it was when you realised that your father was suffering from cocaine poisoning! You did realise it, you know!"

Lomas refused to meet the Inspector's eyes. He shuffled uncomfortably and broke a cigarette between his fingers. Then he forced himself to look up.

"I thought it was self-administered," he muttered, "until the interview with you after his death—when you told the truth to Gertrude. Even now I have only your word for it that he was poisoned. I knew, but I kept it a secret. It was just over three months ago. I called at the shop. He was in the living-room, and I went through to him. His manner was peculiar. He was extremely excited. Twenty minutes later he was a changed man, depressed and irritable. He even broke into tears. I advised him to see a doctor, but he said he would have no doctors messing about with him. They had not been able to save my mother, and so on, and so on.

"I went across to see Old John, and I asked him what was wrong with the old man. He replied that he wasn't a doctor and couldn't pretend to diagnose, but he suspected acute indigestion as the root cause of the trouble. It was affecting his nervous system. He also said, in reply to a question, that while my father was not stuffing himself with patent medicines he was taking too much bicarbonate of soda. Of course," Lomas added apologetically, "he was using it in another way, as we know."

"Those teeth were giving him trouble, too?" Knollis murmured helpfully.

"They were in a shocking state. He'd rotted them with persistent sweet-chewing."

"And you suggested dental treatment!"

"It seemed wise. The lack of pain would help to reduce the physiological need for the stuff."

"That was very considerate of you, Mr. Lomas!"

Lawrence Lomas flushed. "Oh well, blood's thicker than water when all's said and done."

"He agreed to your suggestion? Readily?"

"With regard to his teeth? Yes. He obviously thought it a good idea, but he always liked to believe that good ideas were his own invention. I had to broach the subject very carefully."

"Just as you did when suggesting that he should leave the whole of his estate to your sister, eh?"

"Eh?"

Lomas looked up, startled.

"Oh, I see what you mean. The usual method to be used with my father was to plant the seed and wait until it matured in his own mind. Once he became convinced that it was his own conception there was neither rest nor peace until it was put into execution. My mother taught me that wrinkle. She had learned to understand him—she had to do so, or her life would have been an even worse hell than it was."

"And he rose to the bait?" suggested Knollis.

"The bait?" Lomas asked in a curious voice.

"I beg your pardon! That was clumsily put. I mean that he accepted the notion about dental treatment?"

"He came down a week or so later. I almost regretted my move then. He was a baby where pain was concerned. You see, he had hardly ever known what illness was. He never had anything worse than a cold in his life."

"And appendicitis," Knollis reminded him.

"I'd forgotten that. I was away from home at the time, thank the Lord! He must have been the worst patient in the world."

"So that, taking all in all," said Knollis, "your mind was prepared to be disgusted when he rolled out of The Ferryman on Monday night?"

Lawrence Lomas nodded slowly. "Yes, Inspector. That was the last straw. He humiliated me before the one person in the world who means anything to me, and so I ignored his presence and refused to acknowledge, even to myself, that he was my father."

"Why did you choose to spend your evening by the river?"

Lomas laughed. "I am courting her, Inspector, and one naturally takes a girl to the loveliest spot possible for one's wooing. I hope I'm not too old to possess a few romantic ideas. It was a grand evening, the scenery was all that could be desired, Nora looked lovely, and well—you probably know how I felt!"

"I'm a little forgetful," said Knollis. "It is twelve years since I did my courting. But you didn't arrive at the spot until fairly late in the evening, did you?—"

"We drove round for a time, stopping at various beauty spots on the river, and then dropped in at The Ferryman for a drink."

Knollis glanced at his notes.

"There must be some mistake. The landlady is prepared to swear that neither yourself nor Miss Gretton entered the inn on Monday evening. Can you account for that?"

Lomas shifted his weight. "As a matter of fact, drinks were brought to the car, so actually we never did go in the inn. Just a matter of words, you see, Inspector."

"How long were you with your father when you examined him on the bank?"

"No more than a minute. No more than a quick glance was necessary to see that he was in a critical condition."

Knollis prepared to leave.

Lomas licked his lips.

"Inspector! You don't think that Ericson had anything to do with my father's death, do you?"

"I don't know. Why?" asked Knollis shortly.

"Well, he had access to my father's books, and—I can't express myself adequately, but I have a feeling about him!"

"Intuition can be most reliable," said Knollis. "I will convey your suggestion to Sir Wilfred Burrows."

CHAPTER XIII
THE THEORIES OF
INSPECTOR KNOLLIS

THE INSPECTOR faithfully kept his promise to Lawrence Lomas, and mentioned his 'intuitions' to Sir Wilfred Burrows, but not quite in the way that Lomas expected. He and Dawes went straight to the Chief Constable's office when they left Desborough—after a second call on Jenkins, the tailor—and there Knollis put forward his views on the case.

"I've developed a theory that fits all the known facts," he explained. "Unfortunately, I need further facts before I can prove it conclusively. I think, however, that this state of affairs will soon be remedied."

"You sound hopeful," said Sir Wilfred. "Suppose you unfold your theories, and then we can judge."

"It starts with Dodson and his death. Dodson could have been murdered for but one reason. He knew too much. Find the murderer of Dodson and we have the killer of Ezekiah Lomas. You agree there?"

"I suppose that does follow," the Chief Constable mused. "You are suggesting that Dodson saw the death of Lomas and recognised the culprit?"

"Dodson *must* have seen it. That is why he skipped. Then he came back, and he died. That is Point One in the indictment. Next we have a matter of gents' natty suitings. Two men in one case with the same style of dress may rightfully be regarded as coincidence, but three men in the same case with identical suitings, gloves, and hats surely suggest something more. I don't believe in coincidence—"

"You always were a suspicious man," Sir Wilfred remarked.

"That's as it may be," retorted Knollis. "I still don't believe in coincidence. Coincidence in books is disbelieved mainly because the writer has failed to draw attention to the fact that there is a link somewhere that makes the apparent coincidence a matter of logical inevitability. Two identical happenings in real life are called coincidence for the same reason, because the link is not readily discernible. Providence is said to work in a wonderful way, its wonders to perform, and because a certain thing happens at A just when the same thing happens at B it does not follow that they are disconnected events. They appear to be so because the link is not seen by the observers. I firmly believe that. I'm building my theory on the principle, and I must stand or fall by it." Sir Wilfred scratched his head. "It sounds like abstruse philosophy to me, and I never could grasp abstract ideas. I like something solid to go at, whether it's an idea or a meal. Still, go ahead. I'll listen."

"We'll suppose then," continued the Inspector, "that Dodson saw a person we will call A administer the coup de grace to Lomas, and that he thought he was B. Now further suppose that B happens to be his employer, or friend, or a combination of both . . ."

Dawes interrupted with an objection.

"Can we have names?" he pleaded. "It's years and years since I did algebra."

Knollis smiled. "Have it your own way, Dawes. I'll start again. Lawrence and Ericson wearing heather tweeds may be a coincidence, but Lawrence, Ericson and Lester wearing heather tweeds suggest something more sinister. The wearing of tweeds by all three suggests intention on the part of one, and maybe two, of the trio.

"Dodson was in tow with Ericson, acting as liaison officer between Ericson and Gretton. On the night in question he is walking in the direction of The Ferryman. And here we pause to ask a question! It was nearly closing time. Even if Dodson hurried he could only have scraped into the inn a few minutes before ten. Being a drinking man—as we can assume from the existence of his other interests—we now wonder whether he was walking in that direction for some purpose more important than the buying of a drink. At all events, the question remaining unanswered, he sees a man in a heather suit administering the death blow to Lomas in some subtle manner—"

"Suggesting that Lawrence Lomas killed his own father?"

"For the moment, yes," Knollis replied to Sir Wilfred's question. "We are seeing the events through Dodson's eyes at present. The man then disappears behind a tall hawthorn bush and reappears at the other side with Gretton, who is also a member of the same gang as Dodson. They walk toward the car, hurriedly. They were fetching help for a dying man, although Dodson did not know that. He hurries to Lomas's side and sees that he is either dead or dying. He realises that these two were the only people, other than himself, who were on the towpath at the time. He believes then that they are making good their escape. What is more, he realises that it is nearly ten o'clock, and that Lomas will be found when the customers leave the inn. He further realises that it is in his own interests to dispose of the body, and so out comes the razor and Lomas goes in the river, to be carried away by the current.

"Dodson then hears the car bumping along the tow- path and hides in the willow beds, only to be surprised when he sees that it is Lomas, and not Ericson, who is with Nora Gretton. We don't know what went on in his twisted mind, any more than we know what quirk of character made him carry a cut-throat razor in his pocket—although razors are used as an offensive weapon by men of his type—but we can assume that he panicked and made a dash for it. He was a primitive type and responded to the primitive urge to escape. Later, several days later, he returned to the cottage, because all his worldly goods and chattels were there. Here again, being a primitive type, he responded to a primitive urge, the urge to return. Some person who understood his mentality thoroughly realised that he would, return, and was waiting for him, and Dodson died and went in the river."

"Yes, I quite understand your reasoning so far," commented the Chief Constable.

"That is Point Two," continued Knollis. "Point Three concerns that unhappy girl, Marjory Ericson. We have learned from Nora Gretton that she met a man at a dance, a man who taught her to sniff cocaine. There is but one clue to his identity, a single clue given to Gretton by Marjory herself. Gretton understood her to say that he came from Leicester. As the centre of the game seems to be in Burnham or Desborough, and as neither of them are in Leicestershire, then I refuse to accept the obvious interpretation of the clue."

Knollis slowly filled his pipe and stared vaguely at the table before advancing his theory a stage further.

"You see," he said eventually, "we are again faced with what appears to be a peculiar coincidence. On the one hand we have Marjory Ericson knowing a dope-peddler who comes from Leicester, and Roger Ericson looking for the man who supplied his sister with cocaine, and on the other we have a man named Lester who is supposed to be trying to prove that Roger Ericson drowned his own sister. Well, Sir Wilfred, I just don't believe it!"

"I see! I see!" Sir Wilfred murmured unconvincingly, while Dawes gave an appreciative grunt.

"One remark in parenthesis," said Knollis, as he lit his pipe and spoke between puffs. "I've sent Forster and Bates to Norwich to make inquiries about a dope boom that died about the time that Ericson sold his business. Now then, we've looked at the events on the towpath through Dodson's eyes, so let us look at the events at Overstrand through the eyes of Marjory Ericson. Unless you can step inside the skin of the people concerned you can't understand how they thought and felt.

"We start from the moment she entered the sea. Roger had left her, and driven in a homeward direction. She swims out, and, we will assume, relaxes mind and body as the water caresses her. Now imagine what she would think and feel if she suddenly saw her brother walking down the beach in a bathing costume! Can't you imagine her swimming back, walking up the beach to meet him? Can't you imagine her surprised voice saying 'Why, Roger!' or words to that effect! I can. If it was Roger, and if he had returned with the intention of murdering her it would have been necessary for him to lure her back into the sea—and he would have found it necessary to concoct a hell of a story to account for his return and for the remarkable presence of the bathing costume. He couldn't explain it away by saying that he found it in the car, or that he had brought it down in order to bathe with her, had changed his mind, and had changed it again. The whole thing would have sounded suspicious from the start, and raising of suspicion was the last thing the murderer desired. One trace of suspicion in Marjory's overwrought mind, and she would have run screaming to the hotel. What is more, he daren't have murdered her on the beach because of that old lady on the terrace. *He* didn't know that her sight was unreliable! What is more; where is the motive? Ericson is a rich man, and Marjory's five thousand wouldn't mean a ha'penny to him. We have only Lester's evidence that Ericson wanted her money in a hurry, and we can't accept that. No, Roger Ericson was not guilty of his sister's death—not directly, that is!"

"Not directly?" asked the Chief Constable. "Then you do think that he was indirectly responsible?"

"Of course he was, inasmuch as *he supplied the dope that was directly the cause of her death!*"

"I understand that you are suggesting that Lester was responsible, but why, Knollis? I can't see a motive."

"No, I'm stuck there, too," interposed Dawes. "We don't even know that Lester was in Overstrand or the immediate district on the day of her death. Mind you, I grant that he'll have a dud alibi if he was, but even then—"

"That will be the next job for Forster and Bates when they return from Norwich and Cambridge," said Knollis. "I think they will prove that Ericson was running dope years ago. Indeed, he may have kept up the game after retiring from legitimate business. He is a young man, and I can't see him accepting a life of inactivity after years of intense activity of an adventurous nature—which dope-running would be to him. Roger was peddling dope! So was this X who came from Leicester, or this Lester who came from Cambridge—have that which way you like. Lester and Ericson may have known each other, in fact Lester told me that they were casual acquaintances, but it does not follow that either was aware that the other was engaged in the snow traffic. Indeed, knowing the secrecy that enfolds it, we can assume that the possibility was highly unlikely."

"That is very obvious," said Dawes. "It's like a secret society, nobody knowing anybody else except by a number."

"Good," said Knollis. "I'm glad you agree. Now then, Lester interests a pretty girl in cocaine and feeds her until she cannot manage without it, and you know that to be the normal procedure. He had produced another customer, and may be feeling pleased with himself. And then, by some queer stroke of fate—only unexplainable because we can't see into the workshop of Providence—he learns that Ericson is the Big Boss of the game. He has introduced his boss's sister to cocaine! And Fate has punished Ericson in a strangely ironic way! You can accept that as logical? Good enough!

"Lester has to sit down and do the major thinking act of his career. If either of two things happens he will be in a predicament. If both happen he is for it! He must not let Ericson realise that he is one of the gang, and he must not let Ericson learn that it was he who served Marjory with the stuff. Both are possible. Both are probable. Lester has to think about his own skin, and cover himself in every possible way. He has to seal Marjory's mouth, and so she takes a step towards the grave!"

He paused to probe his pipe, but Sir Wilfred urged him on impatiently. "Go on, Knollis! Go on, man!"

"Well, still looking at it from Lester's point of view, I think he learns that Marjory is taking a holiday by the sea, at a quiet spot on the Norfolk coast. Perhaps he encouraged the idea. He is standing by to the north of Overstrand, waiting, and prepared to wait a long time. He was not so near to the hotel that he was likely to be recognised, but near enough for his figure to be recognised as that of a man. The obvious connection then springs into the mind of anyone who saw him and the girl together. Roger had a car. Roger took his sister to the sea. Roger is the sole beneficiary. Who else can the man be but Roger? Was she likely to bathe with a stranger within an hour and a half of reaching Overstrand? She, a girl obviously suffering from some deep trouble? No, she was bathing with her brother. She died, and so her brother ran away.

"Lester hatched a pretty plot. As the representative of the Forsyth Insurance Company he sold her a huge policy. He was wise enough not to mention Roger's name, but he did suggest that the legatee be her next of kin. Now do you see where my theory leads?"

"It's likely, Knollis! It's likely!"

"It's a cinch," said Dawes with more certainty and enthusiasm. "The case is in the bag. The Forsyth people will be able to verify so much of the story. Investigating on their behalf! Do you think he suggested the possibility of foul play, Inspector?"

"Of course he did. Now you will begin to see where my remark about parallelism comes in. Roger Ericson is peddling dope. By a queer twist of fate, or a deliberate act of Providence, his sister becomes his victim. He suddenly decides to mop up the whole business. He learns that a certain Ezekiah Lomas is the main distributor and so he decides to buy the business so that he can trace the people who have been working under him. He undertakes the role of investigator, hoping to wipe out the game and at the same time eradicate all traces of his own previous activity. Afterwards he will pay attention to the one who initiated Marjory. That is one half of the parallel.

"Lester murders Marjory for reasons which we have seen, and then undertakes the role of investigator hoping to incriminate Roger Ericson, his unwitting enemy, and eradicate all traces of his own acts."

"It almost looks like another coincidence," said Sir Wilfred in a doubtful voice.

"Of course it does," Knollis replied triumphantly. "That is the whole point! It looks like one, but the link is Lester's mentality. He is an imitative type. He copied Ericson's method because he is of limited intelligence, although possessed of a certain low cunning. It is possible that he murdered Lomas, hoping to incriminate Ericson. If Ericson was charged with Lomas's murder, then the Forsyth people would have come forward with their doubts regarding the death of his sister. And Ericson wouldn't have a leg to stand on. And Lester could have murdered Lomas if Lomas knew of his connection with the traffic."

"Ericson suggested himself as investigator to the Medal people," Dawes muttered to himself.

"And Lester suggested himself as investigator to the Forsyth people," said Knollis.

He turned as the telephone bell rang. The Chief Constable lifted the hand-piece.

"It's for you, Knollis. Slater."

"Hello, Slater. How does it come? Any luck?"

"Luck?" came the reply. "I'm no chemist, but I've tasted enough bicarbonate of soda to keep me free of indigestion for life. The chemists back my unprofessional analyses. There isn't a Medal agent in the district who has more than five grains of snow in the bottom of the bottle. I've still a few to visit, but I thought you'd like a preliminary report."

"Good going, Slater," said Knollis. "Sorry you've such a dull job."

"It's good fun, Inspector," replied Slater, "but one thing is puzzling me."

"Yes?"

"Isn't there too much of this stuff flying about? I mean, it looks as if somebody has planted it with the idea of raising suspicion."

Knollis chuckled. "So you've thought that one up, eh? What do you make of it?"

"Somebody trying to pass the buck."

"That is the right guess, Slater. Listen; when you're through with that job I want you to take train to London and go to the head office of the Forsyth. Find out who suggested the doubts about Marjory Ericson's death, and who suggested Lester as the investigator."

"And the answer will be Lester in both cases?"

"I think so, Slater. The success or failure of the case depends on the answers, so I'll wish you good hunting!"

Knollis passed the news and Slater's comments to his companions. Then he got into communication with his own department. "Find Ericson and invite him in for questioning. Arrest him for peddling dope if he refuses. Now get the Cambridge police and give me a ring when you are on."

"That was the one point that struck me from the time Gretton unloaded all the snow at Lomas's shop," he said as he lowered the instrument. "There was too much of it about, and it was concentrated at one point, the shop. It looked as if somebody wanted to divert attention from some other source, the source that supplied Ezekiah Lomas. They dumped the stuff on his own doorstep, filled his medicine chest with it, mixing it in his sugar, coated his Turkish Delight, and generally blew it about so much that it temporarily blinded us, speaking metaphorically.

"Three people were capable, and also had the opportunity. Lawrence Lomas, Roger Ericson, and Lester. I doubt Lester's opportunity, but there can be no doubt in the other two cases. Ericson was visiting Lomas frequently, and even though the shop-girl could not vouch for frequent visits we have to remember that she left the shop at six each evening. Steadfall could vouch for his non-appearance after seven, *but nobody could prove or disprove whether Ericson was in the habit of calling between six and seven, and the same applies to Lawrence.* Add to this the fact that Steadfall can prove that Lomas had at least one bad bout each week!

"Here's another point, too. Lester told me that he met Lomas staggering from The Ferryman in a drunken state, and that he was carrying a glass in his hand, a glass half-full of what appeared to be neat whisky. Lester could have held the old man up, doped his drink, and then forced it down his throat. Lester was the man in the willow beds, and he, as well as Dodson, saw Lomas die!"

"I hadn't thought of that angle," Sir Wilfred confessed.

"And Lawrence Lomas could have killed his father as he bent over him. The hawthorn bush hid him from Nora Gretton. I still don't think that Ericson was responsible. It would not have suited his purpose. If Lomas died too early, then the business might pass into other hands, and Ericson didn't want that to happen. It was all in his interests to have Lomas alive and capable of selling the business."

He was called to the telephone again, and plunged into a volume of explanation to his counterpart in Cambridge.

"Two of my men are due to call on you shortly, but I'd like you to go ahead and do the job now if you will. Yes, it's Ericson. Search his house for evidence that will prove his connection with the snow traffic. I'm very sure of his guilt. Know anything about a fellow by the name of Lester? L. e. s. t. e. r. Yes. Eh? Very interesting. Thanks a lot! And you'll ring me when the job is through? Good."

Knollis smiled at his companions.

"Lester went along a fortnight ago and told them his suspicions about Marjory's death. That helps considerably, doesn't it?"

As Sir Wilfred passed no comment, he continued: "We have three main lines of inquiry. One follows Ericson back to his sister's death. One follows Lester to the same point. The third follows Lawrence Lomas back to a point three months before his father's death."

"Why three months?" asked the puzzled Dawes.

"Because several things happened three months ago. It was round about that time that Lomas was encouraged to make a new will. It was round about that time that Lomas was encouraged to endure dental treatment. It was round about three months ago that Gretton and Lawrence Lomas came together. But run through the evidence for yourselves!"

"Meaning that Lawrence was planning his father's death even then?" gasped Dawes. Then he stared. "But that lets the other two out completely."

"You must admit, Dawes, that only two events connected with this case happened outside that three-month limit!" said Knollis patiently. "I mean the death of Marjory Ericson, and the marriage of Jennifer and Ezekiah—and those are our two basic factors. If—don't you see that once you have disentangled the main threads the whole case is simple? You can represent it by a circle which is divided into three parts. The first dividing thread represents Lawrence, the second Ericson, and the third Lester. Lomas was the centre, the focal point, and all three were only joined by a thin trail of cocaine, represented by the circumference. Lomas would have died even if he had not traded in cocaine, but Ericson and Lester would not have come into the case at all—"

"Mr. Roger Ericson," said a voice at the door.

Ericson stood there with a uniformed constable at his elbow. Knollis waved him into the room and dismissed his escort.

"I'm glad you were able to come," he said affably as he pushed a chair forward. "I have a theory about this case which I would like you to hear."

"I was pleased to come," smiled Ericson. "Your men were most persuasive. I could do nothing else in the circumstances, could I?"

"My men are trained to have a winning way with them," Knollis replied dryly.

"I was coming along in any case," said Ericson. "I came into possession of a most interesting piece of information this morning, and I'm sure you will be interested."

Knollis cocked a suspicious eye. "We'll deal with that later. You may change your mind by the time I'm through."

Ericson shrugged his broad shoulders. "As you wish, Inspector. I am your guest."

"Several years ago," the Inspector began, "a certain gentleman in East Anglia was making a pretty penny by running dope, probably from the Continent, but that is pure supposition."

"It sounds interesting, Inspector. I must hear more of this," Ericson said lightly.

"It is. Now this gentleman was also in business, a legitimate business that was doing well. But the illegitimate business was doing so much better that he decided to retire from the one and concentrate on the other, so he sold out and retired to a certain respectable city. His sister lived in the city and she came to live with him—he arranged that as part of his background of respectability. She saw little of him and so she amused herself by going to dances, sometimes alone and sometimes with a girl companion. At one of these dances she met a gentleman with charming manners . . ."

Ericson was staring through the window at the evening sky and the wheeling pigeons.

"Come, Mr. Ericson," Knollis said reproachfully "you are not listening to me!"

Ericson shook himself and gave a wan smile.

"This gentleman remarked, we may assume, that she was listless, and he, we may assume, suggested a means whereby she could be filled with new life. Most of us are touched with the romantic brush, and she was no exception. His suggestion spelled adventure, and so she agreed. She sniffed cocaine for the first time in her life—cocaine which had been supplied indirectly by her own brother. The first sensations were agreeable, but as she repeated the act again and again she soon found that she was unable to do without it. Now that is exactly how snow-addicts are formed. This charming friend told her how to get hold of the stuff, and from where, and after that he saw less and less of her. He was looking for fresh customers.

"In due course she took a holiday by the sea, or intended doing so. Her brother drove her down to Overstrand and stayed about an hour at the hotel. Half an hour after his departure she went to bathe, and shortly after entering the water she noticed a man approaching from the north—the hotel was south of her. It was either her brother or the charming male friend of the dance. He swam with her, and he drowned her, and then returned to his car and drove away. As I have said, it may have been her brother or the male friend of the dancing nights."

Ericson met Knollis's eyes.

"I called at several places on the way home. I can prove that I never returned to Overstrand, Inspector."

"So you agree that my story is accurate so far?"

"I admit nothing," Ericson retorted.

"That's a pity," said Knollis. "It means that I must continue. Well, this brother probably thought that she had committed suicide and so he decided to wipe up the whole traffic. Anonymity is one of the main rules of this game, and it is highly probable that he did not know a single one of the people to whom he supplied the dope. That being the case, he had to investigate. By some means he discovered that a certain Ezekiah Lomas of Burnham had been distributing to the trade for years. So he advertised for a business in Burnham, and when Lomas rose to the bait he made an offer for the business as a going concern, hoping by this means to get in touch with his anonymous colleague and—er—settle the account.

"On the night of Lomas's death he interviewed him, and left him, and Mr. Lomas walked out to The Ferryman to keep an appointment. He did not know it, but it was to be an appointment with death. The appointment was faked, a hoax, and it was arranged by this East Anglian gentleman who wanted to make sure of Mr. Lomas's absence while he searched his house for the particulars of the cocaine transactions—which he found, I might add! And that in itself proves that he was not the killer of Mr. Lomas, and one suspect is removed from the list. The only way in which this gentleman can clear himself is by coming forward of his own volition and admitting all the facts."

Ericson nodded slowly. "Yes, Inspector; I see that." A moment later, after a slight pause, he said: "So my sister was murdered! I was given a hint to that effect, but I could see no motive. I thought that she committed suicide as a result of her miserable condition, or that she failed to reach the shore because of bodily weakness. In either case I meant to avenge her death."

"Who gave you this hint?" asked Knollis.

"A fellow I knew at home. We were mere casual acquaintances. He thought the circumstances suspicious."

"You never learned the name of the man who introduced your sister to dope?"

"I'd give everything I possess to learn that," said Ericson. "And if she was murdered, then it must have been by the same fellow. Marjory was shielding him, and no persuasion on my part would encourage her to reveal his name. That being so, I cannot understand why he should . . ."

Knollis leaned back in his chair and folded his hands across his jacket. "It will cost you up to fifteen years' penal servitude to learn it, Mr. Ericson. You know how our hands are tied? We are not given much latitude. If we suspect a man, and have reasonable grounds for belief in his guilt, then we must charge him, and after that we can ask no questions other than those intended to clear up any hazy point in any voluntary statement he may have made. There is no third-degree in this country. And so I am going to let you walk out of this room as you came in, a free man, with no stain on your character. I'm satisfied that you did not murder Ezekiah Lomas. You are free until I can prove definitely that you have been engaged in the dope traffic, and then I shall get you!"

Ericson did not move from his seat, Instead, he passed a hand over his eyes. "You suggest that you know this man. I'll give you fifteen years of my life for his name."

"It would be unethical to force you into such a bargain," Knollis said smoothly. "The clue is already in your hands. It was given to you by Miss Gretton. Your sister gave the clue to her. And it is possible that I have misinterpreted it, and so I cannot accept your offer even if I would."

Ericson sat bolt upright.

"I know what Marjory told Nora! She said a man from Leicester. That is what has puzzled me all along. *There never was an agent in Leicester!*"

"Steady!" warned the Inspector. "I'm trying damned hard to be fair with you, and in the face of my own—"

Ericson waved him into silence.

"The man from Leicester? The man from Leicester? Leicester? Good God above! *George Lester!* Am I right, Knollis? Answer me, man!"

"You are trying me to the utmost, Ericson," said Knollis slowly. "Before you go any further I think it is only fair that I should tell you that two of my men and the Cambridge police are at this moment searching your house. If they come away empty-handed the bottom falls out of my case."

Ericson flushed, and then went deathly white. "Then—then the game is up! Like an overconfident fool I kept accounts of the transactions. I—I think I'll make a statement. Yes, I ran the traffic. The stuff came from the Continent. It was landed at night at a remote spot on the Blakeney Marshes. . . . So it was Lester, the double-crossing rat!"

"Once again, trying to be fair," said Knollis, "I should tell you that I firmly believe that Lester had no idea that Marjory was your sister when he first met her. He didn't know you as the ringleader, did he?"

Ericson shook his head. "No, although I knew of him. And now, as you have played square with me, here is the information I promised you. I went to the Victoria Station this morning to see about a train home. Gertrude Lomas was in the booking-hall, bullying a porter who was wheeling several large trunks towards the luggage lift. I was going to marry her, but it was so evident that she was making a getaway that I kept out of sight until she had passed the barrier. Then I examined her luggage. It was bound for Harwich and the Hook of Holland "

The Inspector jumped to his feet, overturning the chair. "I said all along that the vital events occurred three months ago, and I was so blind that I couldn't see the most vital factor of the lot!"

He pushed the telephone across to Sir Wilfred Burr- rows.

"Ring Fountains, sir. I'll be swearing down the thing if I do it. Ask 'em why she cleared out—and I know the answer!"

Sir Wilfred obliged, gravely. Three minutes later he informed Knollis: "Her notice had expired. She gave them a quarter's notice, saying that she had taken a post in Switzerland for the good of her health."

"How true!" commented Knollis. "Now ring Morgan and Caine and see what has happened at that end."

Sir Wilfred did so. Then he pushed the instrument away and said solemnly. "She touched them for a six thousand pound advance and left a post-dated cheque for four thousand for Lawrence."

"And what do we do *now*?" murmured Dawes.

"Take my statement," said Ericson, "and then you are free to get after Lester—the skunk!"

"You're a cool chap," said Knollis grimly. "I'm surprised that you don't want to get away to settle him for yourself. That is the usual procedure, you know!"

"That wouldn't do," Ericson said quietly. "It would be over in a few minutes if I dealt with him. Lester has a vivid imagination and few brains. So he will have the long wait in custody, the suspense of the trial, and then those long three weeks before he goes to the scaffold. And that is how Marjory died! Mental anguish for months, and then a violent death. It will be much more appropriate!"

"Please take Ericson's statement, Dawes," Knollis said coldly.

CHAPTER XIV
THE ELIMINATION OF MR. LESTER

ROGER ERICSON's statement caused the Inspector no surprise. In one detail only was he further enlightened; Lomas had been lured to Willow Lock by a cryptic message from a mythical member of the dope ring which offered him a ridiculously high figure for the business—so that his cupidity and greed had in the end brought him to his death.

When the reports came from Cambridge Knollis was supplied with ample evidence of Ericson's guilt. Speaking to Forster over the telephone he said: "Turn to Lester's trial now. Find out whether he danced, where he danced, and if Marjory Ericson danced at the same places. Ask the Cambridge people to help you. Get a warrant and go over his house. Get me the date of Marjory's death, and find out where Lester was supposed to be on that date. You may learn a lot from his insurance account books. Find out what his weekly income was, and if there was an increase or decrease in business for the week of her death. And jump to it, please. Every hour is of the utmost importance now. Good hunting!" Slater came in a little later, and his 'samples' were sent to the laboratory, after which he was despatched to London to interview the Forsyth people.

The Inspector ordered a meal for Dawes and himself, Sir Wilfred having gone home for dinner. He used the telephone again while the meal was before them. "I don't think we need stir from the office again," he said with deep satisfaction as he lifted the instrument.

He gave instructions for Lester to be brought in for questioning, and then asked for Fountains, and Mrs. Gregory.

"I understand that Miss Lomas has left you," he said. "Was her departure very sudden?"

"Well, it was and it wasn't, Inspector," came the refined voice of Mrs. Gregory. "Miss Lomas gave her notice three months ago. Actually, she should have left me last week, but asked permission to stay for a few days on account of her father's death. Then she suddenly decided to pack, and left a few hours later."

"I see," said Knollis ambiguously. "Have you any idea what she had in view when she gave notice? I mean, was she taking another situation?"

"No, and that was the peculiar thing about it, Inspector. She had nothing of the kind in mind." Knollis hesitated, and then made up his mind. "I'm wondering if you could possibly spare the time to run over here, ma'am? I'm exceptionally busy, and I cannot find time to get out to Fountains. You have interested me immensely, and—"

"My curiosity is aroused, Inspector. I will be at the Burnham Police Station within the hour. I take it that you have certain suspicions?"

"Uncertain suspicions would be nearer the mark," chuckled Knollis. "I thank you, ma'am."

He occupied himself with his notes until Lester was brought in. Lester was cheerful, almost defiantly cheerful.

"I'm beginning to wonder which of us is doing the work in this investigation, Inspector," he said. "You seem to find my information interesting."

"So it is," the Inspector retorted. "I'm doing the work, too, in case you didn't know! Anyway, you appear to be holding a few clues that would be useful to me. Over Marjory Ericson, for instance; what made you suspicious of the nature of her death?"

Lester gave him a curious look, as if he was attempting to read his thoughts, but Knollis's face was not one that could easily be read.

"I was out that way on the day she died," he said at last. "My business took me into Norfolk."

"This is interesting," murmured Knollis. "Tell me more, Mr. Lester. You are not going to tell me that you saw Ericson on the beach with her?"

"I'm not at all sure, Inspector."

Lester leaned forward as if about to impart information that was confidential.

"You see, I passed Ericson as he was coming from Overstrand. It also happened that I took the coast road. I never could resist the sea, and so I left my car and walked on the cliffs. I saw Marjory Ericson in the sea, and also saw a car on the beach. A man was walking from it towards her.

"He was in a bathing costume. She came from the water to meet him. I realised that I was interrupting a *tête-à-tête*, and went back to the car, then driving north about my business."

"How far from the coast was Ericson when you passed him?" asked the Inspector.

"Oh, eight to ten miles, I should say."

"Really!" murmured Knollis. "Now one other question. How did you know that the girl in the water was Marjory Ericson?"

He smiled for he saw that he had startled Lester for the first time. The man was definitely scared.

Lester hesitated. "Well, I didn't—then. But when the news of her death came out I realised that it must have been her."

"Queer, isn't it?" muttered the Inspector. "But for your finer feelings you would have stayed, and would have seen a murder. In fact, you might have been able to save her life, eh?"

"I—I suppose so," stammered Lester.

"And the man? Did you recognise him?"

"Well no, not actually. It was afterwards that I found myself wondering about him. It looked a lot like Ericson!"

"Marjory took out a policy with your company. You told us that. Did she transact the business through you?"

"Well, no. I am a district inspector. One of my men handled the business, and I investigated it before advising the company to accept her as a good risk."

"She was medically examined?"

"Who? Marjory Ericson?"

"Who the hell do you think we are talking about?" snapped Knollis. "She is the only person under discussion. Was she, I ask, medically examined?"

Lester looked round as if for a means of escape from the trap that Knollis was laying for him. "She—she—"

"She was not medically examined," said Knollis. "And that is strange. She takes out a policy for several thousand pounds and is not examined by a doctor! Still," he added airily, "I'm an ignorant man and I know little of such matters."

Lester took his remarks literally. "Yes, of course," he said with a perceptible sigh of relief. "She had a rooted objection to being naked before any man, even a doctor."

"And of course there are no women doctors," Knollis said facetiously.

"Or—or women!" exclaimed Lester.

"You must have known her very well indeed if she confided to you such matters," said Knollis.

"You don't understand, Inspector," Lester said desperately. "She was keen on the policy, but she simply couldn't bear the thought of an examination! She would have refused the business, and so I persuaded the company to pass the clause up. She appeared to be in good health—"

"Despite the fact that, as was shown at the inquest, she was a nervous wreck as a result of narcotic habits, and was therefore a rotten risk for your company!"

"Well, she paid the deuce of a high premium, Inspector!"

"Not five thousand pounds?" Knollis asked gently. Lester laughed uneasily. "Well, no! Hardly!"

"And you believed that you were doing a spot of good work for the Forsyth?"

"It was a dam' good premium, Inspector!"

"It will be a dam' good pay-out, too, Mr. Lester!" Lester was silent, so Knollis knocked the nail home.

"A fine stroke of business indeed! You allowed a girl in desperate health to take out a policy that was bound to cost your company a matter of several thousand pounds before the second premium payment became due. Some business man!"

Lester's lips became a straight line.

"How much did she pay you to overlook the small matter of the medical examination, Mr. Lester? Or perhaps it was for forging a doctor's certificate? Which?"

"I don't accept bribes, Inspector Knollis!" Lester said with forced dignity.

"Only money for mixtures of bicarbonate of soda and cocaine, Mr. Lester!" Knollis mocked him.

Lester was on his feet then, shaking a fist in the Inspector's face. Knollis regarded him stonily as Dawes dumped him back into his chair.

"You can't accuse me of trafficking!" he shouted.

"Do you dance?" asked Knollis.

"Dance? What the devil has that to do with it? What do you mean by dancing?"

Knollis shrugged his shoulders.

"Well, it depends. There are two ways of dancing—on a ballroom floor, and at the end of a rope. You do the first kind if you are peddling dope, and the second if you are guilty of murder. Marjory Ericson danced on a ballroom floor and became a snow addict. Some other person is going to do the rope dance before the year is out."

"You mean that you are accusing me of murdering her!" Lester asked in an awed voice.

Knollis smiled. "Good lord, no! But I am accusing you of peddling dope, or procuring, or several other pretty offences."

"But the whole thing's absurd!" Lester protested. "I told you, when you visited me at The Ferryman, that I was investigating her death. How the deuce does my case cross this Lomas case? Tell me that!"

"I will," said Knollis, unperturbed. "You passed Lomas in the passage, or the doorway, of The Ferryman?"

"I told you that."

"And he was carrying half a glass of whisky?"

"Why, yes, I told you that, too."

213 | THE DEATH OF MR. LOMAS

"Then that was where you crossed the Lomas case," said Knollis with a light smile.

Lester sagged in his chair. "Joking, eh? Lord, but you frightened me for the minute. I thought you were trying to frame me."

"Peculiar sense of humour, mine," said Knollis. "Now you went back into the saloon bar after that incident?"

"Yes," said Lester with renewed courage.

"You are a liar," said Knollis. "You were in the willow beds when Lomas collapsed. I know you were there because you were seen!"

Lester reluctantly admitted the truth of the assertion. "Yes, I followed him until I saw Lomas and Gretton on the bank. Then I retreated to the path in the beds."

"And saw everything that happened?"

"Yes, Inspector."

Knollis drew a deep breath.

"Then you will kindly come clean—even if I have to scrub you. I've been messing about all week because my one material witness fails to come forward. Of course," he added, "you are under no compulsion!"

"It's the same thing," said Lester cynically. "I followed Lomas—"

"He was still carrying the glass?"

"Yes, I'm coming to that in a minute. When I saw Lomas and Gretton—"

"You speak as if you know her intimately!"

"I've seen her about the town at home," Lester said lamely. "Anyway, Lomas got up and ran to meet his father. He took the glass, forced the contents down his throat, and threw the glass in the river. Then the old man pushed him aside and staggered on, collapsing a few yards beyond where Gretton was lying.

"Lomas waited a few minutes and then lay beside Gretton. He stayed there until the two barges passed and then went to his father. He felt his pulse and hurried back to Nora Gretton. She rose and they went back to the car."

"And what did you do?"

"Me? I hurried to the inn, entering the bar parlour by the rear entrance as if I had come from the lavatories."

"This is all extremely interesting," mused Knollis. "Reverting to my insinuation with regard to the business of peddling dope, you would not object if I was to obtain a warrant and run a fine tooth comb over your house?"

Lester paled, and gaped. "Search my house? But there's nothing there that could possibly interest you?"

"You keep books?"

"Why yes. I'm a business man."

"And run your business on business-like lines?"

"I—well, I hope so, Inspector."

"Then there would be no object in searching your house?"

"Of course not," said Lester as he once more recovered his self-control. "It would be a sheer waste of time."

"And since there would be no object in searching your house, I take it, similarly, that there would be no objection if I did so?"

"All this is getting paradoxical," Lester complained. "What would you expect to find if you did that?"

"I think I'll tell you," said Knollis. "I should expect to find proof—but perhaps you would be interested in a theory I have elaborated?

"You see, Mr. Lester, we have definite proof that both Ericson and Ezekiah Lomas were concerned in the cocaine traffic, and we have to work backwards from that fact. Peculiarly enough, it leads straight to Marjory Ericson and the evening or night when she met a certain man at a dance. He persuaded her to sniff cocaine, and then again, and again, and again, ad infinitum, or almost! She then realised that she could not do without the stuff. She was given the address of a Burnham tradesman who would supply her. A new customer had been provided with life-membership of the unholy fraternity.

"So far, so good. But a difficulty arose when this peddler found that he had been supplying the sister of the Big Boss. Awkward, wasn't it?" the Inspector asked the white-faced Lester. "He knew that he was for it if the truth reached the Big Boss, and so he decided to close Marjory's mouth for ever and ever.

First he had to arrange that suspicion, if it arose, should fall on the Big Boss, and so he arranged a motive. He persuaded the girl to insure herself and make a will—all her worldly wealth was to go to her next of kin. That done, the rest was easy. All he had to do was remove her to some quiet spot where a murder could be made to look like accident or suicide, or murder by her own brother, and then arrange an alibi for himself.

"We will assume that he suggested a seaside holiday for the sake of her nerves. He planted the idea that her brother should save her the fatigues of travel by running her there in his car. Now—as soon as she went to bathe, and her brother had sheered off, he slipped into a bathing costume or swim-suit and joined her in the sea. She died."

Knollis paused for his version of the story to sink in. He continued:

"The mind of a man alters after he has committed a capital crime. It all seems so easy and straightforward before the act is committed. Little doubts creep in afterwards. Has everything worked out as planned? Was he seen? Was he recognised? It is an old tale, and we meet it time after time. It has brought many a near-perfect crime into the full light of day. I think it happened here. The murderer of Marjory Ericson wondered, and wondered, and wondered. That wonderment produced something akin to panic in his mind. Instead of letting well alone he began to tamper with his well-made and well-executed plans.

"You are listening, Mr. Lester? He began to play the age-old game of passing the buck—incriminating someone else. He expressed doubts to his company and asked to be allowed to investigate her death, hoping to be able to prove her brother guilty. Then, when Roger Ericson came to Burnham, he followed, turned an acquaintanceship into a pseudo friendship, and learned a great deal while both were in residence at The Ferryman. Altogether a pretty chain of thought, but it didn't work, Mr. Lester!"

Lester ejaculated an involuntary "Oh!"

"Our man was a plain damned fool, with a strong instinct for imitation. He saw that Ericson was wearing a suit similar to

Lawrence Lomas's, and so he went to Lomas's tailor and had a suit made in the name of a man old enough to be his father. The tailor thinks he can identify the man. I am sure that he can!

"Our man hoped to take advantage of a coincidence, hoped that if he was detected while engaged in any illegal enterprise he would be mistaken for Lawrence Lomas or Roger Ericson. All the way through he was at the mercy of his imitative instincts, copying Ericson's methods. Instead of allowing coincidence to draw the scent away from himself, he drew it towards him, heaping suspicion on suspicion."

The Inspector rose and placed a hand on Lester's shoulder.

"George Lester, I am detaining you on suspicion of being concerned in the death of Marjory Ericson, and on suspicion of being concerned in the cocaine traffic run by another who is now detained."

"You can't do it!" screamed Lester. "You can't prove a thing against me! You have no evidence!"

"When my men have finished searching your house I shall have more evidence than I want—and they are doing that now, at this very moment! Take him downstairs, Dawes."

Lester opened his mouth, closed it again, and allowed himself to be led away.

Mrs. Gregory came in shortly afterwards, and Knollis expressed himself as satisfied with the information she was able to give him.

"So she gave notice three months ago?" he said. "Can you tell me why she did so?"

"I can only assume that her brother's visit had something to do with it, Inspector."

"He called about the time that she gave notice?"

"He called often," said Mrs. Gregory. "They talked earnestly as he led her to his car, and there seemed to be an air of tacit understanding between them. Gertrude was constantly remarking that there was a silver lining to every cloud, and that every dog had its day. I did not understand, and of course I did not ask her to explain. But I was convinced that the manner of her brother and herself was—well, shall I say conspiratorial? When she gave me her notice of intention to terminate her agreement I came to the conclusion that her brother had found a more desirable position for her, although I had always been confident that she was happy with me. Er—am I to assume that there was—well, foreknowledge of her father's death, Inspector?"

"I'm afraid so," said Knollis in reply. "More than that I cannot say at the moment. By noon tomorrow the whole truth will be known, but before that I dare not risk a guess."

Talking the matter over with Dawes half an hour later Knollis said: "I'm still at a loss with regard to the method Lomas used for the distribution of the snow. Can you suggest anything?"

"Only that we question the Desborough Road sub-postmaster about Lomas's outward mail," said Dawes.

Knollis slapped the table. "What an ass I am not to have thought of that! We'll go now. By the way, Dawes, you realise the truth about the Bridge Hotel appointment? It was Lester who first met Lomas there. He went back to The Ferryman, and Lomas went into the Bridge with Ericson. Lester had been following old Lomas round the city, and it was he who jumped on the bus after Ericson had left him."

"I was sorting that out in my mind," said Dawes. "I reached the same conclusion."

The sub-postmaster was reluctant to divulge information, but was at last cajoled into revealing that Mr. Lomas never sent small packages or bulky envelopes through the post. "Apart from the books he sent out from that postal library there was nothing except letters."

Knollis blinked. "Postal library!"

"You didn't know about that, Inspector? He used to send books all over the country. I often wondered how he made it pay, but he was a mean man and he wouldn't have done it if it wasn't possible to make a profit."

"Postal library!" Knollis repeated. With a muttered word of thanks he almost ran from the building, Dawes on his heels.

"I barked my shins on that box of books when I first visited the shop! I wonder . . ."

The box was still standing in a remote corner of the storeroom, a black box with a hasp and padlock, and *Postal Library* stencilled on its lid in white paint. Knollis soon found a way of unlocking it, and then he and Dawes stared at the miscellany of titles that met their eyes. There were books on archaeology, pigeon-fancying, tennis, chess, geology, and at least two dozen other subjects.

"Queer," said Dawes.

"Very queer," said Knollis.

He chose a book on electro-magnetism, and opened it. The fly leaves and the title pages were intact, but the pages bearing the text had been cut, a small square out of the middle of each page, so that the whole assembly formed a small box, with the front cover serving as a lid.

Each book in the box had been served in the same way. At the bottom of the box they found two lists.

Knollis went through them carefully, exclaiming when he came to the name of Marjory Ericson and the date when she had first joined Mr. Lomas's "library." Knollis sat back on his heels and smiled. "The gods are good to us, Dawes. Very good indeed. And to think that I literally ran into the most important clue on my first visit. It just shows the weakness of man's strongest effort, and the virtue of patience! Get your gloves, old chap. We are bound for Desborough. I want a chat with Lomas's mechanic before he goes to bed. I prefer to question him away from his place of business."

"You think he knows something?"

"No, I don't think he knows anything."

"Then you think he saw something?"

"It was what he didn't see that counts, Dawes," said the Inspector. "If he can tell us what he did see, we can guess what he didn't see, and our good friend Whitelaw will be able to verify—or nullify—our guess. The main point right through this case, Dawes, has been the overflow of cocaine."

"I don't get you," said Dawes with a puzzled frown.

"No?"

Knollis was concerned with his own thoughts. He shook himself. "Slip down to the box and ask Whitelaw to meet me at the office in an hour's time if possible. Oh, and you'd better warn Bunny that we are about to make an arrest. He was in at the beginning and so he'd better be in at the death. Hop it, Dawes, my friend!"

Dawes closed his mouth, and obeyed.

CHAPTER XV
THE DEATH OF MR. LOMAS

The dental mechanic received Knollis and Dawes with engaging diffidence, apparently doubtful whether he was to regard their visit as an honour or otherwise. He invited them to be seated, and remained standing himself. "I cannot imagine what I can do for you," he murmured.

"Very little, I'm afraid," Knollis said candidly. "Mr. Lomas was taking dental treatment at his son's surgery, and there are just a few matters regarding this which I think you can clear up or otherwise corroborate."

"Anything I can do, Inspector. . . ."

"Mr. Lomas was attending weekly?"

"Oh, yes."

"Having a tooth extracted each week?"

The mechanic grinned, and regained some of his confidence as the conversation turned on his own trade. "Almost on the instalment plan," he murmured. "Mr. Lomas had lost two by misadventure and so the scheme was likely to extend over thirty weeks."

"Thirty-two teeth per mouth, eh?" said Knollis.

"In the adult mouth, Inspector."

"What sort of a patient was he?"

The mechanic grinned again. Lomas seemed to be an amusing memory. "A child of five had more guts."

"You assisted at each operation?"

"Oh yes. He had gas. Couldn't bear the thought of a needle pricking his gums."

Dawes flashed a significant glance at the Inspector, but Knollis did not heed him.

"He disturbed the serenity of the surgery, eh? Wanted attending to there and then, as soon as he entered the building? Was that the idea?"

"Exactly, Inspector. He came in a twitter, remained in one, and departed in the same petulant mood. Nervous as a cat. Most disturbing."

"Tell me," said Knollis; "what is the usual procedure on the arrival of a patient for extractions. I suppose there is a set procedure?"

"You've never had an extraction, Inspector?" the mechanic asked with some surprise.

"Years ago," Knollis replied evasively. "I've almost forgotten what happened."

"Well, Mr. Lomas seldom varies his procedure. I suppose he came to it by trial and error. He examines the mouth, sprays the gum—freezing it, as we call it, and then leaves the patient for a few minutes. He then returns, sterilises his instruments—"

"Aren't the instruments sterilised immediately after the departure of the previous patient?" Knollis asked.

"Oh yes, of course, but Mr. Lawrence is most particular. All instruments are twice sterilised. Quite normal, really."

He waited for a further question, but Knollis signed him to continue.

"He injects the novacaine or whatever he may be using, and again leaves the patient while the anaesthetic does its work. On his return he performs the extraction and again sterilises the instruments while the patient is making a great show of the small amount of blood released."

"And that is that?"

"That is that, Inspector."

"And Lomas Senior always disturbed the procedure by his haste to get the job over and done with?"

"He did! On several occasions Mr. Lawrence had to leave the instruments used on a previous occasion until his father's extraction was over and done with."

"Can you drive a car?" Knollis asked suddenly.

"No, Inspector, nor any other motor vehicle. Why do you ask?"

"Never mind that now. Any idea whether Mr. Lomas will be at home to-night?"

The mechanic glanced at the clock. The hands were pointing to eight. "No, he will not, Inspector. He told me that he was taking Miss Gretton to Willow Lock—a celebration supper. He and Miss Gretton are engaged to be married. A very nice young lady is Miss Gretton. Mr. Lawrence is a lucky man."

"He is," said Knollis. "Remind me to slip along and congratulate him, Dawes. Well, I think that is all, and I thank you for an interesting talk."

As they drove back, along a road lighted by a low-riding summer moon, Dawes asked a question: "One thing gets me groggy. You never asked about the procedure in Ezekiah's case. He had gas."

"I know," Knollis said gently. "Surely you see by now how he was killed?"

"By the hypodermic that was fished from the river. But even then it isn't clear. I don't see how you arrive at your conclusions. They are always right, but you get 'em when there is no apparent evidence. And what is still more unsatisfactory, you never explain how you get there!"

"There's no magic in it, Dawes," Knollis mused. "I'm blessed with patience and a too-vivid imagination. I put myself in the skin of the person concerned and try to imagine how I should set about the job if I possessed their particular type of mentality. I've done that with 'em all; Lawrence, Ericson, Lester, Gretton, and Gertrude, not forgetting Ezekiah as well. I generally find that there are about three ways in which a job could be done, but only one of them that would appeal to the person concerned. Lester was the easiest meat of all. He responded to his primitive urge to imitate, and only a plain unimaginative fool could have let him slip from the net. Gretton is my only difficulty, and she bothers me. Not having much of the feminine in my make-up I can't quite see *why* she fits in. She works for Ericson and plays with Lawrence, and I'm not at all sure that she hadn't solved the 'man from Leicester' clue and was passing the tip to me. I'm beginning to think that she is deeper than she appears, that she has rumbled the whole game from A to Z and is wiping the score clean in her own way. Well, we have Ericson and Lester, and Lawrence Lomas will shortly follow."

"You are satisfied that he murdered his father?"

"Perfectly satisfied. Who else could have done the job? Ericson sent the old boy to Willow Lock so that he could scout round the premises, and I've no doubt at all that he was in the shop when Lomas died. Lester was in the willow bed, and his yarn about Lawrence forcing the stuff down his father's throat was bunk. He had previously told me that Ezekiah threw the glass down at the doorway and that he, Lester, carried it indoors."

"His tale was all hooey," said Dawes with a nod. "I thought so at the time. He was trying to push Lawrence in up to the neck. That was very obvious. Lester must have been in the willow beds, but while he saw what Lawrence did to his father he wouldn't realise what was happening."

"That is the point, Dawes. Neither would Gretton realise what was happening. We have to remember that while it was light, it was not full daylight by any manner of means. Lawrence chose the safest time of day for his action. I believe he learned from Gretton that his father was going to Willow Lock, and he made preparations accordingly."

"How was it done?" persisted Dawes. "Whitelaw said it was not taken subcutaneously, and that passes up my private opinion about the method."

"Whitelaw, doctor or no doctor, was wrong," Knollis said grimly. *"The stuff was injected subcutaneously.* Every minim of cocaine that went into Ezekiah Lomas, with the sole exception of amounts he may have taken himself, was injected with the help of this hypodermic syringe in my pocket, and every dose but the last one was injected in Lomas's surgery, right under the nose of the mechanic!"

Dawes stared through the windscreen, at the rapidly approaching suburbs of Burnham. "You mean that he was needled while under the gas, Inspector?"

"Of course! How else could it be done without Ezekiah being aware of it? Eliminate the impossible, and whatever remains must be the answer. That is an old axiom."

"My God!" exclaimed Dawes. "What an audacious trick!" He thought a moment, and then said: "And Gertrude Lomas was in the plot?"

Knollis nodded sorrowfully. "She conceived it! Or so I believe. I slipped up on Gretton, and I did it again on Gertrude, and all because I cannot understand the ramifications of the female mind. Understanding of Lawrence is easy. I know him like my own brother. Ever since a child, as the evidence shows, he has sponged on his mother and his sister. His sister was forking out even from her meagre earnings at Fountains. I'm as certain of that as if I'd seen her doing it. Lawrence didn't cadge because he needed it, but because it was an ingrained habit. The plot against his father bears the same mark. He got his father to alter his will, making his sister the sole beneficiary—"

"But that's what Lester did!" Dawes exclaimed.

"Lawrence knew Gretton before he started poisoning his father. Isn't it extremely likely that Gretton should have told him the story of Marjory's accidental death in the hope of surprising him into an involuntary betrayal of his knowledge of his father's illegal business?"

"Yes, it is," said Dawes.

"And having put himself in the clear, by removing the monetary motive, he began to undermine his father's health by pumping him full of cocaine. He was a crafty devil, and when I say 'devil' I mean it. He knew that his father was trafficking. And he knew that when his father found himself growing morbid and depressed he would turn to his own stocks for solace. That happened. Lomas Senior knew that something of the sort was happening, and he was using snow as an antidote—poor devil, and I mean that, too! He knew it when he visited Bunny, and he knew that either the bane or the dote was killing him by inches. He could not bear the mental agony of the bane, and so he dare not leave off the antidote."

"It's going to take a lot of proving," said Dawes.

"If those people at the laboratory know their knitting we have the case in the bag. If Whitelaw can find those needle marks in Lomas's mouth then Lawrence is for the high jump. The scientific evidence is almost of more importance than our evidence these days. Put old Waywood Lockson in the box for the Crown and the jury will eat his expert, dry-as-dust evidence. What is more, I think Lester will be only too pleased to say exactly when he saw."

"And what did he see?"

"Lawrence produce a syringe and give his father an elephant's dose of coke."

"And that was how it was done!"

"That was how it was done! Y'know, I'm wondering how much Gretton knows about Ericson. Does she suspect him? Anyway, here we are. Jump out. Whitelaw should be waiting for us."

The doctor was waiting. He was almost apologetic as he shook hands with Knollis. "There's something wrong, Knollis. I told you that the stuff was not injected . . ."

"It needed laboratory experts to prove otherwise?" said Knollis. "I expected that, and it is no reflection on you. Our man was anticipating an ordinary post-mortem examination and nothing more. The stuff was injected." Knollis expounded the same theory that Dawes had heard during the drive from Desborough. The doctor listened with open amazement, and shook his head when the story was told.

"It sounds all right, Knollis, but there isn't a scrap of evidence. The theory is a good one, but there is one snag, a bad one. Lawrence Lomas gets away with it. There isn't a single puncture in the man's mouth."

"Oh my Gawd!" exclaimed Dawes.

"Nor in his nostrils!" added the doctor.

225 | THE DEATH OF MR. LOMAS

Knollis refused to be discouraged. He fetched a sheet of paper from his desk, wrote a few words on it, and folded it. As he handed it to the doctor he said: "We are going out to Willow Lock to arrest Lawrence Lomas. If you care to follow us when you have taken another look at Lomas's body you'll probably be in time to hear Lawrence confess that he killed his father in the way I have described on this sheet of paper."

He dragged Dawes away before the doctor could recover from the shock. They found Sir Wilfred Burrows waiting for them, and after assisting him to ease his bulk into the car they went to The Ferryman.

Knollis explained the state of affairs as they went, and in return the Chief Constable informed him that the Cambridge police had telephoned, asking that both Lester and Ericson should be detained. Sufficient evidence had been found to convict both; to hang one and send the other to penal servitude.

"And there is one further item which I do not profess to understand," continued Sir Wilfred. "They said that Miss Gretton could now return and would we pass that message on to her from the Forsyth people."

"Has Slater started for London?" asked Knollis with a happy grin.

"Yes. Why, Knollis?"

"Then he will have a nice trip at the expense of the ratepayers," smiled the Inspector. "And that clears up the last point. Nora Gretton was a Forsyth agent working with the Cambridge police. Thank heaven for that!"

She was hurrying from the inn as they drew up. Knollis slipped from the driving seat and intercepted her. He delivered the message and met her broad smile with a friendly laugh.

"Candidly, you've been a darned nuisance, Miss Gretton, but I expect your evidence will cancel that out! We've got Ericson and Lester under arrest, you know!"

"I expected that from your message," she said. "Lester did kill Marjory, but it was Roger's beastly stuff that led to her death. And now Lawrence . . ."

"I'm just going to arrest him," said Knollis.

"I saw you from the toilet room, Inspector, and . . . and if you don't mind very much I won't stay. I don't want to be there. I—I rather like him . . ."

She sniffed tearfully. "I'll walk home along the tow-path. The river is smooth-flowing and peaceful. Now that I've avenged Marjory I need peace more than anything in the world. . . . Good-bye, Inspector Knollis."

"I'm sorry," said the Inspector gently.

Lawrence Lomas sprang to his feet as the three men entered the room. "What the hell is the meaning of this? Am I never to be left alone again?"

"Never again," Knollis replied solemnly, "until the chaplain comes for you. You killed your father by injecting cocaine into his mouth while he was under an anaesthetic in your surgery!"

"I didn't! I didn't!" Lomas hissed viciously. "I defy you to prove that I killed him. There isn't a puncture to be found in his mouth."

"Your sister has left the country, Lomas."

He drew a deep breath. "Left the country? When?"

"This morning," said Knollis. "Her luggage was marked for the Hook of Holland."

"So—she's—gone!"

"And she'll come back. Wireless telephony is a wonderful invention. She'll take her stand with you, in the dock. She conceived the plan, and you executed it."

"You can't do that," Lomas raved. "I'm innocent! What had I to gain by killing my father? He left all he had to Gertrude."

"And you would do just as you have done since your boyhood, Lomas; swindle her for the lot!"

Lomas sniggered nervously, but before he could reply Dr. Whitelaw walked into the room. He glanced at Knollis, and smiled. "Congratulations, Inspector! I don't know how you do it, but you were right. We found hypo punctures in Lomas's mouth after all. Deuced clever!"

"It's—it's a lie!" shouted Lawrence Lomas.

"It was neat," said Knollis. "Each time you drew a tooth you got rid of your assistant, *and then injected the cocaine in the resulting cavity, and in the other cavities!*"

Lawrence Lomas staggered to the open window, gasping.

"I want air! Air!"

Before Knollis could stop him he had thrown himself out and was limping to his car. They went after him with all speed, but he had thrown the clutch in before they could come up with him. He sped away from them, out of the parking ground, and along the tow- path, gaining momentum with every yard. Dawes ran to the police car, but the Inspector called him back. "Too late, Dawes! I know what I should do in his shoes—and, my God, he's going to do it!"

He hurried after the car, Dawes now at his side, and Sir Wilfred puffing along behind.

"What's—going—to—happen, Knollis?" gasped the Chief Constable.

"The death of Mr. Lomas," said Knollis. "He is nearly at the spot where his father entered the river!"

The speeding car, bearing Lawrence Lomas with it, suddenly swung to the left. For a split second it seemed to hang motionless in space. Then it dropped, sending up a great fountain of water. There came a cry of fear, and a horrid gurgling. The car sank inch by inch until at last it disappeared beneath the surface. Great circles spread to the bank on either side, hurried both up-stream and down-stream, and then an unruffled mirror took their place, serenely reflecting the foolish face of the week-old moon.

Knollis sighed, and turned away. Dawes followed. Only Sir Wilfred Burrows remained, gazing at the silent water.

"Got it, Knollis! I've got it at last. That Emsworth fellow you mentioned! Cousin of mine met him last year at Shepheards' in Cairo! Bless my soul! To think that I should have forgotten!"

THE END

Printed in Great Britain
by Amazon